Born in Dublin, **JENNY O'BRIEN** moved to Wales and then Guernsey, where she tries to find time to both read and write in between working as a nurse and ferrying around three teenagers.

In her spare time she can be found frowning at her wonky cakes and even wonkier breads. You'll be pleased to note she won't be entering Bake Off. She's also an all-year-round sea swimmer.

Also by Jenny O'Brien

The Detective Gaby Darin series
Silent Cry

The Stepsister

Praise for the Detective Gaby Darin series

'Full of twists and turns . . . A fabulous story till the end'

'A clever thriller . . . Mind blowing'

'Keeps you on the edge of your seat.'

'You won't be able to put the book down until the very satisfactory end'

'An excellent start to a great crime procedural series!'

'An amazing thriller from beginning to end'

'This book has everything . . . Full of twists and turns'

'Very, very clever plotting . . . Highly recommended'

Darkest Night

JENNY O'BRIEN

ONE PLACE. MANY STORIES

HQ
An imprint of HarperCollins*Publishers* Ltd
1 London Bridge Street
London SE1 9GF

HarperCollins*Publishers*
1st Floor, Watermarque Building, Ringsend Road
Dublin 4, Ireland

3

First published in Great Britain by
HQ, an imprint of HarperCollins*Publishers* Ltd 2020

Previously published as *Stabbed in Wales*

ISBN: 9780008390181

MIX
Paper from
responsible sources
FSC
www.fsc.org
FSC C007454

This book is produced from independently certified FSC™ paper
to ensure responsible forest management.

For more information visit: www.harpercollins.co.uk/green

Printed and bound by CPI Group (UK) Ltd, Croydon CR0 4YY

This book is dedicated to all of the students at Elizabeth College, Guernsey; to their stories and to the characters they are yet to imagine, create and meet.

Jenny Palmer, Principal of Elizabeth College.

Chapter 1

Christine

Consciousness came upon her slowly, memories flickering through her mind – memories she was afraid to summon from the shadow of sleep.

Christine had never been any good in the mornings, usually only surfacing when the gnaw of hunger and the thirst for caffeine overrode the comfort and warmth of her bed. But this morning was different, not that she could put a finger on exactly how or why.

Reaching out, she picked up her gold-plated watch and squinted at the dial, just about managing to make out the little hand pointing at the six. She decided to ignore the box beside her bed. Without her contacts she was as blind as a bat but, with her head thumping, the thought of even lifting the lid had her resting back against the pillow. She'd need a gallon of coffee with a paracetamol chaser before she could even think about starting her day.

Friday nights usually followed a defined pattern. She finished work around five, which allowed her plenty of time to dash to Asda before returning to her top-floor flat along the West Shore to get ready for the evening ahead, not that it was usually that exciting. Since her divorce, her nightlife had contracted to meeting up with a girlfriend for a few drinks, before returning home to an oven-ready pizza, a bottle of prosecco and whichever boxset she was currently watching on Netflix. Life was predictable and, in truth, a little boring. But boring was as good as it was safe. She rarely deviated from this pattern and any time she did it was usually something she regretted in the morning. It had been a hard lesson to learn when at university that what looked hot and handsome through a cocktail-infused haze invariably turned into the proverbial frog when daylight hit. But last night had been different. There'd been more laughter and more fun than she'd had in a very long time.

Her eyes snagged on the wall of birthday cards, carefully placed on top of her tallboy. She'd been dreading turning thirty. Now the only thing she regretted was the headache from hell trying to dig its way out of her skull with the blunt end of a pickaxe. Turning her head slightly, she stared at one card in particular while she tried to piece last night together. It felt as if there was a cloud between what had happened and what she remembered. No. She frowned, her brain addled with the complexity of thinking. It was almost as if someone had sucked the centre out of her memory only to leave a pale outline. She remembered leaving work just as she remembered the pile of goodies she'd popped in the fridge for later. She even remembered the black silky top and trousers she'd flung on before rushing to leave the flat, the sound of her heels echoing on the stairs. She remembered the man.

Her thoughts collapsed in on themselves, hovering on some-thing lurking in the distance. Turning her head, she focused on the mound buried beneath the duvet next to her, a shady memory pushing through the curtain of her mind. So, that was it; her mouth pulled into a thin smile. For the first time since the divorce she'd dragged some poor unsuspecting bloke back to the flat for a night of passion. Her smile disappeared. She couldn't remember much, hardly anything. His cologne, something light and tangy. The force of his body driving through hers. He had no name and no face. There was nothing else apart from a lingering sense of regret and disgust that she'd sunk so low as to have sex with a stranger.

She shook her head, wondering at the direction of her thoughts. Instead of trying to work out what had happened she should be kicking the body beside her in an effort to clear both her bedroom and her life from whichever stranger she'd invited back. Her ex-husband was her worst mistake and one she was determined never to repeat. If she could get it so badly wrong the first time, there was every reason to suppose that she'd get it wrong the next.

With a sigh, she slid out of bed, careful not to shift the covers or depress the mattress. If he found her standing in the nude, he might think he was in for a repeat performance and that certainly wasn't going to happen.

Walking across the floorboards in bare feet, she was careful not to make a sound, thankful that the door was open and her dressing gown still in its usual place – draped across the back of the button-backed chair. She slipped her arms through the sleeves and tied the belt in a secure bow before making her way into the kitchen and to the percolator that took pride of place on the worktop.

With coffee brewing, she wandered into the bathroom to get the packet of paracetamol that lived in the mirrored cabinet above the sink. Tablets in the centre of her palm, she raised her hand to her mouth only to pause at the sight of her reflection in the mirror. She looked like shit, the bags and shadows emphasising the tiny lines that had only appeared since the divorce. But it wasn't her looks that confused her. It was how she felt. Her head was banging but it was more than that. Her gaze followed the tremor of her hand as she popped the pills into her mouth. She'd never been one to party into the small hours but, on the odd occasion when she had, she'd never felt like this. It was probably her age; after all, she wasn't getting any younger, she thought with a grimace as she remembered her amnesia. If she could only manage to obliterate the grinding pain in her head, she was sure her memory of last night would come racing back. It felt like an evening she probably wouldn't want to remember but she still needed to know.

Back in the kitchen, she was relieved to note there was still no sign of activity from her room. The door to her flatmate's bedroom also remained determinedly shut. She paused, one hand on the coffee pot, the other reaching for a mug. Nikki was usually up and about by now and, as a poor sleeper and early riser, what were the odds that she already knew about the man in her bed.

Christine scowled at any thought that centred around her increasingly unwelcome lodger. Agreeing to allow Nikki to move into the small box room, as a temporary stopgap, was all very well. But not when Nikki had made it clear from the beginning that she wasn't going to make any effort to help around the apartment. She lived like a slob, leaving a scattering of dishes and clothes in her wake and Christine was growing increasingly sick of picking up after her. It was almost like bunking down with a teenager although, as an only child, she'd never had that pleasure. She should have sent her packing weeks ago but the truth was she felt sorry for her. More fool her. Nikki was a problem and one she didn't know how to sort but she was determined to at least have a chat with her as soon as she'd managed to boot lover-boy from her bed.

With that thought uppermost, Christine pushed herself up from the table and reached for another mug. She had no idea if he even drank coffee but, as her mum always said, it was the thought that counted, not the action. She'd let him have his drink before showing him the door and after, she'd do what she'd been putting off for months. She'd tell Nikki that it wasn't working and that she'd need to look for somewhere else to live. Pleased that she'd finally come to a decision, she left the kitchen and walked back into her bedroom.

'Come on, matey,' she said, trying to be jokey.

She grabbed the corner of the duvet, still half fearful of what he'd look like in the cold light of day. After the first sip, she'd managed to come up with a blurry image of tall and dark-haired, but his face was still a complete blank.

'Thanks for last night and all that but I need to be somewhere. I've made you a cuppa—'

There was no warning of what was coming. Her memory was still as absent as it had been earlier and now other thoughts joined that big gaping hole inside her mind, her eyes riveted to the body spread across her bottom sheet – a sheet awash with blood. The pale alabaster skin. The unblinking stare. The mouth open in what appeared to be a silent scream. The cavernous hole in the white T-shirt, which confirmed what she knew already. She'd never touched a dead person before. She'd never even seen one. Her mind shifted to thoughts of her grandfather's recent demise and her refusal to remember him as anything but how he was before dementia had taken hold of both his mind and body.

Christine dropped the mug she'd been clenching, letting it slip through her fingers only for it to bounce once before cracking in two, spewing coffee across the floor. Turning away, she just managed to reach the security of the bathroom before losing the entire contents of her stomach.

Arm stretched out against the tiled wall, she ignored the sight of last night's supper, instead heaving in deep breaths in an attempt to settle both her stomach and her nerves. But no matter how hard she squeezed her lids, Christine couldn't obliterate the memory of the cold foot under her fingertips, the pale pink nail varnish almost garish against the translucent white of her skin and the almost slippery dampness of her flesh. Was it worse that she recognised her as Nikki, the person she'd been planning to berate about her slovenly ways? Seeing her naked like that for the first time, her body laid wide open to prying eyes, made Christine feel embarrassed somehow. She hadn't even thought to pull the sheet up to hide her flesh, not that it would make any difference to her – not now.

For the first time in her life Christine didn't know what to do. She knew that she had to contact the police but that was easier said than done. What would she say and, more importantly, what would they think? She had no idea what had happened; would they believe her?

She reached for the flush before turning to the sink and washing her hands, her attention snagged by the haunted expression staring back at her in the mirror. The stark truth was that she'd gone to bed with a man only to wake up next to the body of her flatmate. Where was he? What had happened to him? But more importantly what had happened to Nikki?

Christine turned away with a sigh. The thing that scared her the most, of course, was what if she was guilty?

Chapter 2

Gaby

Saturday 9 May, 8 a.m. Rhos-on-Sea

DC Gabriella Darin was annoyed at the persistent ringing of her doorbell. She'd switched off her phone the night before and, after a long luxurious bath filled to the brim with her favourite bath oil, she'd towelled and plaited her hair before climbing into bed with her Kindle and a plate of rice cakes in preparation for the lie-in she'd planned – her first in ages. The rice cakes were the only discordant note in her ideal evening, that and the lack of a man to share both her bath and her bed. But her life was a work in progress. After being forced out of her last job for nearly causing the death of a civilian, she was determined to focus on her career before tackling any of the other issues.

Now, she placed her Kindle down on the coffee table beside her mug of tea before pushing to her feet. With this being her first weekend off since she'd moved to St Asaph Station from Swansea, over three months ago, it could only be Amy. But thumping on her door at this time of the morning wasn't really her style . . .

Gaby had been seeing less and less of her friend and colleague over recent weeks, conversations now starting and ending with Tim, Amy's new boyfriend. Gaby was happy for her, more than happy, but she'd be even happier if she was able to find that special person for herself. It would certainly cure the boredom that seemed to have set in since her transfer.

North Wales was stunning with its long stretches of golden beaches, incomparable lush fields and hills coated in green. It was a place to repair her soul of the damage caused by her last case, but it was also meant to be a place to make use of the skills she'd honed after thirteen years in the force. It was just a shame that her new boss, DCI Henry Sherlock seemed to have other ideas. She headed for the hall, trying not to think about next week's interview for the job of detective sergeant. It was difficult not the get her hopes up but, after the mess she'd made of finding Alys Grant, she was lucky to still be in the force let alone involved in the kind of cases she wanted.

The shadow through the etched glass pane in her front door wasn't Amy. If she didn't know any better, she'd think that it was the detective that Sherlock had buddied her up to as part of her induction, but that couldn't be right on her weekend off . . .

'You should know by now that a copper never turns their phone off – not even on their wedding night.'

'Aw, come on, Bates. Give me a break.'

'A break! You want me to give you a break,' DC Owen Bates said, sending her a look before pulling out of her narrow drive. 'At least you were only dossing about at home. I was about to leave the house for a pre-rugby match training session. You might remember that it's meant to be my weekend off too but, with DI Tipping still off sick and half the force down with Norovirus, we had no chance. Henry did say that he'd make it up to us both but when is another thing. It's hard enough with the cuts to manage the workload let alone try to give us time owing. Kate's been nagging me for ages to make some plans for a weekend away but I daren't.'

Gaby threw the bearded Welshman a quick look. Being youngish, free and single, she hadn't spared a thought for what it must be like trying to juggle a partner and young family within the narrow confines of a career in law enforcement. The DCI was as fair a copper as you could get but he couldn't magic staff out of thin air.

Reaching out a hand, she patted his knee briefly. 'When this case is over, Owen, I'll cover for you so that you can make an extra-long weekend of it.'

'You know I'll do the same if you ever manage to get that love life of yours sorted,' he replied with a laugh.

'Ha, that will be the day. So, where to next?' she said, neatly changing the subject. The very last thing she was willing to discuss was her lack of anything bordering a romantic entanglement.

'The West Shore, across from the play-area.' He shot her a look. 'Sherlock isn't able to make it, but he asked me to pass on a message.'

'What's that?'

'He wants you to head up this one, Gaby. Well done. It must be a good omen for your interview.'

She watched Owen turn left onto Gloddaeth Avenue, her eyes sliding to the distant mountains framing the West Shore. If she knew Sherlock, he'd have his reasons for choosing her over Owen but now wasn't the time to puzzle it out. The only hope was that she was up to it. She wouldn't admit it to anyone else but those few short months in Swansea had caused her to question her abilities. If she could miss most, if not all, of the clues during the previous case, wasn't it possible that she could do the same again?

Instead of replying all she said was, 'You were saying about the murder?'

'Yes, looks like an open and shut case, so not something you'll be able to sink your teeth into. The only thing we don't appear to have is the murder weapon. The key suspect, a Christine de Bertrand, must have hidden it. Early thoughts are that it's some kind of kitchen knife. The pathologist said he'd meet us there so we should know more shortly.'

She bit her lip hard, the taste of blood leaving a metallic taste in her mouth. 'Make my day and tell me that Rusty Mulholland is on his hols or, even better – that he's fallen off a cliff?'

It would be a kindness to say that Gaby had a difficult relationship with the red-haired Irish pathologist. She had no idea why he'd taken an instant dislike to her but he could barely look her in the eye without a curl of his mouth or a snarky comment from his lips.

'Ha, no such luck, sweetheart,' Owen said, pulling up behind the CSI van and switching off the engine. 'I really don't get what gives between you two?'

'Nothing gives, Owen, and it's not likely to. Ever. That man is a scourge and the less I see of him the better.'

Gaby compressed her lips, her attention now on the red-brick building ahead with a bright yellow door flanked by a pair of pyramid-shaped topiary bushes, not that she knew the first thing about gardening.

'Well, there's obviously something up, he's as nice as pie to everyone else.' Bates unclicked his seatbelt, urging her to hurry. 'The sooner we can get the body bagged and tagged and the suspect interviewed, the sooner I can sign off.'

Gaby raised her eyebrows but said nothing. There was little point. With no family nearby she knew she'd be press-ganged into giving up her weekend. There was always a huge amount of extra work generated on a case like this. Interviews, witness statements, paperwork galore – the list was endless. But in this instance, she didn't mind. As the two most senior DCs in the unit, it was always going to be either her or Owen and, as he had a toddler and another on the way, she was the obvious choice.

Walking into the middle of the scene of a crime always had

10

her pulse racing and her heart jerking in her chest. It wasn't that she was nervous, far from it. In a strange sort of way, it was the feeling of excitement building. They had a golden hour, that first sixty minutes, to push aside any preconceived ideas and focus on the facts. Securing the crime scene was vital but it was more than that. The first impression of the location. The first impression of the main suspects. Their first words before lawyers turned up to slam the window of opportunity in their faces.

She walked beside Bates to the police van and, reaching out a hand, took the clipboard from the officer standing watch, scrawling her name, rank, date and time in the allocated columns before handing it to Owen. 'You said it was a cut and dried case?'

'Yes, indeed. A modern-day love story gone wrong. All we need to do is find the murder weapon and it's straight to court to bang her up for the twenty-first century equivalent of life – so ten years then.'

She pulled a wry smile at his joke although it was far from funny. 'A modern-day love story? I don't get it?'

'You know what, Gaby, at the tender age of thirty-five I feel I'm too old for this game,' he said, patting his pockets for his phone. 'The world has passed me by on a steam train. Between you and me, if things don't change, I'm going to have a serious think about leaving the force.'

'Ha, that would be impossible, I would have thought. You love the job nearly as much as I do. It's coppers like us, grassroot ones determined to avoid those managerial ivory towers, that keep the streets safe. Somehow, I can't see you becoming a PI or security guard and what else are we trained for? And anyway, what would I do without my partner?' she added, grabbing a white suit from the pile and shaking it out.

'You'd do fine,' he said, shoving his black lace-ups into the blue overshoes provided, before pulling up the hood to his paper suit and tying a double knot under his chin. 'Now not a word to anyone about what I've said, even to Amy Potter.'

'Okay, although as family liaison officer, Amy would be the very last person to share a confidence.'

'Yes, well. I'm going to concentrate on solving this little puzzle before I decide. It shouldn't be too difficult.' He pulled on an extra-large pair of disposable gloves and adjusted his mask before following her up the short flight of steps and into the dark, narrow hall, saying a brief hello to PC Diane Carbone, who was standing guard beside the front door.

'Why's that?'

'Because our suspect murdered her girlfriend in cold blood.'

Gaby had a thing about bedlinen. She didn't mind scrimping and saving on other aspects of her life, but Egyptian cotton sheets were a must. She had a neat stack of carefully ironed, pure white linen in her tiny airing cupboard at the top of the stairs and, unlike almost anyone she knew, she changed her sheets twice a week. Her mother thought it an extravagance with half the world starving and the other half happy to put up with bobbly brushed nylon, but she didn't care. She looked forward to Mondays and Fridays for the simple pleasure of slipping into her freshly made bed.

The bed in front of her must, at one time, have resembled hers. There were still tell-tale signs in the neat hospital corners and lace-edged pillowcases. The owner had taken pride in this room, Gaby thought, her gaze now resting on the scatter cushions in tasteful shades of cranberry and sand to match the throw, which had slipped to the floor in a heap. But all resemblance ended with the sight of the dark-haired woman splayed across the sheets.

Standing at the end of the bed, her hands clasped behind her, Gaby looked down at the naked body, the skin now that distinctive waxy pallor she always thought synonymous with the dead. While part of her grieved for such a young life lost, the other part, the clinically detached one, tried to work out which major artery the blade must have nicked to produce so much blood, thankfully mainly contained within the duvet.

'Hope you're keeping those hands glued behind your back, Detective Darin. Don't want to corrupt the scene now, do we?'

Turning her head, she caught the eye of the pathologist and frowned. Rusty Mulholland. It was a good job that murders in North Wales were a rarity, Gaby reminded herself, curling her fists. Over the last month or so, they'd drawn an uneasy truce mainly because she'd gone out of her way to avoid any of the places he usually hung out. It was when she bumped into him at the station that it became more difficult.

She tilted her chin to look him in the eye, something made difficult by his six-two frame.

'As if, Rusty.' She refused to call him anything other than the nickname the rest of the team called him in deference to his hair. 'Anything you can tell me?' she continued, her calm demeanour unchanged despite his narrowing gaze. She was getting used to masking her expression when he was around.

'What, apart from the fact that we have a dead body? No, not a thing. You should know by now, Detective, that's not how it goes, or haven't you worked with us long enough yet?'

She ignored the sarcasm. She'd have liked to have ignored him completely but the last time she'd tried he'd been even more acerbic. Whatever she said, she couldn't win. He didn't like her and there didn't seem to be a thing she could do about it.

Casting a final look at the body, she was pleased to note one of the constables taking photographs from every conceivable angle. There'd also be a rough sketch of the crime scene in addition to detailed measurements of the room. Rusty, for all his bad manners and abruptness, was good at his job. She'd already clocked that he'd bagged the woman's hands to minimise the risk of both contamination and the loss of any forensic evidence from what was one of the most important parts of a body following a crime. The fingernails were an oasis of DNA debris and within an hour of arriving back at the lab, he'd have arranged for the victim's to be clipped and scraped.

Wandering out of the room, she headed along the hall, flicking a curious eye at the pictures adorning the walls. Modern art wasn't her thing, not that she had either the time or the money to fritter away on non-essentials like food. She frowned. If truth be told, modern art confused her. If she had the money, she'd like to start a collection of local scenes in and around Rhos-on-Sea, a place she was learning to call home following the recent purchase of her cottage. But that was only a pipe dream – her rundown house took most of her salary and B&Q took the rest.

A technician, dressed head to toe in white plastic overalls, diverted her attention from the walls to the kitchen and the sight of DC Bates talking to what was presumably the key suspect. She was pleased that DCI Sherlock had decided to leave it to them. While good at his job and one of the best chiefs she'd worked under, he'd be the first to admit that the day-to-day job of crime-solving was best left to his detectives. His skills lay in managing both budgets and staff.

Gaby paused on the threshold, examining the scene at her leisure. There was no hurry in the way she let her gaze roam around the room before finally landing on the woman sitting on one of the four Bentwood chairs that circled the table. First impressions were important to a copper, and she knew that she'd replay these few seconds time and again in the privacy of her mind, remembering the pale-as-milk redhead, wrapped up in what appeared to be a dressing gown and little else.

She looked somewhere in her early thirties with flowing russet curls that owed little to artifice. Apart from the hair, which was bloody amazing, she also looked ordinary. Somebody you wouldn't throw a second glance at if you came across her in the street. But then again, murderers didn't tend to shout out about their crimes and Gaby would bet her last pound that this suspect would be the same. No. She was innocent until proven guilty, something Gaby sometimes had difficulty remembering.

'This interview has been suspended at 09.25,' Owen said,

14

interrupting her thoughts and she watched in surprise as he switched off the mini voice recorder before gesturing for her to follow him back into the hall. 'I thought I'd do the preliminaries and read her her rights, but all she's done for the last five minutes is stare into space. It's as if she's in a trance. She hasn't even confirmed her name or demanded to speak to a solicitor.'

'She's probably in delayed shock. It's a pretty gruesome scene in there.'

'And one she's made herself so she should be used to it by now,' he said, with a grunt. 'I know she's within her rights to remain silent, but this is ridiculous.'

'Now, now, Owen, that's unlike you. You don't need me to tell you that we can't assume guilt. Don't go making assumptions that we can't question until Rusty has worked his special kind of magic.'

'Ha, I didn't know you cared,' Rusty said, from somewhere over her left shoulder. 'And after all this time, too.' His sneer matched Owen's like a couple of bookends in a bad mood. 'While you're here passing the time of day, I thought I'd let you know I've arranged to take her back to the lab. Early indications are a single stab wound to the chest with the possibility of a nicked aorta. If she hadn't been cocooned in the duvet, I'm guessing the splatter would have hit the ceiling.' He looked at Owen. 'I'll have the report on your desk first thing Monday.'

Gaby squared her shoulders, determined not to let him see how much his cavalier attitude affected her. 'That would be on my desk, Dr Mulholland.'

'Would it now?' he said, opening his eyes wide. 'They've decided to let you off the reins, have they? Well, good luck with that.'

Gaby pulled a face at his retreating back. She hated altercations of any sort but that didn't mean she was going to let him continue to walk all over her. She promised herself there and then that the next time he was rude, she'd tell him exactly what she thought of him.

'I suppose we should get Amy down here ASAP if de Bertrand

isn't prepared to talk to us.' Gaby dragged her phone out of her pocket to search for the number of the family liaison officer only to pause at the sound of her name.

'Oh, I nearly forgot, Detective Constable Darin,' Rusty said, stomping back up the stairs. 'I think you might need these.' He put his hand in his pocket and withdrew a small velvet-covered box, laying it out in the centre of his palm.

Gaby looked from the box and back to his face, for once lost for words. On the one hand he'd told her not to touch anything and on the other . . . 'I do hope you think it was worth disturbing the crime scene before we've lifted any fingerprints because I certainly don't. Of all the stupid, cockamamie—'

He stiffened, his back rigid, his mouth a thin hard line of disapproval. 'What sort of word is cockamamie? And anyway, I think you'll find that it's against her human rights to deny her access to them. I could be wrong, but then again I am only a doctor as well as a pathologist.' He handed her the case before heading back the way he'd come.

'He really doesn't like you, does he?' Owen said on a laugh.

'It wouldn't be the first time a man hasn't . . .' Gaby's voice petered out at the sight of the hearing aids nestling in the bottom of the box.

Chapter 3

Christine

Saturday 9 May, 1.10 p.m. Llandudno Police Station

They hadn't let her out of their sight despite the clock above the door stretching past one. The male detective, whatever his name, had barely allowed her to get dressed before escorting her into the waiting car and taking her back to the station. There was lots Christine could say to him if she could be bothered. Just because she was hearing-impaired was no excuse to shout. Shouting raised decibels but distorted clarity. It also increased stress levels to the extent that all she wanted to do was shout back, something she was pretty sure wouldn't be appreciated under current circumstances. So, she'd worked on her breathing, trying to calm down. Being angry wouldn't help, just as aggravating the police would make it worse. Something had happened between the time she'd crawled between the sheets and climbed out of bed and she'd need all her smarts to figure out exactly what.

The room they'd taken her to was small, about half the size of her kitchen and filled with a table and stackable plastic chairs.

There was nothing to focus on apart from a female police officer leaning against the wall with her arms folded across her chest and a look of boredom on her face.

Shifting slightly, Christine finally forced herself to relive the scene back in her bedroom, something she'd pushed into the corner of her mind while they'd clipped her nails and swabbed her skin. They'd even taken her dressing gown for analysis although what they thought they might find was another thing. Shuffling back in her chair, she hitched up her jeans. They'd taken her belt and her watch, although how she was expected to take her own life with her trusty Seiko was a question she was yet to ask. She'd been photographed and fingerprinted, something that had drummed home more than anything else that she was a suspect in an horrendous crime. And the awful truth? She didn't have a clue how to make them believe that she was innocent.

As a child, she'd hated the sight of blood. When all her friends were watching *Buffy*, she'd be the one hurrying out of the room at the squeamish parts. So much blood in her lovely bed. It almost felt as if someone had let Jackson Pollock into her bedroom with a jumbo tin of red Dulux. All Nikki's blood. She felt sick at the thought of what had happened to her. While not her favourite person, Christine had always felt responsible somehow for how Nikki's life had gone pear-shaped. If it hadn't been for Paul . . . No. She blinked away the thought, forcing her mind to turn back to more practical issues – the past was a place she was determined not to visit. The very first thing she was going to do when they let her go was put the apartment on the market. There was no way she could ever live there again. She'd probably have to go back at some point to collect her things but until then, she'd need to think of somewhere else to stay.

Her mind was a complete blank. She couldn't ask her parents. They were the very last people she could ask. She could no more ask them to put her up than she could tell them that she'd been taken into custody. She grimaced, a picture of her ageing mum and dad floating before her. A shock like that had to be managed but, as an only child, there was no one she could ask to knock on their door for a cuppa and a chat before informing them that . . . what? Their darling daughter was currently being detained at the local nick. Oh, they hadn't charged her or anything, far from it, but she'd watched more than her fair share of *Midsomer Murders* to know the score. They were waiting for a solicitor to be assigned before the interrogation began in earnest.

The question of who to tell about her situation hovered. It had to be someone she could trust and, moreover, someone who would be prepared to tell her parents. The desk sergeant had demanded the name of someone they could call on her behalf but who? Kelly, the girlfriend she'd met up with last night, was always an option but her parents had never met her . . . She frowned. That only left the head at the special needs school where she worked, but she liked Jessica Kinney too much to land this on her doorstep.

She sat back in the chair and crossed her legs. In fact, she couldn't involve her at all. At the first whiff of bad news, she'd be put on suspension or maybe even sacked. The school already took a dim view of parking offences – she didn't dare think about what their reaction would be to a murder accusation. She groaned, plucking a tissue from the new box the PC had conveniently dropped beside her elbow. The only person she could think of was probably the last person in the world she'd ever dream of phoning under normal circumstances. But being suspected of murder was far from normal.

The sight of the door opening had her uncrossing her legs and folding her hands in her lap. She'd deliberately ignored the chair facing the barred window and little patch of blue sky, instead choosing the one opposite the door for obvious reasons. While profoundly deaf, she still managed to hear some sound with the assistance of her high-pitched hearing aids but that didn't alter the fact that the click of a door being pushed open was something she probably wouldn't hear on a good day and, as days went, she'd had better.

'Hello again, you might remember I'm DC Gaby Darin and this is my partner, DC Owen Bates,' the short stocky woman said, joining her at the table. 'We've managed to assign a solicitor – this is Mr Andy Parrish.' She waved a hand towards the bespectacled middle-aged man following them into the room, an old leather briefcase clutched under his arm. 'For the record, Ms de Bertrand, the conversation with be recorded.' She flicked a switch on the microphone set into the wall at the side of the table.

The solicitor, with a brief smile, went to take the chair beside her only to stop at the sound of her voice.

'No. You need to sit opposite.'

'Opposite? I don't understand?' he said, a puzzled expression on his face as he looked at the empty chair to her right.

Christine let out a loud sigh. 'Mr Parrish, I suffer from a hearing impairment. So, despite the hearing aids—' she raised her hand to her hair, pushing it behind her left ear for emphasis '—for me to be able to understand you, I do need to see your lips, unless any of you can sign?' She allowed her eyes to drift to each of them in turn, the sight of their quickly lowered heads confirmation enough. 'Just as I thought.'

She'd been taking a huge risk that none of them knew sign language. While deaf in her left ear since a riding accident when a child, her current state of near total silence was something that had crept up on her over the last couple of years. Yes, she was learning to sign but she was far from fluent. She was also only a beginner at lip-reading – but they weren't to know that. She knew instinctively that telling them she could hear, albeit slightly, was to her advantage.

'If you'd prefer to have a sign-language interpreter present, I'm happy to halt the interview until one can be arranged?' Gaby said, her look frank and with no trace of the embarrassment Christine was used to.

She shook her head briefly.

'For the record, Ms Christine de Bertrand has declined the services of an interpreter at this time.' Gaby flipped open her notebook to a new page and jotted down the date and time. 'Now, please can you tell us, in your own words, exactly what happened in the lead up to this morning's—'

'Before you start questioning the witness perhaps you should caution her in my presence,' Mr Parrish interrupted, pointing a finger at the microphone. 'And I'd like it noted for the record that anything Ms de Bertrand has said to you, or any of your officers, up to this point is inadmissible as evidence.'

'Understood, loud and clear, Mr Parrish,' Gaby said, a smile frozen on her face. 'DC Bates, if you could do the honours, please.'

Both hands on the table, Christine glanced down at what was left of her nails and the chipped dark red nail varnish, taking little notice of the barely audible words the bearded man was reading from a piece of white card that he'd pulled out from his pocket. She'd always prided herself on her hands, and her rainbow selection of varnishes, which she renewed daily, were a source of both discussion and amusement for her pupils. She'd never wear red again. She raised her head back to Gaby.

'Now to repeat my question,' Gaby said, only to be interrupted.

'Don't bother! Which part would you like? The part where I went to bed with a bloke or the one where I discovered my flatmate dead under my duvet?' Christine replied, staring back.

'How about from the beginning. Let's say, when you returned home from work. I take it you do work?'

'Yes. I'm a teacher at St Francis's, at least I was. Innocent until proven guilty won't hold much water with members of the school board.'

'Let's skip the school part and talk about arriving home from work,' Gaby said, rolling her pen between her thumb and forefinger.

'I usually leave at five o'clock on a Friday and, after a quick dash to Asda, I showered and changed before heading out to meet up with a friend for a few drinks – yesterday was my birthday.'

'Congratulations,' DC Bates said, without even the glimmer of a smile. 'So, your friend and the bar staff would be able to confirm that, would they?'

She shifted her head, a frown appearing. 'Sorry, can you repeat that please? It would be helpful if I know when someone else is speaking . . .' She spread her hands.

'Of course,' Gaby said, shooting the other officer a quelling look. 'My colleague asked whether your friend and the bar staff would be able to confirm that?'

'Kelly certainly could – not sure about the bar staff but probably,' she said, swallowing hard. The problem wasn't with their memory . . . She wasn't even sure which pubs she'd been in.

Her mind seemed stuck in a loop. Over the course of the morning she'd managed to dredge up a hazy recollection of the new drinking game Kelly had started, which involved copious amounts of Mojitos. But her inability to recall most of the subsequent events, including the lead up to her one-night stand, was a first, and more than scary – bloody terrifying.

Lifting her hands, she cradled her forehead and silently condemned last night's excesses. They were usually much more restrained in their drinking habits but celebrating her milestone birthday by getting smashed had seemed a good idea at the time.

'You said that you went to bed with a man,' Gaby said, flicking a look at Christine's ring-less hands. 'Your boyfriend, partner, husband—?'

'I'm not married, not anymore.' She pushed her hair away from her face, annoyed that she hadn't had the foresight to bring a scrunchie. 'The thing is we had too much to drink, way too much—'

'A couple of girls out on the lash in Llandudno on a Friday night isn't that uncommon,' Gaby interrupted with a smile. 'Safety in numbers and all that.'

'Yes, but I can't really remember much after meeting up with Kelly,' she said, her gaze resting on her solicitor who was busy tapping away on his laptop, a sheaf of papers pushed to one side. 'I can't really remember much more apart from what I've told you already. The next thing after the drinking contest was waking up this morning.'

'Can you at least tell us something about him?'

'There's nothing, no memory of what happened between us, if indeed anything did,' she said, wiping her fingers over her face before dropping her hands back to her lap. 'Dark hair; short, dark hair,' she continued, almost to herself, struggling to search through her mind for even a glimmer of something else but it was useless.

Gaby lifted her head from where she'd been writing in her notebook. 'So, fast-tracking to this morning, can you tell us exactly what happened from when you woke up?'

'There's not a lot to tell. I felt a bit disorientated – too much alcohol.' She pulled a face. 'I certainly wasn't in the mood to deal with having to face some random bloke over my bowl of corn-flakes.' She paused, trying to see it from their point of view and suddenly not liking the impression she was giving. 'You're prob-ably thinking that I'm a bit of a slapper but that's not the case. Hooking up isn't something I do now. Yes, when I was younger, but I can't remember when I last took a stranger home to my bed – it must be years. I felt awkward, uncomfortable even. I have a nice flat, somewhere I feel comfortable and, to be honest, when I woke up, I couldn't believe what I'd done. He could have been anyone . . .' Her voice cracked, willing them to understand. 'I needed to get away from the reality of the situation, so I left and went into the kitchen – coffee was called for, in large amounts.'

DC Bates lifted his hand. 'Leaving a stranger asleep in your bed? Why didn't you wake him?'

'I've told you, I wasn't thinking straight. It was like there was a fog . . . Everything was hazy, and my head was banging. I put the coffee on and headed into the bathroom for a pee and paracetamol.' She put her hand up to her hair and tugged at a corkscrew curl. 'You think I always go about looking like someone's plugged me into the mains? This is usually blow-dried before being ironed into submission.'

Mr Parrish gained her attention by tapping his index finger on the side of his laptop before speaking. 'Are you sure you're happy to continue the interview, Ms de Bertrand? If you're not feeling up to it, we can always postpone until later.'

She managed a smile out of relief that he had a tongue in his head. She'd been starting to get seriously worried about who they'd dumped her with. 'No, let's carry on. The sooner it's over, the sooner I can leave.'

Christine caught the tail-end of a look passing between the three of them and felt her stomach fall to her knees. Gripping her hands together to stop them shaking, she dropped her head a moment, trying to understand what was going on. It wasn't some awful mistake. It wasn't some nightmare dream that she was going to wake up from with a sigh of relief. The reality was that her flatmate had been found dead in her bed and she was the number one suspect.

'So, I take it I'm not going to be allowed home any time soon? What about bail or something?'

'Currently, you're helping us with our enquiries into what is a complex and very serious case, so I'm afraid bail doesn't come into it,' DC Darin said, glancing up from where she was busily scribbling in her notebook.

'But I'm still a suspect, is that right? The only suspect?' Christine said, her gaze fixed on the detective's face. 'So, how long are you going to keep me here – in case I need to feed my dog or something?'

'Do you have a dog, Ms de Bertrand?' Her voice was sharp.

'No, not anymore but you weren't to know that,' she said, not quite believing how her life had derailed so quickly. Her parents had led her to believe that the good guys always came out on top – but they'd lied. She was stuck here without even a toothbrush or a clean pair of knickers for however long they decided to keep her – years if they charged her and she was found guilty. But despite all that, she was a lot better off than Nikki. Her mind, as if on a puppeteer's string, pulled her back to the image of her death-cold body bathed in all that blood. She felt her throat tighten with the threat of tears but managed to swallow them. Now wasn't the time for tears. Tears wouldn't help her and they certainly wouldn't help Nikki.

'So, presumably, reading between the lines, I'm the main suspect in a murder and, never having been in this position before, I'd like to know what happens next?' she asked, her arms now folded across her chest. 'How long am I to be kept here without being formally charged?'

'Not long. You'll be taken into custody but, as they don't have the facilities in the Llandudno branch, you'll be transferred over to St Asaph's station and to their custodial suite.'

'But that's miles away. How do you think—?'

'This isn't a holiday,' DC Bates interrupted with a wave of his hand. 'Someone has died in your bed and, until we can ascertain what exactly happened, we need to ensure we know where you are. Now we still have some more questions,' he said, his look pointed. 'You've told us up to leaving the stranger in your bed and going to the bathroom. What happened next?'

He was making it sound as if in some way she was at fault and, hugging her arms across her suddenly trembling body, she probably was. But if there was a rule book to follow under the current set of circumstances, she was yet to find it.

'I went back into my room . . . I'd made him a coffee.' Her words were a mere thread of sound. 'I wanted him gone, you see, and I thought that was the best way, kinder than showing him the door. I called out something, I can't remember what, but there was no answer. After a moment I pulled back the duvet and—' The image of Nikki's body seemed to have leeched from her thoughts to behind her eyes, causing her cheeks to pale. 'There was blood everywhere, so much blood. I ran then. I had to get away. I only made it to the loo in time.'

'And what can you tell us about your relationship with Nikki Jones?'

Christine shifted her head in the direction of the bearded detective, scowling at the way he'd clicked his fingers almost under her nose to regain her attention. 'Not a huge amount. I knew her from university but we'd lost touch. I bumped into her again and offered to put her up for a bit. She seemed . . . well, she seemed to have fallen on hard times. If you want the truth, I felt sorry for her, not that I'd ever have told her. She wasn't the type to accept charity.'

The tiny bit of energy, flowing through her veins and muscles, was fast diminishing. With her hand on her forehead, she now asked. 'How long am I to be kept at the station?

'A few days at most.'

Mr Parrish lifted his briefcase and popped it open, placing his laptop and papers inside. 'The maximum length they can detain you without a formal charge is seventy-two hours.'

'But that's three days, what am I going to—?' All colour drained from her face, not that there'd been much to start with. They thought she was a murderer, all three of them, even the solicitor who now couldn't quite meet her eye. Oh God, what the hell was she going to do. She could tell the interview was over by the way they spoke directly into the microphone before switching it off and standing to their feet.

'It shouldn't be long, Christine, if I may call you that?' DC Darin said, now standing by the door. 'I'll send an officer in with some tea while we arrange for your transfer.'

'Wait.' Christine hugged her arms more tightly across her chest, trying to retrieve both her courage and her pride from where they were hiding. She couldn't do this alone, not now. She needed help but would he be the right one to ask after everything she'd done to him? She was about to find out, one way or the other.

'You said you'd inform someone about what's happening to me. I'd like that person to be Paul de Bertrand, my ex-husband.'

Chapter 4

Paul

Saturday 9 May, 5 p.m. St Gildas Independent Boarding School

Beddgelert

The school bell rang at the same time each evening at St Gildas, one of the oldest independent boarding schools in Great Britain. Within seconds the corridors were filled with the echo from six hundred pairs of boys' shoes racing into the refectory in time for supper. Like most boarding schools, life at St Gildas was governed by rules and regulations and no child wanted to be late in case they missed out on the Saturday treat of toad in the hole and chips.

The teaching staff followed at a more leisurely pace, tucking a copy of the evening paper under their arms as they passed the long mahogany table that filled one corner of the Jacobean-styled main entrance. These housemasters and mistresses had every reason to feel smug at their place amongst one of the top ten boarding schools in the country. Cocooned within their ivory tower, two miles south-west of the village of Beddgelert, the outside world rarely had the audacity to interrupt their orderly existence and any unsavoury intrusions were swiftly brushed under the antique Persian rug that took pride of place in the headmaster's office.

The headmaster, Paul de Bertrand, was a lucky and relatively recent addition to the school, an addition the board was pleased to embrace with his prior experience both as an educationalist and university lecturer. The only fly in the ointment was when his wife had upped and divorced him within months of taking up his tenure because, of course, a married headmaster was so much more desirable than a divorced one. But, over the last couple of years they'd muddled along, occasionally partnering him with a suitably well-bred woman, at one of the many dinner parties he had to attend, with a view to her slipping into his erstwhile ex-wife's shoes. So far it hadn't worked.

Arriving at the table at the head of the room, Paul inspected the sea of boys, a wry smile on his face. Life was as good as it could be under the circumstances – circumstances he couldn't spend too much time thinking about or he'd go mad. The divorce rankled. He thought about Christine's desertion first thing in the morning and last thing at night, without fail, and it was as much of a mystery then as it was now. The thing about having the ideal marriage was that he had no idea when or even how it had started to crumble. Up to the day he'd found her gone, a crappy note left propped up on the mantelpiece, he'd thought their life perfect. Now he had no expectations or ambitions. Now he had work and Ruby, their five-year-old miniature schnauzer – that was all.

He pulled the newspaper out from under his arm for something to do while he waited for his meal to be served. With a couple of staff due to go on maternity leave, there were still supply teachers to find and references to plough through. Afterwards he'd sit in his private lounge with a glass of port by his side and a book on his lap . . .

It took one glance at the headline glaring out from the front of the paper for him to unfold it, the cold hand of fear tracing its way up his spine.

'It's your favourite again, sir. These Saturdays do come around with an increasing regularity,' Maggie, one of the dinner ladies, said before placing his plate in front of him with a smile.

He didn't see her smile, a smile that quickly changed into a frown before she turned on her heel and made her way back to the kitchen. He didn't see anything other than the headline laid out in front of him.

The body of a young woman has been found on The West Shore. Her flatmate is currently assisting the police with their enquiries.

'Headmaster?'

'What? Excuse me, sorry. I was miles away,' he finally said, looking up into the face of Eddie Taylor, the sports master.

'No problem. There's a call for you, they wouldn't leave their name.' He handed him a piece of paper. 'If you could phone this number – they said that it's urgent.'

Chapter 5

Paul

Sunday 10 May, 9.25 a.m. St Asaph Police Station

'Where is she?'

'Good morning, sir,' the custody sergeant said, looking up from the computer monitor perched on the desk in front of him. 'How can I help?'

'I'm looking for Christine de Bertrand. She was transferred here yesterday from Llandudno. You wouldn't let me see her last night but I'm . . .'

'Ah, yes,' he interrupted, pulling a print-out towards him and running his blunt-cut nail down the list before lifting his head. 'And you are?'

'Paul de Bertrand, her . . . ex . . . husband.'

'Right. Unusual name, if you don't mind me saying. French, is it?'

'No. It's Chinese,' he snapped. 'Of course it's bloody French.'

'There's no need to take that tone here, sir, or I might have to arrange for you to join us.'

'I'm sorry.' He placed both hands flat on the desk, staring down at the officer whose tone of voice had dropped along with his professional smile.

Of all the situations Paul had found himself in over the years, this one ranked right up there with the most difficult. But by the look on the officer's face, if he didn't moderate his behaviour pretty smartish, he could find himself booted out or, even worse, arrested – neither of which would help Christine's cause.

He heaved a breath, making more of an effort than he'd made in a very long time. 'Look, it's been a bit of a shock, all right. I haven't heard from her for nearly six months and to get a call like that out of the blue.'

'Yes, sir. If you'd like to take a seat while I check in with the detective in charge of the case.'

'I don't want to see any detective. I want to see my ex-wife,' he said, his voice rising.

'All in good time, Mr de Bertrand.' The sergeant tilted his head in the direction of the chairs lined up against the wall.

The one thing Paul de Bertrand wasn't, was stupid. With a BA in classical civilization, an MA in late antique and early Byzantine studies and a PHD in Assyriology, he'd quickly learnt that life was a game and, as with all games, there were rules that must be followed. The only problem was he didn't know which game he was meant to be playing. The throw of the dice. The turn of a card. The positioning of a chess piece. With twenty years' experience in teaching, he was a dab hand at games. He won some. He lost some and learnt from the experience. This wasn't a game he could afford to lose.

Sitting down on one of the blue plastic chairs, he scrolled through his choices only to realise that he didn't have any. The phone call hadn't said much, only that Christine was assisting the police with their enquiries. If it hadn't been for the evening newspaper, picked up from the sideboard on his way into supper, he might have been tempted to leave her to her own devices.

After all, she'd been the one to walk out on their marriage. No. It hadn't been their marriage she'd walked out on – it had been him. She'd abandoned him like an old sock and the thing that hurt the most was he still had no idea why. There'd been no indication that things weren't right between them and certainly no precipitous act like an affair. He'd never even noticed other woman and as for her . . . he was as sure as he could be that there wasn't another man involved but as for another woman—?

Removing his glasses, he pressed his hand to his forehead, trying and failing to shut out the morning's headline that had shouted out in four-inch Helvetica script.

Lesbian Bloodbath in Llandudno.

How could he have gotten it so wrong? He'd be the first to admit that he found women confusing and Christine more confusing than most. The truth was he should never have looked at her and as for marrying her . . . He sighed, scrubbing his hand across his jaw. It still rankled that she'd never told him her reason for walking out. One minute they were planning where they were going to spend their holiday and the next, he was staring at empty wardrobes and shoe racks. The letter she'd left had said everything and yet nothing. She'd refused to see him or even answer his calls and, to this day, he still didn't understand.

Replacing his glasses, he found the custody sergeant focused on him, one hand gripping the phone. He would have laughed at the thought of anyone taking notice of a balding headmaster, but he didn't find anything remotely funny about the current situation. It was beyond tragic. Ignoring him, he took off his raincoat and, folding it neatly in half, placed it on the seat beside him before glancing at his watch. As headmaster of an exclusive private secondary school, Sunday was his quietest day but he'd still be missed in the refectory at lunchtime. He sighed a second time. The deputy would be more than happy to step into his shoes. He was already nipping at his heels. This situation would only make it worse.

'Mr de Bertrand?'

The woman standing in the doorway was short and stocky, her dark hair ruthlessly dragged back from her face and secured in a thick plait. He didn't know what he'd been expecting but it certainly wasn't her.

'Actually, it's Dr. I thought he was going to take me to my . . . to see Christine?'

'That's not how it works . . . Dr. I'm Detective Constable Gaby Darin,' she said, her handshake firm. 'I've been in to check on Christine and she's fine but I'm afraid it's not possible for you to see her at present.' She gestured for him to follow. 'If you could come this way. I have a few questions.'

The room she took him to was small and windowless with only four chairs and a table. It was bare, characterless and cold, the walls painted a dull cream, the floor covered in some wood-effect lino. He sat down on the hard chair offered and wondered about Christine. Was this the type of room they had her holed up in with no home comforts and nothing to do except think? Were they trying to break her, to force her into some kind of confession? For all their differences, he knew murder wasn't something she'd ever be capable of, even under the most extreme of circumstances.

He shifted his head from where he'd been staring at the wall. 'So, why can't I see her? Surely that's against her human rights?' he said, leaning forward, his arms folded on top of the table, his eyes unwavering. He was used to dealing with all sorts in his job. In fact, part of his week was taken up with irate parents, underperforming teachers and recalcitrant students. Dealing with authoritarian civil servants was a sideways step as far as he was concerned.

'No. Her human rights are being taken care of just fine by the PACE Act of 1984,' Detective Darin said, offering him a thin smile.

'But what possible threat could there be in my seeing her?' he replied, tightening his jaw. 'I wouldn't expect to be left alone with her or anything.' He spread his fingers. 'It's not as if I'm smuggling anything in. You can search me, if you like.'

'Oh, don't be under any illusion that we wouldn't, Dr de Bertrand – search you, that is. No, the reason you, or indeed any of her family, friends or acquaintances, are unable to see her currently is because of the risks involved.' She leant back in her chair, crossing one leg over the other, her trouser leg riding up to reveal a glimpse of calf. 'While I'm sure you're a law-abiding citizen, we've been burnt by similar law-abiding citizens in the past. You wouldn't believe the tricks people get up to. As I've already said, I've been to check on your ex-wife and, apart from suffering from a bad case of boredom, she's fine.'

'Did she give you a message for me?'

She widened her gaze. 'No, and I'm afraid even if she had, I wouldn't pass it on in case it held some hidden message.'

'Oh, for God's sake.'

'I don't make the rules,' she said, lifting her palms. 'Now, while you're here, I'd like to ask you a few questions, if I may?' She only carried on at the sight of his slight nod. 'Is there anything you can tell us about Christine's relationship with her flatmate?'

He shook his head briefly, curling his hands into fists. 'No. Nothing.'

'Nothing because you don't want to assist us or nothing because—?'

'Nothing because I didn't even know she had a flatmate.'

'But she still asked us to call you to let you know she was in custody?' she said, her eyebrows arched.

'Yes, but . . . look, Detective, Christine and I have what's probably termed a difficult relationship. If it wasn't for needing help with Ruby, I probably wouldn't even have been told where she'd moved to.'

'Ruby?' she questioned, her pen hovering over her notebook.

'Our miniature schnauzer,' he said, almost laughing at the sight of her stiffened shoulders. He had enough on his plate already without having the added worry of a child. 'We agreed during the divorce that I'd have her. She's an anxious dog and leaving her for long periods of time while Christine went out to work wouldn't have been an option.'

'And when was the last time you saw your ex-wife?'

He picked his words carefully while he searched through his head for what to share of the last time he'd seen Christine. He'd run over that meeting many times because of the uneasy feeling that she hadn't been totally honest with him. He could have sworn by the way she'd examined his face, the deep flush on her cheeks, that she'd still had feelings for him and yet her words were a continual echo of how far their relationship had veered from those dizzy early days.

He cleared his throat. 'I had to go away to a conference in Brussels at the start of December so I dropped Ruby off for a few days. When I picked her up was the last time.'

'Okay.' He watched her jot something down on the corner of her pad, before lifting her head. 'This conference – it was in relation to . . .?'

'My job as headteacher of St Gildas Independent Boarding School.'

'Right. And how did you find your wife?'

'Pretty much the same as ever,' he said, trying not to think about the cloud of freshly washed hair and far too thin face. He'd thought then that she looked tired, under a strain of some sort but nothing that the detective needed to worry about. 'I didn't stay long. She'd already brought Ruby down. I don't know if you know much about dogs, but she was leaping all over us. Probably over-excited at having us back in the same room. The woman from the ground-floor flat came out to see what all the commotion was, and I left soon after. We haven't been in touch since.'

'Okay, thanks for that. We'll catch up with the neighbour later to see if she remembers your visit. So, that was the last time you were in touch?'

'Yes, apart from sending cards at Christmas and birthdays.'

She studied him for a moment, her face relaxing into the glimmer of a smile. 'I know this must be difficult but if there's anything else you can tell us about Christine that would have an impact on the investigation and perhaps help her . . .?'

'There's nothing to tell. She's the most mild-mannered of people. I don't understand what could have happened but I'm one hundred per cent sure she's not guilty.'

The detective underscored something twice on her pad before continuing. 'You've probably seen the newspaper headlines this morning. Care to comment?'

'If you're asking me if she's gay then it's an emphatic no.' He pushed away from the table and stood to his feet.

'Please sit down, Dr de Bertrand.'

'Why? Am I under arrest or something?'

'No, you're free to go. But I had thought you'd like to assist us in finding the truth,' she said, not breaking eye contact. 'If there's any information that you think might have an impact on our investigation, I do suggest that now's the time to tell us.'

He sat down abruptly, brushing his hand over his head, his bright blue eyes steady. 'I can't even begin to guess at what happened but the one thing I do know is that Christine would never . . . She's not gay, all right. We had a very healthy sex life and there was no suggestion, ever, that she didn't enjoy being with me.'

'What about other men?'

'Excuse me?'

'Other men either before, during or after your relationship broke up?'

He opened his mouth to speak only to close it again but not before dragging air into his lungs from the suddenly claustrophobic room. While he could fully understand why the question needed to be asked, it was still a kick in the ribs. He wasn't completely sure how or why their marriage had descended into the final farce of those last few weeks but those dark days, the worst days of his life, weren't something he could discuss. One minute he'd thought himself the luckiest man alive and the next . . . the next he'd been deserted and facing a letter from her solicitor seeking an immediate divorce due to 'irreconcilable differences'. He still had no idea what those differences could be but it was laughable to think that another party was involved. Surely, he'd have known. Surely, he'd have sensed some change but there'd been nothing to indicate she was anything other than blissfully happy.

'I can't answer about before we got together but, to the very best of my knowledge, she was faithful throughout our marriage,' he finally replied. 'And, before you ask—' he removed a folded handkerchief from his pocket and started to polish his glasses '— so was I. As to other men, after we separated and then divorced . . . who knows. But by then she was entitled to sleep with anyone she liked, and I certainly wouldn't have been someone she'd have contacted with a list of her conquests. She knew how I felt and the one thing she's not is deliberately cruel.'

'You say you knew how she felt – how did the separation make you feel?' she said, staring down at his hands and where he'd balled them around the arms of his glasses.

He extended his fingers before replacing his glasses on his nose and his handkerchief back in his pocket. 'Devastated, if you must know, not that it has any bearing on anything. As far as I was aware our life was good, better than most. We both loved life at the school. There's a great satisfaction in watching how children can blossom and grow in the correct environment.'

'I'm sure. So your wife is a teacher too?'

'Yes. She taught history to the senior boys before our divorce.'

'I'll be frank with you, Mr de Bertrand. The thing that's puzzling me is, if your marriage was so perfect and there wasn't another party involved, why the break-up?'

'Sorry, your guess is as good as mine – that's the one thing she refused to discuss.'

She settled her pen down on top of her notebook and shifted back in her chair. 'Okay, that'll be it for now. We're about to release the name of the victim to the media but you'll know it already,' she said, standing to her feet.

'Actually, that's where you're wrong, Detective. As I said earlier, I didn't even know she had a flatmate so how on earth would I know her name? While I sent Chrissie cards, to keep the lines of communication open, she didn't acknowledge them. She could have stuffed her flat to the brim with all and sundry and I'd have been none the wiser.'

'No, only one. A Miss Nikki Jones,' she said, her look intense. 'A former student of yours, I believe, Dr?'

Chapter 6

Nikki

2008
Cambridge

Coming to Cambridge University was both the best and worst of decisions.

Nikki hoiked her rucksack up her back and straightened her shoulders, her attention on the large expanse of grass ahead. She was either brave or stupid to think she could cope with the added strain of attending such a prestigious college. But despite her misgivings and yesterday's five-hour train journey, she'd managed to get this far.

Pulling out the slip of paper from her pocket, for what seemed like the millionth time, she read the directions to the lecture theatre. If she had the nerve, she'd ask one of the other many students bustling around – by the look of them, they all knew where they were going. Her ignorance was mainly down to her reluctance to attend Fresher's Week. But for someone like her – with all her insecurities – that was never going to happen, her hand instinctively pulling her sleeve down over her wrist. Heaving a sigh, she peered at the red-brick building laid out in front of her before making her way back to the entrance and the porter's lodge. It would mean she'd be late, the one thing she'd been trying to avoid, but that couldn't be helped.

'Hello there, you look a bit lost. Can I be of any assistance?'

She glanced up from the slip of paper into the face of the kind-looking man hovering in front of her and let out a sigh of relief even as colour stole up her cheeks. She wasn't used to people noticing her – in fact, she went out of her way not to put herself forward in any given situation. But getting a place here was a new start. She had to draw a line under— No. She had to draw a line through the past just as she had to escape from under her mother's clutches. This was a new beginning.

'Yes, thank you. I'm totally lost. I'm looking for . . . the Classics Department.' She stared down at the paper again, missing his look of amusement. 'Lecture theatre three.'

'Ah, what a coincidence. I'm heading that way. I still remember what it was like on my first day too but that daunting feeling soon passes. Give it a couple of days and you'll be a dab hand at finding your way about. I'm Dr de Bertrand, by the way, one of the course lecturers, so you'll be bumping into me in one way or the other over the next three years,' he continued, raising his left eyebrow.

'I'm Nikki, Nicola Jones.'

'Well, Miss Jones, welcome to Cambridge University and St Augusta's College in particular.' He walked around the circular lawn to the side of the campus and the building straight in front of them. 'We're tucked out of the way here, near the library,' he said, pushing open the door and gesturing for her to go on ahead. 'Mostly the rest of the college leave us to our own devices – something we're very happy with.' He led her down a long corridor only to pause outside a pair of wide-double doors. 'This is where I take my leave, but I'll see you inside shortly.' He offered her another smile before turning on his heels and moving through the next door, which had 'Private' etched in gold letters.

Nikki lifted her head, the round handle smooth under her fingertips, her thoughts in panic mode.

Here goes nothing. The first day of the rest of my life.

Chapter 7

Gaby

Sunday 10 May, 10 a.m. St Asaph Police Station

There was something father-like in the tall, thin man in charge of the squad room. DCI Sherlock was an old-school copper with old-fashioned values and a way about him that had all his staff jumping over more fences than the average gymkhana. Gaby would do anything for him except perhaps *willingly* give up her long awaited first weekend off in three months.

Despite being 10 a.m. on a Sunday morning, the incident room was busy, busier than a usual weekday. Gaby settled in her chair, smiling across at her friend, Amy Potter, who'd accompanied her when she'd left her job in Swansea and joined the North Wales MIT. She raised her eyebrows at the sight of her new hairstyle. Amy changed her look almost as often as her top and today her hair – which last week had been captured back off her face in a sleek ballerina bun – flowed down her back in a slick of honey-blonde. Of Owen Bates, there was no sign, his toddler having fallen foul of the norovirus rampaging through North Wales.

'Thank you everyone for coming in on your weekend. We'll try and make it up to you,' DCI Sherlock said, picking a stray bit of fluff from his trousers before placing his hands in his pockets. 'As most of you will now be aware, following the headlines in the evening newspaper, we have a murder to solve. DC Darin will be meeting with the next-of-kin straight after this briefing for a formal identification but we're pretty certain that it's thirty-year-old Nikki Jones. We also have a woman being held in the custodial suite helping us with our enquiries.' He scanned the room, his gaze landing on each of them in turn. 'On the face of it, it looks cut and dried but, as we know from other investigations, that may not be the case. Before I hand you over to DC Darin, please remember that we need this cleared up quickly – we could very well have a murderer on the loose.'

Gaby stood and made her way to the front of the room, well aware that all eyes were following her progress. This was the first time she'd overseen a case, but she wasn't scared, far from it. After all, this was what she'd been working towards, all those years pounding the beat in Liverpool. Even the disastrous couple of years in Cardiff and those months in Swansea hadn't deterred her from her goal. Okay, so it didn't look that exciting an investigation to cut her teeth on. Everyone, including her, believed the woman they were holding was as guilty as hell. But presumed guilt meant little. It was her responsibility to back up each theory with clear-cut facts and it was the responsibility of her colleagues, currently shuffling in their seats, to help.

'Firstly, I'm well aware that this is Sunday so I'll be brief. As you all know by now Nikki Jones was discovered dead in the bed of her flatmate, Christine de Bertrand, early yesterday. Owen and I interviewed de Bertrand in the presence of her solicitor before she transferred across to the custodial suite. She's a thirty-year-old special needs teacher who suffers from profound hearing loss – she's also denying all knowledge of how the victim ended up dead in her bed.'

'It was probably a lovers' tiff,' DC Malachy Devine said with a sneer. 'Not that I know anything about the inner workings of a lesbian's mind.'

'There's always at least one insensitive jerk on any team – you're it,' interrupted DCI Sherlock, glaring at him from the other side of the room. 'And it's that kind of attitude that will have us up in front of the IOPC if we're not careful. We're going to have enough problems with the media as it is without our own work colleagues adding to the gossipmongers. You should know by now, Devine, that the sexual orientation of the parties involved is immaterial to anything except the actual investigation. Have you all got that?' He folded his arms across his chest before firing a look at Gaby. 'Carry on, Detective.'

'Thank you, sir,' she said, her smile fading. She'd known as soon as she'd walked onto the crime scene how it looked – she was beginning to think that Sherlock hadn't been doing her any favours in choosing her to act as lead.

'We're still waiting for Dr Mulholland to perform the autopsy but it looks like a single stab wound to the heart,' she added, pressing her hand to the centre of her chest for effect. 'De Bertrand was examined by the police doctor on arrival at the station and was found to be covered in blood from the back of her neck right down to her heels but, surprisingly, none on her front. There was also none visible on her hands, probably down to her washing them before the police were called to the scene. She even admits having done so in her statement. Either way, it's unlikely that she'd have been able to remove all traces, if indeed there was any blood in the first place – her nail clippings will give us the definitive answer we need.' She walked to the first in a line of whiteboards pinned to the wall, tapping the mugshot photo of Christine de Bertrand with her knuckles.

'De Bertrand claims to have gone to bed with an unidentified man she met the night before, and that she has no idea how Nikki ended up between her sheets instead. So, on the face of it, we have a straightforward case of de Bertrand murdering her flatmate and somehow trumping up a story about a tall dark stranger. But as we all know appearances count for very little in our game. We need to dismantle her statement, lie by lie or, alternatively, find the man if he exists.' She snapped her notebook shut before replacing it in the pocket of her jacket. 'We have some outstanding issues, not least of which is the murder weapon: a blade of some sort. Hopefully, Dr Mulholland will be able to give us more details tomorrow so that we can narrow the search but it's imperative that we find it. I have a couple of PCs trawling through the rubbish bins and hedges in the surrounding area as I speak. Another biggie, is the fact that Christine de Bertrand is adamant she went to bed with a man and woke up with a woman.' She lifted her head, sliding her eyes over to DC Devine. 'I have to say that I disbelieve her. It's the kind of ridiculous, jumped up excuse that the guilty use to muddy the waters for us hard-working detectives. One of the first things we need to do is ascertain the truth of that statement,' she said, keeping her expression unaltered at the sight of his fancy gold cufflinks peeking out from the sleeve of what looked to be another new suit.

She felt far from easy about the detective, mainly because of the size of his disposable income. Bent coppers were a reality and one she would not tolerate. After what had happened in Cardiff and the way she'd been drummed out of the area for flagging her concerns about a team member on the take, she was probably being oversensitive. There could be a hundred and one honest reasons for Detective Devine's apparently healthy bank balance – something she'd best remember.

'Mal, de Bertrand claims to have been out drinking with a Kelly James. I have the address but not her telephone number, as de Bertrand's mobile appears to be missing, but it should be easy enough to track down.' She tore a sheet from the back of her notebook and handed it to him before turning to the woman seated on his left.

Marie Morgan always seemed to put her at a disadvantage with her carefully styled blonde hair and model looks. Even today, on her weekend off, she'd still appeared in the office within twenty minutes of being called and without a hair out of place. It had only taken Gaby a couple of days to realise that she was also a hard-working grassroots detective willing to put in the hours that the job demanded.

'Marie, I'd like you to chase up what the CSI team found in the flat. Both girls had laptops for a start and then there's all those birthday cards dotted about. I want every one of them traced back to the sender. I also need you to get cracking on all the CCTV cameras from Mostyn Street to the West Shore,' she said, handing her a small 10x10 photo of Christine. 'We may be lucky but, you know as well as I do that a good image from any one of these is as rare as hen's teeth. To be honest, I'm more interested in any information about the man she's meant to have taken home, if indeed he exists. All she can remember is that he was tall and had dark hair, which is little help.'

Gaby moved back, resting her hip against the edge of the table. She'd made a comprehensive list in the front of her notebook of all the key points she wanted to say but she was determined not to refer to it for a second time. Having an orderly mind, she'd annotated each task as a numbered bullet point, and she knew which she'd yet to discuss.

She turned her stare back on DC Devine, hoping against hope that he wasn't going to be a thorn in her side during the investigation. She'd already given him one job. Now she was interested in seeing how he'd perform under pressure – there was no room for wasters in the department. 'In addition to interviewing the friend, Mal, I need you to interview the occupants of the two other flats in de Bertrand's building,' she said, before switching her attention to DC Jax Williams. Jax was the newest member of the team, his keener than keen answering grin showing none of the disillusionment that Malachy and the older members of the group displayed. 'I do hope you have a warm coat, Williams, and a liking for all things furry?'

'Ma'am?'

'As we all know from the numerous complaints with regards to dog excrement, the West Shore is a haven for all things on four legs and a little birdie has tweeted in my ear that it's the place to go for Saturday morning walkies,' she said, struggling not to laugh at the sudden downward curve of his mouth. 'I want it to be your number one priority to haunt that shore from 6 a.m. onwards so that we can catch up with as many of the dog owners as possible and see if they saw anything odd. Keeping on the birdie theme, we'll be killing two of them off at once as I'm hopeful that a police presence will have a positive impact on the number of complaints.' She picked up her mobile from where she'd placed it on the table in front of her and tucked it into her jacket pocket, her voice not showing any of the relief that was flowing through her veins.

'We'll reconvene here midday Monday following the autopsy.'

Chapter 8

Paul

Sunday 10 May, 11.55 a.m. Oswestry

Christine's parents lived in Oswestry, a quaint market town on the English/Welsh border that was far enough away for the local media frenzy to pass them by but not too far for Paul to avoid breaking the news in person.

Pulling up outside their house was an exercise in restraint – restraint because of the memories that threatened to breach the defences Paul had erected since their divorce. Divorce wasn't easy at the best of times, but he'd liked Christine's parents, not only because they were his in-laws. Their relationship had been far deeper than the usual and one he missed to this day. By contacting him, albeit through a police officer, his ex-wife had tasked him with breaking the very worst of news.

He tried not to allow his mind to dwell on the glow of hope that burnt bright within his chest at the thought that she'd chosen him. While he wouldn't admit it to anyone but himself, he'd always assumed there was another man waiting in the wings ready to step into his shoes. How was he now meant to behave in the knowledge that she'd dumped him for no other reason than she could? He'd always known he was too old and stuffy for her effervescent, bubbly personality, an opinion which was shared by the boys at the school. He'd have pulled them up on their comments about *how old de Bertrand has managed to pull such a dolly bird* if he hadn't believed that, on some level, they were right.

He opened the back door of the car, much to the excitement of Ruby who'd spent the last couple of hours cooped up on the back seat with only her rug for company. 'Come on, girl, they always had a soft spot for you and hopefully it will help to break the ice somewhat.' He ruffled her head before attaching her lead, watching in amusement as she headed for the nearest lamppost.

The gate creaked when he pushed it, the paint peeling under his hand and, stepping back, he noted the changes to the property with a frown. The outside of the pebble dash family home had a general air of neglect with crooked gutters and missing tiles. In the old days, he'd have spent a week of his summer holidays pottering about, happy for once to get his hands dirty with the type of work he rarely had a chance to immerse himself in. The school was well-maintained by a small team of handymen and gardeners and he was barely allowed to prune a rose before someone or other interfered.

The long ping of the doorbell was swiftly followed by the sound of a door closing and, after a couple of seconds, he found himself face-to-face with his ex-father-in-law for the first time in almost two years. Paul's first thought was that he'd aged; his white wispy hair barely a memory, the skin on his face mottled and careworn. But, give him his due, Dennis, after a brief stare, recovered enough to draw him into a swift embrace.

'Oh, my boy, it's been too long, and Ruby,' he said, dropping his hand for the dog to sniff. 'Come on in, Hazel is just boiling the kettle.' He gestured for him to follow. 'You sit yourself down in the lounge and I'll go and warn the missus.' He paused on the threshold, his smile apologetic. 'You know what she's like – seeing you after so long, while welcome, is going to be a shock.'

The lounge was as he remembered with the same cream-striped wallpaper and large three-piece suite that Hazel and Dennis had owned for as long as he'd known them. Even the TV was the same and with what could have been the same snooker match on the screen. If it wasn't snooker it was either football or tennis, depending on the season and whichever one of them managed to snaffle the remote first. His mouth pulled into the semblance of a smile, his attention drawn to the mantelpiece and the display of family photos lined up between a pair of silver candlesticks and an old mahogany clock that always ran ten minutes fast no matter how many times they adjusted it. But he wasn't thinking of either clocks or candlesticks at that precise moment, his gaze flowing from one photo to the next, each one displaying Christine in a variety of poses. A little black and white snap of her lying stretched out in her pram. Her first day at school, a toothy grin displaying a distinct absence of front teeth. At her prom, her glorious hair stacked up high, dangly earrings catching the light. And finally, a photo he hadn't expected. A photo that stopped him in his tracks, a deep sadness swamping all sense, thought and feeling. Picking up the frame, he stared down at the couple captured for all time, the sight of their laughing faces almost too much to bear. Their wedding day. A day he'd never thought would come to him. He was years older than Christine, a good ten, and completely set in his ways but one look into those electric-blue eyes and it was like he'd been kicked in the stomach. He could almost imagine himself back in the sun-drenched courtyard, dappled late afternoon light filtering though the bougainvillea-filled trellises, the only noise the chink of champagne glasses, the only smell the slight echo of her scent – a scent he couldn't bear to smell even now. Her face. Her beautiful face, framed with fiery red hair dripping in ringlets, the colour emphasised – if that was possible – by the pure white of her gown. He could almost feel the silky tresses running across his skin.

Placing the frame down, he nudged it back in place with a fingertip, his frown reappearing. Where had that love disappeared to? It was the very last emotion radiating down his spine and causing his hands to ball into fists. Hate was the only word suitable to describe what he was feeling now. If he could, he'd wrap his hands around her lovely neck for what she'd done to him. They said that love and hate were opposite sides of the same coin . . .

The rattle of the inevitable tea tray dragged him back from the past, a deep blush splayed across his cheeks at the direction of his thoughts and, with a shake of his head, he strode across the room to take the tray from his ex-mother-in-law's hands. She couldn't quite return his smile, something that saddened him. He'd prided himself on the relationship he'd forged with her parents and, at the risk of sounding trite, he viewed them as friends more than anything – friends who now had difficulty meeting his eye.

'Well, this is all very nice. On your way back to that school of yours?' Dennis said with a cheerful grin. 'We've missed your little visits, haven't we, Hazel?'

Hazel remained silent, all her energy taken up with pouring out cups of tea and passing round the sugar bowl.

Paul gripped onto his drink, trying to pull his thoughts together; he'd obviously overestimated his ability to both start and end difficult conversations. As headmaster, challenging conversations were the norm and not the exception. He'd lost count of the number he'd had with both staff and parents, but it was the awkward discussions with pupils that hurt the most, especially those where the end result was always going to be either suspension or expulsion.

Clearing his throat, he rested his cup back on the coffee table and gestured for them both to take a seat. 'Dennis, Hazel . . . my dears. I have something to tell you, something you're not going to like. Something that's so far from the realms of normal, as to be nonsensical.' He stopped speaking, taking the cowardly way out by staring down at Ruby's head where she was snuffling in the middle of some rabbit-filled dream or other. 'Christine has been involved in an altercation at her flat. She's okay but . . . but the police seem to think that she might have been involved in the death of her flatmate. I know it's ridiculous but until this mess is sorted, she's being detained at St Asaph police station.'

'They've arrested her?' Dennis interrupted, taking hold of Hazel's hand as if his life depended on it.

He lifted his head. 'Not exactly. More like detained her while she assists them with their enquiries,' he said, looking at their interlaced fingers. 'She asked me to come – to explain, but I wasn't allowed to see her or anything.' He lifted his cup to his lips, eyeing them both over the rim. 'I know it's been a shock – a shock for all of us – but there must be some simple explanation. I'll make us another drink while we talk about it.'

One mug led to two and a gentle request to stay for lunch, something he couldn't really spare the time for but, instead of repeating one of his standard excuses, he found himself reaching for his phone and calling Noel Barnes, his deputy. Sitting in the painfully familiar south-facing dining room, with views over the back garden, he could be forgiven for thinking that some magical force had turned back the hand of time but it only took one look at his ex-mother-in-law's wary expression to realise that some things were impossible. He placed the fork on the centre of his plate, unable to eat another bite, determined like never before to get some answers to the questions that had been tripping him up ever since she'd walked out.

Taking a breath, he fixed on her face, his jaw clenched. 'The one thing I can promise is Christine's innocence. Despite everything that's happened between us, I think you can still probably guess that my feelings haven't changed.' He stopped, swallowing the lump that had suddenly appeared and when he continued, his voice had fallen a key. 'There's no way she'd be party to any of the stuff the gutter press will probably accuse her of and I'm sticking by her until she's freed – whether she likes it or not.'

He sat back in his chair only to lean forward again as he intercepted a look between them, a look which had him press his hands flat against the table. 'What is it? What aren't you telling me?'

'We can't . . . it's not our place—'

'Oh, for heaven's sake, Hazel, if you know of something that might help, it's your duty to say.'

'It's not what you think, Paul.'

'How the hell do you know what I'm thinking?' He ran his hand over his head. 'Look, I'm sorry, all right. I have no right . . . It's—'

'It's just that you love her as much as we do, son.' Dennis wrapped his arm around Hazel's shoulder, hugging her tight. 'This travesty has gone on for far too long, love. It's about time he finally knew the truth.'

He couldn't leave them straightaway. If he was being honest, he had trouble leaving them at all. They were lost, the pair of them, like he was lost.

He unlocked the car and opened the back door for Ruby before settling in his seat, a wave of tiredness enveloping him. Just when had he become the grown-up? He'd known instinctively that they'd turn to him in the same way they'd turned to him in the past but, for the first time, he had no answers to their questions. It wasn't a case of calling out the plumber or electrician anymore. Now they were in the big league and he no more knew what to do than they did. He'd promised them that he'd keep in touch, the only positive thing that had come from the meeting.

Pressing the ignition, he started the car, his brow wrinkling. There'd been something nagging him since the divorce – something gnawing away at both his self-confidence and faith in humanity. He'd expected awkwardness in this, their first meeting. After all he had no idea what fairy-tales Christine had told about the break-up of their marriage. She could have made up all sorts of stories to disguise the truth. But the one thing he'd never felt was uncomfortable around them. He'd worked hard in the beginning to gain their acceptance. He had no illusions that they'd thought him too old and, as her tutor, probably not the most suitable of individuals for their daughter's hand. But he'd thought all that was in the past.

Glancing over his shoulder, he checked that the road was clear before pulling out. The one thing he'd never have guessed at in a month of Sunday's was the truth. His chest heaved at the futility of the situation because now it was immaterial. She obviously hadn't loved him enough to trust him and, with her decision, they'd all lost. Him, Ruby and Christine.

Chapter 9

Gaby

Sunday 10 May, 4 p.m. St Asaph Hospital

Gaby was hoping for at least Sunday afternoon off if only to sort out her washing. But, with half the force still off sick and the other half trying to cope with the sudden influx of work, she was the only one free for what was viewed as one of the most unpleasant jobs of all – accompanying the next-of-kin when they went to ID the body.

Slamming her car door shut, she walked round to one of the many side entrances to the hospital, this one marked private, all the time trying to remember if she had a clean white shirt hanging up in her wardrobe for her interview tomorrow. But, after the Saturday from hell, she couldn't even remember if she had any teabags left let alone the state of her ironing pile, and teabags were far more important than whether she had to wear the same shirt two days on the trot. Her expression altered at the direction of her thoughts, a wave of guilt flooding her face with colour. Even now, a grieving mother was sitting in the pathology department, trying to pluck up the courage to perform a task that no parent should ever be asked to carry out. Her troubles were minor in comparison. She'd make do – it wouldn't be the first time.

She stopped on the threshold, putting a hand up to her trade-mark plait, tied off with a coordinating navy band to match her trouser suit, before glancing down at her watch. She should have been off duty hours ago, but these things couldn't be rushed. People's grief couldn't be managed like a MacDonald's drive-through and she'd be here for as long as it took. She couldn't remember how many viewings she'd been present at now, which probably said a lot – certainly more than ten but probably less than twenty. At a guess, she'd hazard eighteen. Eighteen lives lost – eighteen lives too many. Some old. Some young but, whatever the age of the victim, it was always the survivors that hurt the most. She grimaced, her hand reaching out to push the door open. Of all the jobs she had to do, this was the one she found most difficult.

The autopsy viewing suite at the hospital was situated in the basement, well out of the way of the day-to-day patient-focused activities. No one wanted to think about what happened in these rooms and that included her. But a depressing environment for such a depressing task didn't help and Gaby couldn't complain at the welcome she'd received or indeed the facilities – the hospital had done its best with the limited resources available. The waiting room, with plush blue fabric sofas and coordinating sea-themed walls was nice enough, not that anyone would be interested in interior decorating at a time like this.

The woman sitting in front of her was a surprise and Gaby had to struggle not to raise both eyebrows at the neutral expression and orange face that had been baked to an overripe grape in the hot Spanish sun. Penny Jones-Steadman wasn't what she'd been expecting with her tight white jeans and body-hugging T-shirt, the picture of a leopard emblazoned across the front, the ears and nose carefully picked out in glittering sequins. The shoes were six-inch spikes in red with nail varnish and lipstick to match. Gaby noted the contrast between her plain suit and low-heeled loafers in a coordinating shade of navy with a heavy sigh. While she liked clothes and loved shoes with a passion, she'd never have the nerve to wear anything so blatant even with her recent two-stone weight loss. Perhaps she should start?

'Thank you for flying over at such short notice,' she said, a brief smile on her lips, her attention on the expression flickering across Nikki's mother's face. 'It shouldn't take long. They'll bring your daughter into the viewing room next door.' She hesitated, taking time to choose her next words carefully. 'I feel I must point out the temperature.'

'I always feel the cold here so it's not going to make a blind bit of difference,' Mrs Jones-Steadman said, wrapping her arms around her middle.

'No, I don't mean about the room. It's your daughter. If you feel the need to touch her . . . I must warn you that she'll feel . . . cold.'

Mrs Jones-Steadman stared; her lips compressed into a thin line. 'I get the picture. Let's get it over and done with, shall we?'

The viewing room was another place where the fundraisers had been busy. While essentially a bland square box of a room, it was painted in calming yellows, which toned in with the tongue and groove ceiling and wooden flooring. There was even a flower arrangement in the corner, a recent addition since the last time she'd had to attend. No one could make this any easier, but the staff did what they could under the circumstances.

They'd laid Nikki out on a hospital trolley, one of those expensive stainless-steel hydraulic ones that raised and lowered at the push of a button. The pathology porters had wheeled her body into the wooden frame, masked with yellow curtains, that was a permanent fixture in the centre of the room. So, in effect, it looked as if she'd laid down on her bed for a rest. The only part visible was her head resting on a pillow, a yellow counterpane pulled up to her chin.

'That's her.'

'Excuse me?'

'I said, that's my daughter.' She pulled the door open. 'Is that all, or is there anything else you want from me?'

'Oh, right.' Gaby shot a brief look across at Nikki before following her mother back into the seating area. Of all the viewings she'd attended this had to be the shortest. Her thoughts returned to the last time she'd been here, to the fisherman's wife, almost prostrate with grief. Despite working in the force since she was a teenager, she'd never understand what made people tick and, staring at the bitter expression on Penny Jones-Steadman's face, she didn't particularly want to learn.

'I need you to sign here,' she said after a brief pause, gesturing to the form she'd prepared earlier. It was obvious the usual platitudes were meaningless to someone like Nikki's mother and without them she was at a loss. There was no emotion expressed and no wish to prolong the identification. Gaby couldn't begin to work out what must be going on in her head and that more than anything puzzled her.

'I'm not sure when we'll be able to have the body released for burial . . .'

'Well, you have my contact details in Málaga,' Penny replied, groping round in the bottom of her bag for a pen. 'I'm heading to Manchester shortly – I don't want to miss my flight.'

You don't want to miss your flight? Don't you care at all? But instead all Gaby said was, 'What time do you have to be at the airport? I can give you a lift if you like.'

'Only if it's not out of your way?'

'No, it's the least we can do after having dragged you all this way. My car's in the unloading bay next to the entrance.'

She pulled her keys from her pocket, careful not to leave the signed declaration behind. She didn't want to drive the two-hour-plus round trip to Manchester, but she felt she had little choice, not if she was to find out any more about Nikki.

The roads were empty for a change, which was the only positive thing Gaby could take from the trip. So much for her dedication to the force, she scowled, remembering both the teabag and shirt situation that had yet to be resolved.

'So, how long have you lived in Spain, Mrs Jones-Steadman?'

'Call me Penny. Steadman and Jones were my ex-husbands' names, therefore ones I can do without hearing every couple of sentences,' she said, ruffling her hair with her hands. 'I moved when Nikki was eighteen so twelve years now.'

'And were you in regular contact with your daughter?'

'Do you have children, Officer?' Penny turned in her seat to glare at her.

'No. Not yet.'

'Well, it's hard to sit there condemning me when you don't know what I've been through with that girl.'

Gaby eyed her briefly before returning her attention to the road ahead. 'Why don't you tell me? Anything, any background about the – about your daughter that might help the investigation would be very welcome.'

'I'm probably not the best person to ask. I haven't heard from her apart from the odd text in well over a year.' She flipped the visor down, checking her hair in the mirror before continuing. 'If I didn't have the dogs to look after it would be a lot easier, but I can't leave them for more than a night or two.'

'Do you have many pets then?' Gaby said, sliding her another look.

'About a hundred.' She laughed at the obvious look of dismay on Gaby's face. 'There's no need to drop me off at the nearest funny farm, Officer. I run a dog sanctuary. There are lots of dogs abandoned in that part of the world and I try and do what I can to fill the gap.'

'Really? That sounds amazing but hard work, I'm guessing. Did Nikki give you a hand when she used to visit?'

'That would be difficult.'

'Why's that?'

'Because she never visited. Travelling wasn't really her thing. In fact, I can't remember if she ever travelled outside the UK.'

'That's unusual these days.'

'Yes, well, Nikki was nothing if not unusual.'

'In what way?'

'In every way miss – er, sorry. I can't remember your name?'

'Darin. Gaby Darin.'

'Well, Gaby, is it normal to spend all day sitting in front of the television eating to the extent that you get so fat you can't even get up out of your chair?'

But surely not recently, Gaby thought, switching on the wiper blades to clean the windscreen. Nikki certainly hadn't been fat when she'd seen her lying across Christine's bed. If anything, she'd been thin, far too thin. Obviously, something had happened for her to decide to change her life in such a dramatic fashion. But she'd had the wherewithal to get a job, a job she wouldn't have been able to hold down if she'd refused to move from her chair. She flicked on the indicator before pulling over into the next lane, thoughts pinging in all directions. What could have been the motive for the attack or was it as simple as the newspapers were saying, a love affair gone wrong? Maybe Christine had decided to go back to her husband only for Nikki to go berserk, the blade puncturing her chest in the ensuing struggle.

She continued driving in silence, playing out all the possible death scenarios in her mind as if watching a cine-camera stuck on fast-forward. But none of them seemed to fit. There was something about the case that didn't make sense – the only problem was she had no idea which part.

'What about when she was younger?' she finally said. 'Her dad, for instance?'

'She adored her father. Like two peas in a pod they were. When he walked out it felt as if she'd joined him – she did in spirit,' Penny said, her fingernails beating a silent tattoo against her thigh. 'They were always planning something, whispering in corners. I wasn't surprised when he found someone else, our marriage had been dead for years but for him to do that to Nikki . . . I could never forgive him for that and, when I remarried shortly after, Nikki hated my new husband. She hated school and she hated me. She blamed me for everything, her only solace the bottom of a biscuit tin. By the time she'd finished her A levels and managed to win a scholarship to that fancy university, we'd well and truly had enough of each other.'

Gaby stared into the distance, the lights of Manchester clearly illuminated on the horizon. What must Nikki have been feeling, deserted by both parents when they went on to new partners. A troubled young woman left to flounder in the world. She'd like to know about the intervening years since she'd left college. What had she done? Where had she been? By the antipathy seeping out of the woman at her side, she knew she'd have to look elsewhere.

'What about the school? Couldn't they do something?'

'You're having a laugh. The school was useless. Look, Gaby, you can judge me all you like but the truth of the matter is that my daughter was dysfunctional. Oh, she was bright, perhaps too bright for her own good, but without the common sense she needed to survive in this rat hole of an existence. I tried everything to help but she kept pushing me away and there's only so much a parent can take.' She lifted her bag onto her lap and started searching for her passport and ticket. 'You'll never know how much I regret failing my daughter, but Nikki was on her own path to destruction long before I decided to move to Spain.'

Chapter 10

Gaby

Monday 11 May, 9.20 a.m. St Asaph Hospital

Gaby should have known that her Monday was going to be worse than usual. The autopsy had been scheduled for eight o'clock, while the teabags and the white blouse issue had yet to be resolved. But, not only that, there'd been a pile-up along the A55, which entailed a long detour in addition to an emergency stop to fill up the car. Despite her interview lined up for later, she could just about manage wearing the blue frilly blouse with lace ruffle at the collar and cuffs instead of one of her plain work ones but driving on thin air was, as yet, outside of her current level of expertise.

She ran along the dingy corridor to the autopsy suite, situated in the bowels of the state-of-the-art hospital. The untidiness of the place never ceased to amaze her. While the front-of-house reception area looked immaculate, obviously the NHS budget didn't run to spending much-needed money on areas that weren't routinely available to the public.

Before pulling open the door, she glanced down at her service-able wristwatch but whichever way she looked at it, she was late – the one thing she couldn't abide in others. And it was bound to be another black mark against her by the caustic pathologist.

Grabbing a gown and pair of blue paper-thin overshoes she hurried into the lab, offering a brief apology as she went.

'I wouldn't expect anything different, DC Darin,' Rusty Mulholland said, barely lifting his head as he carried on rummaging around in the now open abdomen.

Gaby felt colour flood her cheeks but not from embarrassment. After losing her weekend and most of last night, she was in the mood for an argument. The only thing stopping her from telling him exactly what he could do with the mass of intestines he was currently placing on the weighing scales, was the presence of the mortuary assistant and pathology porter. She ground her teeth, curling her nails into her palms as an added precaution. No. She'd bide her time until they were alone before letting rip. To speak to her like that in the presence of his colleagues was one step too far even for him. He must be the most pompous arrogant know-it-all it had ever been her misfortune to meet but to tell him would mean an all-out war and she had no intention of starting something she didn't have the time to finish.

Instead of replying, she heaved a couple of deep sighing breaths, forcing herself to look at something other than the tall, gowned figure hunched over the trolley in the centre of the room.

As rooms went it was nothing like the glamorous autopsy suites normally seen on television. Here there was no fancy overhead lighting or theatre-like equipment. The walls were painted a drab grey as was the floor, with one length of wall given to industrial stainless-steel sinks with shelves above. There was even a toilet in one corner for the disposal of bodily fluids it was far too early in the morning for Gaby to even contemplate. She dropped her eyes to the drain, which split the floor in two, before shifting them upwards and to the trolley. Autopsies were messy businesses and, unlike operating theatres where everything had to be sterile, this was all about protecting the staff from the risks involved in cutting open a dead body. Instead of healing the sick, their remit was one of pure discovery. Each body had a tale to tell, and it was up to the chief pathologist to pull together the fragments until the story was complete.

She turned her head away from the large Y-shaped excision that extended from the centre of each shoulder blade to just south of the navel, and back to the victim's head, her hair contained in a paper hat. It was hard during procedures like this to remember that, only a couple of days ago, Nikki had been a living, breathing person and not the mass of blood, tissue and bone currently splayed out in front of her. Death had no dignity assigned to it, especially when it was part of an active investigation. Her colleagues simply did what they had to – solving the crime was key.

As in any other profession there were good and bad staff that made up a team and, no matter how much she disliked him, she couldn't argue that Rusty wasn't good at his job. She watched as he spread the skin back over the abdominal cavity to line up the blade entry site against the perforation of what looked like the heart. There was no need for him to be quite so gentle or quite so diligent in preserving Nikki's dignity with a green sheet carefully positioned over the lower part of her body. But that was him all over. Kindness personified to the dead, less so with the living.

After another half an hour or so of excavating the inside of the abdomen, Rusty stepped away from the table and removed his gloves. His heavy-duty apron, gown and goggles came next, swiftly followed by his rubber overshoes. Heading to the first sink, he covered his hands with copious amounts of pink Hibiscrub.

'Thank you, Dean and Ollie, for your assistance. I'll leave you to close,' he said, pulling off his microphone and switching off the wall-mounted voice recorder.

She stood watching, her hands clasped in front of her, her eyes boring a hole into his back. It felt as if she was invisible, which wasn't a feeling she was comfortable with. She didn't know what it was about him but as soon as she walked into a room, all she got was his stony face and the sharp edge of his tongue. It wouldn't be so bad if he saved up his snappy comments for when they were alone, but people had started to comment and after all, what could she say? It wasn't as if they'd fallen out or anything. She'd never spent enough time in his company to know the first thing about him and, given the way he treated her, she had no intention of changing that.

'I suppose you'd like to hear what my findings are, DC Darin, especially as you missed the preliminaries?' he said, beckoning for her to follow him into his office, situated at the other end of the corridor. It was a small room dominated by a large desk and wall to wall shelves packed full of books and files. 'Tea or coffee?'

'Excuse me?' She stood motionless, unable to process what must be the first conciliatory gesture he'd ever made towards her. She'd been all set on telling him exactly what she thought of him – now she didn't know what to think.

'You look as if you've had a tough weekend of it,' he said, focusing on the frilly blouse before finally meeting her gaze, his head tilted in the direction of the kettle. 'Surely you have time for a drink while I fill you in on the details? Tea? Milk and sugar?'

She watched him as he added a tea bag into a second mug, her temper downgrading from boiling to simmering in an instant. She had no idea why he was putting on a nice act, but she was pretty certain she was about to find out.

'Here.' He thrust the mug into her hand with barely a look. 'And do take a seat.'

'Thank you,' she said, the words catching in the back of her throat. 'You were going to tell me what you've learnt?'

'Of course I was,' he said, folding his frame into his swivel chair. 'The blade entered through the sixth intercostal space, about here.' He placed his hand against his chest. 'It punctured the left ventricle of the heart to a depth of twenty millimetres, which accounts for the large amount of blood loss, thankfully contained mainly by the duvet.'

'Yes, thankfully so,' she repeated, cringing at the memory of the sopping bedding. "Is there anything you can tell me about the implement used?'

'A kitchen knife wouldn't do it. The knife, and yes, I do think it was a knife, had a double edge. This interests me, not least because I don't think I've ever seen anything quite like it,' he said, staring into the distance. 'A pointed tip and edge, which sliced through the chest cavity like a knife through butter. My normal guess would have been a kitchen knife, something long and thin like one used to fillet fish. But that in no way explains the state of her rib,' he added, frowning again. 'If I didn't know any better, I'd say that there were two knives but that doesn't tally with the evidence of only a single thrust. In effect we're looking for a double-edged knife, one side razor-thin and the other saw-like.'

'What about her rib specifically?' Gaby asked, lifting her mug and taking a long sip.

'Just that it was almost shredded where the knife hit.' Removing his glasses, he rubbed the red marks staining either side of his nose. 'I'll get my books out and see if I can add anything.' Picking up his mug, he drained it in one and said, 'Fancy another? That didn't even hit the sides.'

'Thank you. That would be lovely. As you say, it's been a difficult weekend, made more difficult by me running out of teabags.'

'I can't think of anything worse,' he said, a smile appearing – probably the first smile he'd ever directed at her. 'I can't even think of leaving home before I've had at least two mugs.'

After a couple of minutes, he placed her refilled mug on the side of the desk before settling back in his chair.

'I take it the main suspect is this Christine person?'

'What? You don't think she would have been capable?'

'On the contrary, she'd have been capable all right. It wouldn't have taken that much force to kill the victim. But what it did need was either a huge amount of luck or an in-depth knowledge of the chest cavity to position the knife so exactly. And, after twenty years in medicine, luck doesn't do it for me – I couldn't have done better myself.' He ran his hand across his jaw before continuing. 'As we both know, knife crimes are particularly messy and usually the perpetrator has to make at least a couple or more attempts to get the desired result. The knife was slipped through the intercostal space like a dart hitting a bullseye. Here, let me explain it a little better,' he said, peeling off the top Post-it-note and starting to draw. 'The heart is basically a pump, situated very slightly left of the sternum, or breast-bone.' The tip of his pen was pointed at the drawing. 'Of the four chambers, the left ventricle here is under the greatest pressure as its job is to drive blood around the body and, if you consider that the body contains five litres of blood and the heart pumps exactly that amount around the body each minute, that accounts for the amount of blood in the bed.'

'So, basically most of her blood drained away,' she said, her voice little more than a hoarse whisper. 'Would she have known . . .?'

'After the initial thrust, probably not. Death would have been pretty much instantaneous.'

'That's something at least.' She stared at the drawing, a shudder running down her back.

'Take another sip. You look as if you need it.' He pushed her mug towards her.

'Thanks. I'm not normally such a wimp but I've never been that good around blood.'

'I would have thought you're in the wrong job, then?' he said, another smile on his face.

'There's blood and then there's gallons . . .' she replied with an answering twinkle.

'Actually, to be exact, five litres are only a little over a gallon but no one's counting, except me.'

She rolled her eyes, reluctant for once to make the snappy

comment resting on the tip of her tongue. She couldn't believe they were having what passed for a civilised conversation, even if they were talking about the goriest of topics. In all probability it was only a blip and, the next time they met, he'd be as beastly as ever. But it was good while it lasted.

'What you're saying is that the positioning of the knife wasn't a lucky accident? That the killer must have had some degree of knowledge of anatomy to insert it quite so exactly?

'In a nutshell. Yes.'

'So, what else can you tell me about the victim?'

'There are a few more things that might be of use but the knife is, I'm afraid, indisputable. I'm still waiting for the full toxicology report, but she had been drinking. Her blood alcohol level, at 160 micrograms of alcohol per 100 millilitres, was double the limit. And a preliminary examination of the contents of her stomach confirms that she'd eaten within the last hour prior to her death – I'd hazard a guess at pepperoni pizza. There was also no evidence that she'd been sexually assaulted or that intercourse had even taken place recently,' he continued, his left eyebrow arched. 'Which disproves the gutter press's theory about three-in-a-bed. The one other thing of note, which may give you some insight into the type of person she was, is that she had a history of self-harming. I'll try to have my full report for you tomorrow but, by the state of her arms and the varying degree of healed scar tissue, I'd say the self-harming started as far back as her teens.'

Gaby opened her mouth to speak only to close it again. Self-harming was a condition she hadn't come across in her working life before, which would necessitate more research than she had time for. Unless Rusty had some contacts? After all, he kept reminding her that he was a qualified doctor. She narrowed her gaze, staring at the framed photo of a boy decked out in some posh school uniform that took pride of place next to Rusty's phone. Another thing she hadn't known about him and something to file for future reference.

She sighed, forcing herself away from the photo and back to the drawing of the heart beside it. She'd come here for information but all the visit had given her were problems and a bucket-load of additional work, all of which had to be carried out within the next few hours or she'd have to release their main suspect. Not main suspect – the *only* suspect unless Christine's supposed lover materialised.

'So, any pointers where I should start investigating about self-harming?'

'Surely a good place to start would be with the family?'

Gaby shook her head. 'I met with the mother yesterday and she never mentioned it.'

'No, well, I'm not overly surprised. There's a stigma surrounding this sort of thing and some youngsters are adept at hiding such issues from parents,' Rusty picked up the empty mugs and walked to the counter, all trace of his earlier affability rapidly disappearing. 'I'll put you in touch with a friend of mine at the hospital, a psychiatrist. She'll be able to answer more of your questions. Well, if that's all. I do have a report to write.'

'Sorry.' She pushed to her feet. 'Thank you for everything, including the tea.'

'Oh, the kettle's always on for coppers like you. I'll be in touch . . . with the report.'

Gaby cast him a look before reaching for her bag and heading to the door. Something had shifted between them. She had no idea what, but unarmed neutrality was a great improvement and one she was going to welcome, if not with open arms then at least with a willingness on her side to meet him halfway.

Chapter 11

Christine

The office was the same shape and size as her small sterile cell but, instead of a room full of cops, this time all Christine had to face was her solicitor. But after a second night in captivity, she craved company nearly as much as she craved caffeine. There was a lot she'd give right now for a mug of decent coffee and a decent pillow that didn't leave a crease in her cheek the size of a crater.

Andy Parrish looked the same, his starched white shirt a perfect foil for his paisley tie and conservative grey suit. She, on the other hand, looked worse than something the cat had dragged in. She'd been allowed a shower, a shower where her head and her feet were visible to the female officer standing outside the saloon-style door. They'd even lent her shower gel and one of those cheap black combs that could be found on the shelves of every supermarket up and down the country. It had taken her over an hour to fix her hair into something not resembling a mop, and now it hung past her shoulders in a tangled mass of curls. But, without her hair straighteners, there was nothing she could do about that and, with no access to a mirror, she could only guess at how she looked in the same clothes she'd been wearing since she was first taken into custody.

'We'll have to stop meeting like this, Mr Parrish,' she said, watching him open his laptop and mess around with the keyboard for a few seconds.

'You might as well call me Andy. You'll be seeing a lot of me over the next few days, Christine.'

She tilted her head. 'So what else do you want to know about me apart from my full name?'

He smiled. 'Christine Elizabeth de Bertrand née Greene, age thirty. No previous convictions, not even a speeding fine or parking ticket.'

'That's hardly likely as I gave up my car when I moved back to Llandudno,' she said, before adding, 'And anyway they were never in the right place at the right time to catch me. I'm an arch-criminal in disguise.'

'Well, now they have and it's up to me to try and secure your release.' His smile faded, his eyes narrowing as he searched her face. 'They're treating you well? Able to sleep all right? I've been told the beds are less than comfortable.'

'What, can't you tell I've had ten hours followed by a full English with extra toast and marmalade on the side?' She raised a hand to her hair. 'I don't mind so much about the bed or the mushy cornflakes but what I wouldn't give for a wide-toothed comb and a bottle of hair conditioner.'

'Which brand?' He withdrew a small notebook from his inside pocket and laid it down on the desk in front of him, removing the attached pen with a flourish.

'Any, I'm not fussy. I didn't think it would be allowed?' she asked, her words hesitant for the first time since entering the room. 'They wouldn't even allow me a belt for my jeans and as for shoe-laces . . .'

'I may be wrong, but I've never heard of anyone managing to commit suicide with a bottle of conditioner and a wide-toothed comb.' He returned the pen to the side before shutting the notebook and lifting his sleeve to squint at his watch.

'I wouldn't know where to start and anyway,' she said, crossing her arms over her chest. 'If I tried, they'd think it confirmation of my guilt and that would mean somebody else getting away with murder.' She shook her head briefly. 'The thing I don't understand is why someone would want to do this to Nikki? I might end up having to spend the rest of my life behind bars for a murder everyone seems determined to think I've committed. Where's the justice in that?'

'It's all very well moaning but that's not going to get us anywhere. If you're as innocent as you say you are then we need to encourage the police to look in the right direction so that they can find out what really happened.'

She unfolded her arms and rested back against the chair. 'If you don't think I'm innocent then why the hell are you going to all this trouble? I'd have thought my innocence would be a prerequisite to taking the case?'

'Ha, what made you think that, Christine? I've lost count of the slime-balls and scumbags I've had to represent over the years.' Andy paused, rifling his hand through his hair before continuing. 'Although, it must be said that, this is the most unusual of cases. You're an enigma. All the clues point to you being the only suspect, however, call me naïve, but I do think that there might be an alternative explanation.' He set his notebook aside, returning her stare with one of his own. 'Let's assume for the sake of argument that you are the murderer.'

'Let's not!' she said, pitching a nervous look at the closed door behind him.

'Don't worry about them. The microphone is switched off and anything you say to me is like speaking to a priest. I'd be struck off if I shared a client's confidence. So, tell me about your relationship with the deceased. How long did you know her? How did you come to be sharing a flat, that sort of thing?'

She heaved a breath, expelling it slowly before speaking. 'We met at uni. We were on the same course.'

'And that was?' he said, now tapping away on his computer.

'We were studying classics at St Augusta's College, Cambridge.'

He whistled through his teeth. 'St Augusta's College, hmm. I thought myself lucky to get into Manchester.'

'Yes, well. I only applied on a whim, never thinking for a moment that they'd accept me,' she said with a smile. 'I was lucky, or at least . . .' She hesitated, taking a moment to think it through. 'I thought I was lucky. Now I'm not so sure.'

'So, you met at uni and what else? Did you share a room? Were you good mates? Is that how she ended up sharing your flat?'

'No, no and no,' she said, glancing at the clock above the door. 'It's complicated and I gather you don't have a great deal of time?'

'Christine, I'll make time, all right.' He picked up his phone from the table before continuing. 'Do you mind if I . . .?'

'No. go ahead,' she said, deliberately averting her attention from where he was laboriously texting out a message with his index finger, only refocusing when he'd set his mobile back on the table.

'Your . . . ex-husband has been in touch by the way.'

She took a moment to process his comment. Paul getting in touch with her solicitor. Why? She tried to read Andy's expression, but it was as bland as his exterior.

Instead of asking the question he was probably expecting, all she said was, 'Oh.'

'He's been in touch with your parents too.' He fiddled with his tie. 'You do know you won't be able to see anyone while you're here and that I'm unable to relay any messages?'

'The detective did say.'

'Yes, well, he . . . I thought you'd like to know that he's

concerned.' He tightened the knot on his tie before giving a small cough into his hand. 'So, you were going to tell me about Nikki Jones?'

She dropped her eyelids, her thoughts travelling back to their first meeting.

Chapter 12

Nikki

2008
Cambridge

Day one of the rest of Nikki's life went pretty much as any of the days previously. Oh, instead of the two-up two-down situated in the centre of Barnsley, she was surrounded by the illustrious red-brick walls of one of the oldest, most prestigious universities around. Just as, instead of the flat vowels of the Yorkshire accent, she was exposed to a cultural mix and ethnic richness that had her dizzy with excitement and expectation. But she'd arrived alone with her single suitcase and scruffy rucksack and she was still alone.

She propped herself up against the pillow that evening, trying to close both her mind and her ears to the noises outside her door. There was a first-night party of sorts, all very last minute, arranged by the tall, bubbly redhead in the room next door. Everyone had pooled their stash of precious home-baked goodies and the sound of laughter echoing along the corridors was matched by the thump of music pounding through the walls.

There was no reason why she shouldn't open her door and mingle with the crowd. After all, she was the same: a stranger in a strange place. She even looked the same in her jeans and with her hair tied back in a ponytail. But something held her back. Shyness? Insecurity? Awkwardness? A mixture of all three? Or the realisation that she could never be the same as the herd of what sounded like elephants, racing up and down the halls.

She sat up, shifting the base of her ponytail from digging into the back of her neck. Her gaze focused on her arms where they were resting against her thighs. There was nothing to see, not really. Only a long-sleeved sweatshirt in plain black. But she knew what it was hiding . . .

Pulling back the cuff, Nikki stared down at the faded-to-pale slivers that mapped her flesh like some crazy multi-bypass, a frown appearing. She found it hard to remember how she'd managed to reach a place where cutting herself wasn't the most important thing. Funnily enough, her hated stepfather, for all his pale blue eyes following her around the house, was the first one to realise what she was up to. But instead of running to her mum, to use it as a bargaining tool to ease their increasingly fraught relationship, he'd never mentioned it after that first time and when her mother had finally thrown him out, she regretted that he hadn't tried to at least help her face up to her problem instead of letting her flounder on alone. She'd needed help. It was only now, as an adult, that she realised quite how much.

Instead of reaching for a knife, she searched in her bag and found the bottle she was looking for at the bottom. She poured out some of the clear liquid into her palm, noticing how her hands trembled in anticipation. Massaging oil into her skin, such a simple act, both soothed her mind and settled her anxiety to a level that even she could cope with, her fingertips finding the ridged scar closest to her left wrist. The ugliest, angriest of the lot and the one that had caused her to be admitted to the local hospital for a night. She couldn't believe, after all these years, that she'd managed to get it so spectacularly wrong and it was that mistake that had directed her towards seeking professional help.

The noise outside her door, heralding a pile of partygoers bursting into her room, had her fumbling for her sleeves. But the expression, quickly masked, on the redhead's face told her that she hadn't been quite quick enough. Nikki was used to other people's reactions but that didn't mean they didn't hurt. Surprise. Confusion. Disgust. Horror. Even sympathy – she'd had them all. People amazed her with their attitude – she couldn't begin to list the cruel things that had been said over the years, things she couldn't bear to think about, let alone repeat.

Nikki stood, the varnished floorboards cold under her bare feet, her chin thrust high. Christine, that was it. Christine with her slim body and glorious titian hair. She watched her pushing the couple of lads back out through the door and shutting it firmly in their face before speaking.

'They didn't see . . . anything, if that's what's worrying you?' Christine said, walking across the room and propping herself on the corner of the desk, a bottle of beer dangling from between her fingers.

'I'm not worried about them,' Nikki said, gritting her teeth.

Five-foot-two in her bare feet was no match to her opponent's willowy five-foot-eight or nine. She felt her temper rise at Christine's continued examination. She was in her room uninvited, trailing the smell of cheap booze and cigarettes in her wake and Nikki, for once, didn't know what to do to make her leave.

In an attempt at casualness, she settled back against the bed. 'Say your piece and then leave me alone. You have no right to be here, I certainly didn't invite you.'

Christine's eyes widened. 'My piece? What are you expecting me to say, Nikki? I'm not here to give you a hard time.'

'So, what's keeping you then? There's nothing for you here.'

'Nothing.' Christine looked around at the bare walls and the still unpacked rucksack in the corner. 'I thought that as we're neighbours . . .' She shook her head and suddenly jumped away from the desk, her boots making a dull thud. 'I'm sorry for interrupting,' she said, as if suddenly coming to a decision about something – Nikki couldn't begin to guess what. 'If you need anything, anything at all, all you have to do is thump on the wall, they're like paper.'

Chapter 13

Christine

'I don't know what to say. It's not as if we were friends or anything but I felt a connection with Nikki, if that makes sense?' Christine said, not really expecting a reply. 'She was an oddball. Oh, as clever as you like. You know that saying "too clever for your own good"? Well, that was Nikki down to a tee. Someone uncomfortable in her own skin.' She stared down at her wrists, resting on the desk, a shiver tracing itself across her spine at the sight of her smooth unblemished arms.

Andy touched her shoulder to get her attention and she looked back up into his face, her expression as trusting as a child's.

'Did you know she self-harmed? She'd tried to give up many times, but it was always the same. At the first sign of any stress in her life, she always returned to the knife. I tried to help, but she'd never let me close enough and the one time when I did manage to . . .' She spread her arms wide. 'She ended up dead and I find myself the person most likely to have bumped her off.'

'So, how is it she came to be living with you?' he questioned, 'It doesn't come across that you were the best of friends or anything.'

'You could say that,' she said, her brow puckering. 'But funny as it seems, I did like her. Oh, a lot of that had to do with feeling sorry for the way she lived her life. She was determined to socially isolate herself from anyone and everyone that could have made a difference. The only person that could get through to her was Paul, my ex-husband and even then, she took his kindness completely the wrong way.'

He lifted his head from the laptop where he was typing. 'What way exactly?'

'It's difficult to explain. To be honest, I'm not sure if I understand it myself. I think Nikki mistook his kindness for an indication that he had feelings for her and, when she realised that he was committed to me, she went completely off the rails.'

She focused on his tie, trying to phrase her words in a way that wouldn't make her come across as jealous. Jealousy was the very last emotion anyone would ever feel for Nikki.

'To be truthful, the reason I offered to put her up for a few weeks, until she sorted herself out, was primarily guilt. I hadn't seen her since college. She hadn't been in touch, not that I'd expected it. We were acquaintances who happened to undertake the same course, only that. We didn't even live in the same part of the world, for God's sake, so the chances of us running into each other were remote at best.' She rested her head back against the hard edge of the plastic chair while she waited for him to respond.

'Are you saying that it wasn't a coincidence meeting after so long?

'Who knows? It had been years since I'd last seen her, not since the last few days at uni. We were like ships that passed in the night. Up until bumping into her, I'd pretty much forgotten her existence.'

'Carry on, I'm still listening,' he said, his hands flying over the keys, his diction slow and clear. 'So, how did you meet?'

'That's the funny thing,' she considered, her voice soft. 'I could have sworn that it was an accident. She didn't even know about Paul and me breaking up or my move back to Llandudno.' She lifted a hand, toying with her hearing aid, the high-pitched buzz cutting through the air, interrupting the sudden silence. 'I'd gone into town Christmas shopping if you must know. I'm not that great in crowds.' She tapped her ear.' I don't expect you to understand but these things amplify the background noise nearly as much as the rest of it. I had to get away for a bit so I headed to the prom for five minutes' peace before finishing off. One minute I was staring out to sea, relishing in the sight and sound of the waves breaking against the stones by the pier, the next I was face-to-face with a ghost from my past.'

'Surely a strange term of phrase to use?'

'Not if you knew her like I did.'

Chapter 14

Paul

Monday 11 May, 11.55 a.m. St Gildas School

'Dr Kinnock has phoned, headmaster. He's on his way to see you as a matter of urgency.'

'Show him in when he arrives,' Paul replied, affording a brief smile to his PA before she closed the door behind her.'

Paul noted the time on the antique brass wall clock with a sigh. He'd thought they'd leave him until after his lunch before invading the sanctuary of his office, but he should have known better. The Board of Governors would have called an emergency meeting after that article in the *Mail*, linking the goings-on in Llandudno with one of the UK's top public schools. They would have had no choice but to come and have their say.

He took a moment to glance around the mahogany-shelved walls of his office. He'd known from the outset what the current situation with Christine would mean to his tenure at the college. The last couple of years had been a struggle to say the least. Oh, not in terms of college success. St Gildas continued to retain its stronghold on the top-ten board and, as public schools went, it had a kudos that was both hard to match and impossible to beat. The problem wasn't with the school or indeed school life. The problem lay with him and his attitude to almost everything since his wife had walked out. While he was still achieving and exceeding the targets laid down, it was now at the expense of even a hint of a personal life. He ate, drank and slept the school and only in the darkest trench of his mind did he ever mull over what had happened to change what he'd thought the most perfect of relationships.

He stood from where he'd been sitting, staring into space instead of dealing with the reams of paperwork that sat in the centre of his desk. He still had the report from the bursar and the job description for the post of junior PE teacher to run through, neither of which held any enthusiasm. All he could think of was the last time he'd seen Christine – not that she'd seen him. He'd made sure of that . . .

He was standing in the middle of the room, hands clasped neatly behind his back, when the door was pushed open with only the briefest of knocks. Tilting his head, it took one look at the expression stamped on Dr Kinnock's face to reinforce that this wasn't the usual polite discussion about the budget. The revered doctor meant business. The only unexpected thing about it all, he thought, reaching out his hand to return the handshake, was his own reaction to the impromptu visit. He didn't give a damn. This was a conversation long overdue.

'Ah Paul, this is a worrying business and at a time like this too,' Dr Kinnock said, arranging his jacket before taking the chair offered. 'If I'd known when I met your dear wife that she'd go and get herself into the papers like that and in such a spectacular fashion . . .' He shook his head.

'Actually, she's my ex-wife and, as far as I can see, it should have no impact on the school or my role here.'

'How can you say that, my boy? You know the board were

devastated when you divorced. A married headmaster is so much more desirable than either a single or divorced one. But for her to then go and embarrass the whole school—'

'I'm sure when my ex-wife woke up beside the dead body of her murdered flatmate, the effect on the school would have been uppermost in her thoughts,' Paul interrupted, his voice tinder-dry.

Dr Kinnock withdrew a handkerchief from his pocket and mopped his brow. 'Yes, well, there's no need to be like that.'

'Like what exactly?' he said, determined to retain the semblance of calm despite his mounting anger. 'Someone that I care for deeply is implicated in one of the most heinous of crimes and you want me to be more concerned about any possible effect on the uptake of places? We're full to the brim and booked solidly for the next five years so any possible effect will be negligible, and it will give the Friends of St Gildas something more interesting to gossip about when they cut the sandwiches for the summer fete.'

'I can see I'm wasting my time here, headmaster,' Dr Kinnock said, standing and heading for the door. 'Your current attitude to recent events is disappointing to say the least. I thought you'd have realised by now that the needs of the school far outweigh the needs of one individual.'

'Certainly. No man is expendable. If it makes it any easier, I'd like to tender my resignation, effective immediately.'

Dr Kinnock turned back to challenge him, one hand on the brass door handle, his face suffusing with colour. 'Now there's no need to be too hasty, Paul. You must know, up to this point, we've been delighted with the changes you've wrought but—'

'My mind is made up, Dr Kinnock. Mr Barnes will be fine to act in my absence. If I'd been knocked down by a bus, we wouldn't be having this conversation, and at least it will get you and the board out of – how did you term it? "Such a worrying business." I'll send you my written resignation in due course but, as of end of play today, I'll be on gardening leave.'

Chapter 15

Gaby

'Owen, am I pleased to see you,' Gaby said, throwing her bag on the desk and searching in the bottom for her notepad.

'Not as pleased as I am.'

'Oh, was it as bad as all that?'

'Worse! I've cleared up enough vomit and poo to fill a row of buckets.'

'Oh dear.' She hid her smile under her bent head. 'How's Kate?'

'Luckily it seems to have only affected Pip.'

'Well, that's something at least,' she said, plugging in her laptop and checking her phone for messages.

'She's going to stay with her parents for a few days. She's finding it difficult now she's over six months gone.'

Gaby sent him a look laden with sympathy. While they didn't tend to talk about their personal lives, she did know he was devoted to his wife and two-year-old son, Pip. Not having Kate around, even for a few days, would be bound to hit him hard.

'Don't you worry, Owen. I have more than enough work for you to barely miss them.'

He ran his hand across his beard. 'How did I know you were going to say that.'

'Because you know me so well. Come on, put the kettle on. There'll be just enough time to have a quick drink before the others descend on us.'

'We're out of that low-fat slop you call milk so it's black or full-fat?' he said, picking up the kettle and shaking it before turning it on.

'No milk. I ended up stopping for fish and chips on the way back from Manchester last night so I'm having to be extra careful today.'

'You and your diets! I'll just bet you skipped breakfast,' he added, putting his hand in his pocket and pulling out a cereal bar. 'It's all right, it's the low-calorie sort you always buy. I can't have you fainting from hunger like last time.'

'No thanks,' she said, pushing it away with a brush of her arm.

'The chief's bought doughnuts, the chocolate-covered ones you like.' He held the bar on the palm of his hand, a broad grin on his face.

She flicked him a look before snatching the packet and tearing it open, her attention now on the rest of the team piling through the door. Instead of the briefing, she really wanted to pull him aside and pick his brains about Rusty. The only thing holding her back was a sneaky suspicion that Owen and Amy might be in cahoots over her love life, or lack of. She balled the wrapper in her fist and aimed it at the wastepaper bin. She'd think about what she was going to do later.

'Come on, let's get this over with, and after I'll treat you to lunch. How does a cheese and tomato sandwich grab you?'

'It doesn't but if it's all that's on offer . . . So, what's this about Manchester then?'

'I managed to catch up with the victim's mother before she flew back to Spain.'

'That was a bit foolish to agree to act as her chauffeur. Couldn't you have dropped her off at Llandudno Junction? There's a Manchester train on the hour.'

'Ha ha – very funny, not! After all, what choice did I have? I couldn't very well detain her. She runs an animal sanctuary of some sort and apparently there's no one to cover. I have enough on my conscience already without adding animal welfare into the mix.'

She watched as he shook his head in disbelief. 'For all your brash exterior, you really are the proverbial soft touch, that is if you don't mind me saying, ma'am.'

She aimed a playful punch on his arm. 'I do mind and lower your voice or everyone will hear. It's taken a good three months to get this lot to see my worth.'

Within minutes the squad room was heaving. Gaby couldn't quite decide whether it was because of the presence of doughnuts or because of the case but, whatever the reason, she was pleased at the support from the team, despite the reams of cases they were all trying to juggle. Even Chief Inspector Sherlock had popped his head around the door briefly before heading for a meeting with the chief superintendent.

After the preliminaries were out of the way, Gaby got right down to business.

'I've just returned from the post-mortem. Although we won't have all the findings until tomorrow, Rusty has thrown us a few curveballs.' She rested her hip against the side of the table. 'But, first, let's catch up with what everyone's been up to,' she continued, waiting for Malachy to swallow what remained of his doughnut. 'What about the friend she was out drinking with – Kelly something or other? Did you manage to catch up with her?'

'Kelly James, ma'am,' he said, glancing down at his notepad briefly before lifting his head. 'She popped into the station first thing. Quite distraught over everything especially as her memory of the evening is pretty sketchy to say the least. One of them, she can't remember which, devised a new drinking game with regards to men guessing the correct spelling of de Bertrand's name – for each wrong answer they both got bought another drink. I think there were quite a lot of wrong answers offered.'

'I'll bet there were,' Gaby said, her expression as grim as her voice. 'What else?'

'She remembers there was this bloke but all she could give me was tall, dark and handsome, so that's pretty much half of Llandudno, me included,' Malachy said, a smile breaking. 'After chuck-out, she said that Christine accompanied her to the taxi rank, before starting on the short walk up Gloddaeth Avenue to the West Shore. Her last memory is watching her cross the road by the traffic lights at the roundabout.'

'Good work,' Gaby said, throwing him a smile before continuing. 'And any news from the CSI team?'

'Not much. The laptops are with the IT bods and, as you know, that can take a while. The flat has also been searched to within an inch of its life but it hasn't turned up anything startling. We're delving into both of their finances to see if there's anything strange on that front, but it looks as if Jones had an informal arrangement whereby she transferred three hundred pounds on the first of each month into de Bertrand's account from her waitressing job.' He folded his arms and rested back in his chair. 'I haven't yet had the time to check on her life before moving to Llandudno to work in a café but I'm working on it.'

'Is it me or does the idea of someone with a Cambridge degree working as a waitress seem a bit of a tragedy?'

'What degree?'

Gaby frowned, his answer not the one she'd been expecting. 'I thought someone said that she'd obtained one from Cambridge?'

'Nope. I contacted them. No record of her obtaining a degree. They said she never submitted all of the coursework,' he replied. 'I haven't had time to follow that up yet, but I will and as for the birthday cards . . . We're going to run them by de Bertrand next time she's interviewed but there's one that strikes me as unusual.'

'Go on.'

'De Bertrand was big on recycling and thank God for that. It took seconds to work through the envelopes and then compare handwriting and it looks as if the card sent from the husband was hand-delivered.'

'Was it now? I wonder how many exes are on good enough terms to send each other cards let alone take the trouble to hand-deliver them. Good work, Mal. It's certainly not something she mentioned at interview.' She withdrew her notebook and scribbled something onto the first blank page before turning to face the rest of the team. 'Anyone know whether we've had any luck on the knife front?' Her gaze wandered over the six or so faces staring back.

'Not so far,' Marie Morgan said, with a shake of her head. 'But they're still at it. I've started looking at some of the CCTV footage like you asked but nothing yet. Maybe when we know for definite which pubs she drank in we'll have more luck.'

'Okay. What about the other occupants of the house, Mal?'

'It's a bit patchy.'

'That's not what I want to hear.'

'Well, it's what you're going to get.' His grin lessened the impact of his words. 'The couple in the flat below would have been the ones to hear anything and they were away for the weekend. They're still away but I'll try and catch up with them on their return tomorrow. The ground-floor flat is of more interest though. It's inhabited by a Mrs Ellis, who used to own the whole building before poor investments and rising inflation meant that she had to subdivide into flats. She's lived there for nigh on fifty years and, from the amount she could tell me, seems to spend most of her time staring out of the window.' He put his elbows on the table, cradling his stubbly chin in his hands. 'She didn't know Christine de Bertrand that well. She said she kept herself to herself. Most mornings she'd see her, from her lounge window, heading across the road to the beach for a stroll before work. She struck her as a lonely figure – apart from a couple of girlfriends she never had visitors to speak of. She was always polite when they met in the hallway but never one to stay chatting for longer than the passing of pleasantries.' He swallowed, his Adam's apple bobbing around in his neck. 'She seems to remember one occasion when a man called looking for her. He'd rung her doorbell by mistake. She couldn't give me a description, but she did say that he had a dog with him.'

'That would have been the husband,' Gaby interrupted. 'What did she have to say about the night before the murder? Dr Mulholland estimates that it happened around six a.m.'

'Didn't hear a thing! She normally spends the evening watching telly before turning in at about eleven. She's adamant that she'd have heard the door if they'd arrived home before then, but she takes a sleeping pill every night and she's usually dead to the world until morning.'

Gaby raised a finely arched brow at his unfortunate choice of words but all she said was, 'Did she have anything to say about Nikki Jones?'

'Not a huge amount. Another woman who liked to keep herself to herself,' he said, with a little shake of his head. 'She saw even less of her than she did de Bertrand. A few times in the hall where she appeared to struggle to keep eye contact and as for a conversation . . . I got the distinct impression that she thought her a bit of an oddball. Once she'd come in from work, she wouldn't see or hear from her again until morning.'

'What about weekends?'

'Again, she rarely saw her. De Bertrand was always popping in and out, but she saw very little of Nikki Jones. She called her the little ghost woman because of the way she used to flit in and out of the building.'

Gaby picked up her pen and jotted a note down on her pad.

She was beginning to build up a picture of the victim, a picture that would expand over time. But time was the one thing they didn't have. Sherlock had been adamant that it was a crime of passion but now she wasn't so sure. Suddenly she wished that DI Stewart Tipping wasn't off sick. He'd know what to do.

She heaved a sigh as she walked over to the wall of whiteboards that stretched to fill the space between the window and door. If it came to it, she could always phone him. He'd made that clear the day he'd come in to deliver his sick note. She wondered if he'd known then about DCI Sherlock's plan to let her head up a case. If he had, he hadn't said anything other than to press his hand on her shoulder in a fatherly fashion and remind her to keep in touch. If the paucity of clues continued, she might very well have to take him up on it.

She examined the two headshots in front of her. Neither of the photos did their owners justice but Christine looked a darned sight better than the post-mortem one of Nikki. She'd have liked another photo, one taken when she was still alive but, unusually, none had been found in her room and she hadn't thought to ask the mother when she'd dropped her off at the airport.

Both women were attractive, one with glossy red ringlets, the other with straight brown hair splayed out against the pillow. Two women, one dead, one alive and, if Sherlock had his way, about to be banged up for a very long time. But she had an inkling that she wasn't seeing the full picture. There was something about Christine and that husband of hers that didn't ring true. They could even have masterminded it together . . .

She turned back to the room, the sound of shuffling feet reminding her that she'd been silent too long. She'd think later when, hopefully, there'd be more facts to play with.

'So, who else hasn't fed back then?' she said, her eyes landing on Jax who was making a good attempt at trying to appear invisible. 'Any luck with the dog walking?'

'Actually, I borrowed my m-m-mum's Chihuahua,' he stuttered, flushing bright red at the sound of loud guffaws echoing round the room. Even Gaby couldn't quite hide her amusement at the thought of the six-foot plus blond officer being dragged around the West Shore with something no bigger than his size thirteens on the end of a lead. 'You may jest but it worked a treat.'

'I'm sure. So, what, if anything, did you find out?'

'Well, not a lot actually but I will.' He ran his finger under his collar before continuing. 'I spoke to a Miss Watson, who was in possession of a Cairn terrier. She always walks along the West Shore on weekdays. She's told me about a couple of people to try. There's only one problem,' he said, now staring at his feet.

'And that is?'

'I think it might be a couple of days. She only knows them by their d-d-dogs' names. So, if anyone knows of a poodle called Shirley and a Great Dane called—'

'Okay, the fun's over,' Gaby said, raising her hand to still the laughter ringing out through the room. 'While there's nothing wrong with humour and God only knows we're all in need of a little light relief with the job we do, there's a time and a place for everything and now isn't it. Right then. It's my turn. Dr Mulholland is waiting for the rest of the toxicology reports before completing his report, however, I managed to catch up with him earlier and he's run through the salient points. The whereabouts of the murder weapon is paramount. One of the most important things in the case along with the lack of physical evidence on de Bertrand. Miss Jones was killed by a single stab wound to the chest by someone with an in-depth knowledge of anatomy. Dr Mulholland is adamant that no layperson could have managed to target the right ventricle of the heart so exactly. So the question is, would de Bertrand, a special needs teacher with a classics degree, have the relevant specialist knowledge? And if she had, where would she have hidden the knife?' She stopped to stare across at Marie before walking to the whiteboard and picking up a blue marker. 'As you know, I'm no artist but it was double-edged – one serrated, the other, smooth. Marie, I want the search extended – we have to find it.'

She replaced the cap on the marker and set it on the table. 'There are also a few additional unanswered questions to work through, for one, Miss Jones's background. She has extensive scarring on her forearms that indicate a long history of self-harming.' She focused on her shoes, navy patent and pinching like a bitch but she'd worry about the state of her feet later. Now her mind buzzed with instructions. 'So, we need to find both the knife, and this supposed man/lover – whatever – Christine took home. We also still need to track down any witnesses and interview both de Bertrand's and Jones's colleagues for background. With regards to Ms de Bertrand, we'll leave her to stew for another few hours before re-interviewing and, perhaps by then, we'll have come up with a clearer picture and know exactly what questions to ask.' She lifted her head, her lips stretched into a smile though she felt far from smiling. 'Enjoy your lunch, everyone. I'm on my mobile if you need me.'

Chapter 16

Gaby

Monday 11 May, 2 p.m. St Asaph Police Station

'Take a seat, Detective. I'll be with you in a moment.'

Gaby forced herself to sit right back in her chair instead of perching on the edge. With her hands folded in her lap, she looked the quintessential interview candidate, apart from her frilly blouse, which was the only discordant note, her thoughts again on the pile of washing waiting by the machine. She didn't fidget. She barely blinked as she continued focusing on the top of DCI Sherlock's head as he bent over the open file in front of him. This wasn't the first time she'd applied for promotion up to detective sergeant but the last interview was something she preferred to forget; her mind was reluctant to settle on the fallow period she'd spent in Cardiff. She'd known at the time that it was pointless, the only thing driving her onwards the near-perfect exam results she'd achieved. While she was far from the tallest, strongest or fittest detective, she had other attributes – hopefully they were attributes that would count.

'Right then, sorry about that.' Henry Sherlock raised his head to look at her. There was no smile on his lips or indeed any expression on his face. She no more knew what he was thinking than she did Dr Mulholland – her heart shrunk at the thought. Was she yet again to be disappointed despite the long hours and lost weekends she'd spent behind her desk? If she was, she might as well jack it in except that she'd committed now, the image of her little cottage appearing before her. She'd been too eager. Too determined to make a new life in North Wales – to settle down with . . .

'I've been looking through your file, Gaby,' DCI Sherlock said, his words dragging her back to the interview with a force that made her blink. 'You've applied before, I believe – any idea why you were turned down? I see you took your sergeant exams at the start of last year and came away with a highly commended so it can't be your brain.'

Was it a good thing that he called her Gaby? She didn't know and cared far too much to dwell on it – she might come up with the wrong answer. Reining her thoughts back to the question, she struggled to come up with the kind of answer he'd like. Wasn't that the whole point of interviews? Trying to please the interviewer.

'I had some difficulty settling into the team, sir.'

'As you did in Swansea?' he parried. 'I do know your history, Gaby. You might remember that I employed you on the personal recommendation of DCI Brazil-North. She felt you deserved a chance after what happened in St David's.'

'Yes, well. It was an unusual case.'

'Indeed.' He arranged the papers back in the file, his hands resting on top before continuing. 'I need detectives I can trust. Detectives that are both hard-working and clever. DC Bates is a good man and clear sergeant material of the future but the rest of the team need strong guidance particularly in instances of murder. I need someone in the job that won't be swayed by an attempt to distort the truth such as in the case you're currently working.'

Gaby only just prevented her jaw from dropping and her feet from propelling her body out of the room. If he was telling her what she suspected, she might as well put the house on the market and step away from the force altogether. She'd been told there wouldn't be a third chance. But if that was his attitude, she didn't want the job. Christine de Bertrand was either guilty or innocent. Gaby had no idea which but she was determined to strive for that gold standard amongst all coppers – an open mind. At work, she was very happy to play whichever game he wanted her to but not at the expense of ignoring the rules.

'I'll do everything necessary in this case as with any other to ensure that the right person pays for their crimes, sir, if that's the question you're asking?'

'Harrumph.' He rested back in his black swivel chair, his hands now on the arms. 'Tell me why I should give you the job?' he continued, with the swift change of topic he was known for.

She let the air seep through her teeth. A question she could answer – one she'd prepared for if only she could remember the words.

'Because I'm hard-working, efficient and because I care. I care about finding out the truth no matter what that truth might be.' She twisted her mouth. 'But if you're looking for a yes man, I'm not that person. While I'll listen to what you have to say, I can't promise that I'll always agree. All I can promise is to do my best but, I also know that at times, my best won't be good enough.' She spread her hands, her body language clear. While she cared desperately for a positive outcome to the interview, she wasn't prepared to compromise her ideals. It was best he knew that now or they'd both be disappointed.

Chapter 17

Marie

'So, where do you suggest she could have hidden that knife, Mal?' Marie said, eyeing him over the top of her mug.

'No idea but if we don't find it, we're all for the high jump. Darin's fine when everything's going well but I've heard rumours about what she was like in Cardiff. A real bitch by all accounts, in addition to being a marriage wrecker. Her lover's wife accused her in the middle of a staff meeting. She was so pregnant she was ready to pop all over the squad room floor and Darin didn't even flinch.'

'Well, I speak as I find and, up to now, I've had no cause for complaint.'

'You're bound to say that. Women always stick together, don't they Jax?'

'I-I-I wouldn't like to say.'

'Bloody typical.' Marie slammed the mug down and, picking up her mobile, reached for her bag. 'Malachy Devine, she treats us all the same, as you very well know. Playing the male versus female card won't get you anywhere with either of us and—' she raised her hand, warding off his next comment '—if you're going to spread rumours like that please ensure that they're substantiated by fact. As none of us were actually in Cardiff at the time I'd prefer if we made up our own minds.'

She turned to Jax. 'The air here is a tad too biased for my liking. Catch you later.

Marie stared at the shelf in Boots before picking out a kit at random and placing it in her basket, careful to hide it under the rest of her shopping. While it was unlikely anyone would recognise her in Llandudno, she wasn't prepared to take any chances. They'd been disappointed too many times in the past to share any part of their pregnancy journey.

She headed for the tills to pay before heading back to Llandudno's main shopping street and across the road to Marks and Spencer and the toilets hidden away on the second floor behind the menswear department. There were no thoughts of a special meal and a bottle of champagne cooling in the bottom of the fridge. Those were things that she'd orchestrated for the first couple of attempts. After all they were both young and healthy. Getting pregnant couldn't be that difficult.

Her mindset had changed over the last two years along with the rest of her life and she'd lost a part of herself in the process. Long gone was the fun-loving impulsive girl who'd think nothing of planning a weekend getaway with Ivo, her lawyer husband, Now, she watched what she ate and drank and as for their sex life . . . Locked in the tiny cubicle she yanked down her knickers. But one look at the blood stained bright against the pure white cotton and she slammed the kit back into the packet for burial down the bottom of her handbag later. There were no tears. She was long past the howling rages and inconsolable grief of 'why me'. The tears would come later in the silence of her bedroom while she waited for her husband to drift back home from whatever late-night meeting excuse he could come up with. Their marriage was on the edge and her with it.

Back in the main body of the shop, she paid for a sandwich and a carton of juice before making her way up to the roundabout and Gloddaeth Avenue, her thoughts now directed away from her disaster of a life and back to that knife.

She no more believed in Christine's innocence than Gaby. That's why the search had been kept to the roads branching off the West Shore. There wouldn't have been that much time after the murder to dispose of the knife before phoning the police. But now she allowed her mind to follow a different trajectory, one that included de Bertrand's mysterious dark-haired stranger. What if she *had* met a man in the pub and subsequently taken him back home for the night? How had he gotten into Llandudno? The likelihood was that he'd have driven. So if he'd driven, he must have had a car, which would have been a problem in its own right. Llandudno was always heaving with holidaymakers and now that Easter was only a memory, all the tiny tributary streets that ran between the high street and the promenade were jam-packed with cars.

With a turn of her heel, she headed back the way she'd come, making her way to the car park situated at the back of the Victoria Shopping Centre, her phone in her hand. Before she'd left St Asaph, she'd arranged for a dog handler to join the search party. With a bit of luck they'd have this knife business sorted by teatime.

Chapter 18

Gaby

Monday 11 May, 3.05 p.m. St Asaph Hospital

Straight after the interview, Gaby made her way across St Asaph to the Child and Adolescent Mental Health Service department, or CAMHS, pushing all thought of the less than satisfactory interview out of the way. She should have known better than to get an immediate reply from Sherlock but to be told to wait for a phone call that would determine her whole future was the very last thing she needed right now.

The CAMHS department was situated on the second floor of the hospital, tucked away at the end of a long corridor. After making herself known to the receptionist, Gaby was directed to the waiting room opposite and left to leaf through out-of-date magazines and a copy of yesterday's *Telegraph* that someone must have left behind, neither of which held any interest.

She was examining a collection of pamphlets on an array of conditions from bed-wetting to insomnia when she heard her name called. Standing, she struggled not to raise an eyebrow at the pert blonde filling the doorway. She hadn't known what to expect of Rusty's psychiatrist contact but if she'd bothered to examine her thoughts on the matter, she wouldn't have come up with the cool woman in front of her.

'Detective Darin? I'm Melanie Shaw. Rusty asked me to speak to you. I can only give you a few minutes but that should be long enough – any questions left, I'm happy to answer over the phone or via email,' she said, with a firm shake of her hand.

Gaby pasted a smile on her face to override the sudden feeling of inferiority that coursed through her veins. Everything about the woman was dainty from her finely sculptured cheekbones to her retroussé nose and reed-thin frame. She was pretty in a quirky sort of way, her mouth a little too wide, her eyes slightly too large for her heart-shaped face. But the whole package added up to everything Gaby wasn't, despite her recent weight loss and daily jog.

She smothered a stab of envy as she followed her along the corridor and through the last door on the right. It wasn't like her to feel despondent about life and she was doing everything she could to rectify having piled on the pounds since being almost hounded out of the force. But Cardiff had been nearly a year ago now and the truth was she'd always be a big girl despite the calorie-counting. The best she could hope for was a size 14-16 and that was still a good stone and a half away. So, why should it suddenly matter now? She stared at the knee-length skirt, sheer tights and slim ankles ahead that filled her vision. Now was not the time for self-analysis. She might learn something about herself that she didn't want to know.

The office wasn't what she'd expected, the bright airy space at odds with all her recent experiences of the NHS. The large desk had been pushed up against the wall to make room for the red, fabric-covered sofa and chairs. The artwork was modern and striking, the red and blue patterns reflected in the bright rug that took up most of the floor space.

Sitting on the chair indicated, Gaby dragged her jacket across her chest before removing her notebook and pen from her pocket, suddenly at a loss. Rusty must have arranged the appointment almost as soon as she'd left his office, leaving her very little time to read up on the condition – and the one thing she hated more than anything was not being prepared.

She cleared her throat, stalling for time. 'I'm not sure what Dr Mulholland has told you but—'

'Oh, Rusty never divulges anything relating to one of his little cases whenever we meet, Detective. There's always something much more interesting to discuss.'

I'll just bet there is, she thought, straining to glue a smile onto her lips. She would have laughed if the circumstances had been different. It was almost as if Melanie Shaw was marking her territory. What a laugh. Rusty was the very last man she could ever be interested in. The macho bullshit he came out with was the biggest turn-off. She narrowed her gaze. Her and Rusty? Hell would have to freeze over first and, with global warming, that was never going to happen.

'I never thought otherwise,' was all she said, settling further into the chair. 'The reason I'm here is to find out as much as I can about self-harmers. Why they do it. The drives and urges that make them resort to such extreme measures. That sort of thing.'

'The issues around why people harm themselves are many and complex, but I'll try and keep it simple for you,' Melanie said, lifting her hand and patting her already smooth chignon. 'The main point, and one the media often fails to realise, is that it's all part and parcel of a mental illness, the stress being on the word illness. Unlike the common cold, it's not something you can catch or pass on by being in the same room as a sufferer.'

Gaby scribbled furiously in her notebook, trying to keep up while a list of questions started to pool in her mind. 'So, I'm guessing it starts, what, with teenagers as a cry for help?'

'Oh, very good, Detective, although you're only partly right,' she said, propping her elbow on the armrest and balancing her chin in her hand, her look intense. 'Harmers show up in my clinic as young as eleven but it's certainly not a cry for help. You have to realise that it's something they carry out in the privacy of their own bedroom and, afterwards, hide the scars under long-sleeved hoodies and jumpers.' She glanced at her watch before continuing. 'I could fill a book on the stigma surrounding mental illness and the scars that my patients have to hide for fear of ridicule. The tracks that drug users have are paltry in comparison to the damage caused by a determined harmer.'

Gaby stared down at her notes before continuing. There was something about the case she wasn't getting and the bit about the state of Nikki's arms was just one of the loose ends she wanted to tie off as quickly as possible. 'If there's such a stigma and horrendous scarring then why do it?'

'Ah, if I knew the answer to that question, I'd be a million-aire,' Melanie said, leaning forward in her chair, her hands now clasped on her lap. 'Self-harming is a vicious cycle of emotional release – a bit like those old-style kettles you take camping that whistle when the steam builds. But, as soon as the kettle is put back on the heat or, in this case, the individual is back in the same environment or situation, the whole cycle starts again. This isn't child's play, Detective. Some of these children have emotional scars alongside the physical that would drive you to drink. Having said that, each one brings their unique set of issues along with those scars – it's up to the skill of the healthcare professional to firstly gain the child's trust before even beginning to unravel what's usually a litany of heart-breaking problems. Again, I can only generalise because I don't know any details about the specific case . . .'

'Would it help if I send her medical records over to you?'

'If it's that important.' She flicked another look at her watch before standing. 'I'm sorry that I don't have more time today. You're only here now because I managed to squeeze you in between two consultations as a favour to Rusty. Send over the files as soon as they're released and I promise that I'll look at them,' she said, picking one up from the small pile on her desk.

'I have one more question, well, not really a question as such,' Gaby said, making for the door. 'More of an observation. I guess what I'm trying to understand is the character of the victim. Is it possible to generalise without actually knowing the specifics of the case because I'm beginning to think that poor self-esteem played a huge part? Would that be about right?'

'Rusty did say not to underestimate your intelligence, Detective,' Melanie replied, her smile broadening. 'That's it in a nutshell apart from one obvious omission. There's a huge self-destruct button residing deep inside, which is reflected in the high suicide rates in this sector of the population.'

'Suicide? It's not possible, is it?' Amy said, later that evening around at Gaby's cottage. 'I thought that there was something about the positioning of the knife being too exact for luck to play any part?' She reached for the bottle and topped up her wine glass.

'And there's no knife! Not something Nikki could have staged unless there was an accomplice and that would make it manslaughter at best. Unless the intention was to put Christine in the frame for her murder but that still doesn't explain that blasted knife. What a mess.'

Gaby kicked off her shoes and curled her feet beneath, snagging her toes in the throw, which she'd bought last week to disguise the state of the threadbare sofa.

She'd had to sink every penny she had into cobbling together the deposit for her two-bedroomed detached property along Abbey Road and, if it hadn't been for the sizable handout from her parents, she'd never have managed. She'd only moved in a month ago and the house was still populated with taped up cardboard boxes but that didn't matter. All that mattered was the sense of permanency and commitment that she'd made to North

Wales. It would take a lot more than a few problems with fellow officers to drive her away.

All of her salary now went on the mortgage and she'd had to resort to the local auction rooms to ensure she had the basics like somewhere to both sit and sleep. Nothing matched, from the wine glasses to the mugs on the shelf in the kitchen, the room she'd most like to change with its 1970s yellow-pine cupboards, ill-fitting doors and drab brown tiles. The bathroom, with its avocado suite, was even more hideous but, as she kept telling herself, she spent far more time in the kitchen and the lounge than she did in the bath. At least the sofa was comfy, she thought, even if the rest of the room was a huge disappointment. She focused now on the wood-cladding that covered half the room and the grey shag-pile carpet that covered the rest. The previous owner either rocked the Finnish sauna-look or had a part-time job as a lumberjack but, as her father had said before she'd moved in, she couldn't have everything. The cottage was structurally sound and with the quaintest cottage-garden that surrounded it on three sides. What had attracted her the most though had been the pretty gazebo and large brick-built garage, neither of which she'd had the time or money to think about let alone use. The added income from her promotion would help of course, she mused, remembering the call she'd had from Sherlock, offering her the job and the reason for the impromptu celebration with Amy.

'If the mother was still living locally, I'd send you over to tap her for information,' she said finally, hiding a smile at the course of the conversation, which always turned back to work whenever she was alone with Amy. 'Nikki certainly sounds as if she was one fucked-up kid and, as Family Liaison Officer, you're worth your weight in gold getting information out of difficult customers.'

'I'd have no objection to a week in Spain, although Tim might object unless you could afford to send us both?' Amy pouted at the sight of Gaby shaking her head, before returning to the serious job of loading her sliver of celery with more beetroot hummus than was humanly possible. 'You'll have to tell me how to make this, you know. I'm becoming a big fan.'

'Yes, well, with your boyfriend owning one of the best bistros in the area I don't think my measly little offering can in anyway compare.' Gaby said, topping up her wine glass.

'Talking about men, what's this I hear about the esteemed Dr Mulholland actually being nice for a change, Detective *Sergeant* Darin?' Amy sent her a lop-sided smile. 'And before you ask, it was Owen who told me. He said you were like a cat let loose in a creamery. I thought you hated each other's guts, no pun intended,' she added on a laugh.

'Ha, very funny, Potter. Guts indeed,' Gaby said, breaking into a grin. 'Yes, Rusty did lay off for once. I have no idea what got into him, but long may it continue. However, I wouldn't get too excited. He wasn't that nice, just nicer than normal.' She lifted her glass and chinked it against Amy's before taking a long sip.

'Maybe it's a case of unrequited love on his part but he's too shy to make a move. Did you know the gossip at the station is that his ex-wife divorced him because of the long hours he keeps, screwing him to the floor in the process with the worst divorce settlement ever? There was a boy, too.' She frowned, her pretty face almost hidden by the dim light cast by the table lamp. 'She used him as extra ammunition in the divorce and now he's shuttled between them like an unwanted parcel. Despicable. For an intelligent, not to mention wealthy man like Rusty to fall for a woman with big tits but no integrity is bloody typical.'

'Just where do you get all this from?' Gaby raised her eyebrow and not for the first time at Amy's ability to extract juicy bits of information about her colleagues. She was always the last to hear any whiffs of gossip around the station and she'd certainly never heard any of them utter a word about Rusty. She knew he was newly single but that was hardly surprising if he'd been dumped on well and truly by his ex. She blinked, remembering the photo of the boy on his desk, very similar to the school photos her mother had dotted around the house. She remembered thinking at the time what a handsome lad he was – and he and Rusty were two peas in a pod with the same coppery red hair and gangly frame.

Gaby pushed her wine glass further into the centre of the coffee table, determined to rein in her friend's conversation. Amy, while a dear and one of her closest friends, if not the closest, was a match-maker of the worst sort. Since moving up here she'd bombarded her with a host of potential blind dates. Gaby didn't blind date or internet date. She didn't date full-stop and now certainly wasn't the time to be thinking about Rusty and whatever was going on in his life. The thought that it probably had something to do with the delectable Dr Melanie Shaw squeezed through a gap in her mind before she had time to plug the hole with some emotional putty. That was a thought she was determined to ignore.

'You do know you're wasted as a FLO, don't you? They'd have made good use of your powers during the war as an alternative to scopolamine!'

Amy rolled her eyes before starting to collect the plates littering the table. 'If you're not going to be sensible about the state of your love life then I might as well go.'

'No, leave those,' Gaby said, struggling to her feet. 'And as for my non-existent love life, it's not as if I'm over-run with spare time to go gadding about with all and sundry especially with a possible murderer on the loose.'

Amy looked up from the wine bottle she'd been shaking in the vague hope it might not be empty. 'But I thought you said the feeling round the office was that it was a cut and dried case?

'That's what everyone's telling me but there's still the issue of the perfect placement of the missing knife in addition to the missing man to account for.' She took the plates off Amy and, walking into the kitchen, placed them on the worktop beside the sink, Amy following behind. 'We've also had some of the results back from the lab, which make for interesting reading. Christine de Bertrand's blood alcohol level was three times over the legal limit, which is neither here nor there as she wasn't in possession of a car, but her blood system was floating with Temazepam, a well-known night sedation. They've cross-checked with the inventory from the CSI team and, it's not as straightforward as all that because it's a drug she had in her bathroom cabinet.'

'That's a little odd, don't you think?' Amy said, relaxing against the wall, her arms folded. 'Who in their right mind pops a sleeper right before sex?'

'Exactly. It's beginning to look like she was telling the truth about having no recollection of what happened that night. Intoxicated, drugged up to the eyeballs and deaf is a pretty lethal combo. The level of Temazepam in her blood stream indicate that she would have still been dopy when she woke up – no wonder she couldn't remember. To my mind she's off the hook.'

'Completely. So, what are you thinking then? That it was a date-rape scenario?'

'Possibly. We're still waiting for forensics to get back to us with the results from her swabs and the bed linen. There was nothing obvious which means that, if she did bring a man back, he probably used protection. But, as we already know, every brand of condom leaves a chemical signature so, even if we can't prove anything through DNA analysis, at least we can make an informed guess as to what might have happened.'

'And if by some chance she did murder Nikki in a drug-fuelled drunken rage what would her motive have been?'

'God, you do love to put me on the spot, don't you?' Gaby said, running hot water into the sink and adding a dash of washing-up liquid. 'All I'm prepared to say at this stage is that I think there was a man involved. But who he is or what relevance he has to the case is still a mystery and, harping back to the knife, without any physical evidence, the chances of having a viable case to bring to trial are minimal at best.'

'So she's not guilty then?'

'No, not now we know about the sleeping tablet. But that's not the issue, as you very well know. Now we have to prove it. Rusty will go some of the way – on the witness stand he's going to swear blind that the killer must have had an in-depth knowledge of human anatomy in order to place that knife so exactly.' She shook her head briefly, planting a smile on her face. 'Come on now. I didn't invite you round to bore the socks off you about work. Ring Tim and tell him to pop by on his way past, after all it's meant to be a celebration. If I thought I was busy before . . . And, another thing,' she said, her voice changing from light to serious. 'I really would prefer if you didn't wander the streets this time of night.'

'You think it's that bad then?' Amy pulled her phone out of her pocket and scrolled through her list of favourites, not that she had to scroll far. 'I think you're holding out on me. If de Bertrand isn't guilty then there's a murderer on the loose. Someone that has the knowledge to kill with one thrust so someone that understands human anatomy. A doctor? What about the ex-husband? How does he fit in?' She lifted the phone to her ear and headed across to the other side of the room.

Gaby watched from the kitchen doorway, waiting for Amy to finish her call before continuing where they'd left off.

'All okay?'

'I think so. He's had a crap day at work. Some sort of problem in the kitchen.' She pocketed her phone, her mind obviously on more domestic problems.

'He's all right though?'

'He's fine. Just stressed.' She joined Gaby in the doorway, wrapping her arm around her shoulder. 'Come on, he won't be here for ages yet. So, what do you think about the ex-husband?'

'You should be the last person to ask that question. In our job it's almost impossible to measure the value of a person but, for what it's worth, I liked him. I thought he was genuine.'

'So, he's bound to be the murderer then,' Amy said, picking a tea towel from where it hung from the rail on the door of the oven.

'Mmm, maybe. I've been proved wrong in the past.' Gaby's thoughts winged their way back to the time she'd spent in South Wales and the sudden demise of her boss. She pursed her lips, still unwilling to think about that last case in St David's. A lot had happened since she'd moved up north and thinking about past failings wouldn't help her now. She needed answers not memories, her mind placing Paul de Bertrand in the hot seat. 'There is that issue of the hand-delivered birthday card, isn't there?'

'And he's also a doctor so there's your answer,' Amy declared with a grin. 'There's no point in the Welsh constabulary expanding their workforce with Darin and Potter on the case. We've solved the mystery of *the body in the bed* and all it took was one bottle of wine and a few dips.'

'If only it was that easy, my love, but he's not that sort of doctor. Apparently, his doctorate is in anthropology and, even after a lengthy Google search, I'm still not a hundred per cent sure what that is.'

'Something to do with old bones, isn't it? Tim will know, he spends most of his spare time watching documentaries on Sky. But, if I'm right,' Amy said, her expression suddenly sharp, 'an anthropologist would have a fair idea as to human anatomy.'

Tim was a tall, slender, unassuming man with eyes only for Amy. If Gaby could bottle him and sell him on eBay, she'd make a killing because he was what could be termed the ideal partner. Oh, he wasn't the best-looking bloke on the block by a long way and while tall, he wasn't the tallest. He didn't have time to go to the gym, but his daily jog and demanding job kept both his mind and body in first-class shape. He'd made it to the top of his profession by sheer hard work and deserved all the accoutrements that went with success like the sports car currently pulled up outside her house. But if he lost it all tomorrow, Gaby knew instinctively that he'd still have Amy by his side. He'd knocked on the door and she'd flown across the room to open it, all thoughts of their conversation completely forgotten. For a relationship that only spanned eight weeks she was already planning on what to get them for a wedding present.

'Come on, cut it out or get a room. I'm happy to rent my spare out by the hour – if only it had a bed,' Gaby said, handing him a coffee. 'I've put a drop of whisky in it,' she added with a smile. 'Amy did say you've had a bitch of a day?'

'More than a bitch,' he said, flopping down on the sofa, Amy leaning into his side, his mug resting on the arm. 'For a restaurant that specialises in steak, to run out of meat is unacceptable. I thought we were going to have a stampede on our hands when I realised the delivery from the butcher's never arrived this afternoon. It was only a mercy dash to Asda that saved the day.'

'Poor you.' Gaby picked up the whisky bottle from the top of the old sideboard and placed it on the coffee table in front of him. 'Go on, help yourself. You can always leave your car here and walk home.' She turned to Amy with a smile. 'And, as I've had more than enough, you might as well keep him company – remember, it's my turn to drive tomorrow.'

Chapter 19

Gaby

Tuesday 12 May, 8.45 a.m. Rhos-on-Sea

'I knew we shouldn't have opened that second bottle.' Amy lifted her hands, securing her hair back into a tight ponytail.

'It seemed like a good idea at the time.' Gaby was silent a moment, manoeuvring her car through the entrance to the station, her next words creeping in from the side before she had the time to edit them. 'I've had a card from Izzy.'

Amy's mouth dropped open. 'Izzy Grant? How is she?'

'Good, I think.' She stared at her briefly, the memories of their time together in Swansea filling the space between them. Izzy, whose baby daughter had disappeared. A case that Gaby had solved but only after Izzy's own life had been put in danger too. It was her biggest failure and the reason Gaby had been transferred when moving between police stations wasn't the norm. 'I've been invited to her son's christening.'

'Her son's christening?'

'Yes. Godmothers usually are, you know.'

'Oh Gaby. How wonderful,' Amy said, drawing her into a deep hug before continuing. 'Godmother Gaby. How cool is that!'

'Not quite so cool when the poor little blighter realises who he's named after. Darren Charles Grant.'

'Ha, that's hilarious. I thought for a minute she'd called him Gabriella!'

They parted at the entrance, Amy heading to her office on the second floor while Gaby strolled up to the front desk to ask Clancy, the desk sergeant, if there was any post, only to turn at the sound of her name being shouted from the far end of the corridor. Glancing up, she saw Owen racing towards her.

'Thank God you're early, ma'am. I was about to phone.'

'What is it?' Her eyes widened at the sight of his dishevelled appearance. 'It looks like you've had a night of it.'

'You could say that.' He ran a hand through his hair, only making it worse.

'Has there been a development in the case?'

'No, nothing like that,' he said, throwing a look at the waiting area and the couple of people eyeing them with interest. 'Come on, I'll tell you on the way. DCI Sherlock has called an emergency meeting. They're all waiting in the squad room.'

She secured her briefcase under her bent elbow, trying to match his footsteps stride for stride and failing miserably. Grabbing onto his arm, she pulled him to a halt. 'You've either got to walk slower or carry me and I really don't recommend the latter option.' She glared at him, her voice reflecting her expression. 'Why the hell didn't you phone me last night? I'd have been happy to come in.'

'Sherlock wouldn't let me when I suggested it – some rubbish about you looking tired and needing your off-duty after working all weekend. Believe you me, I'd have been happy with the extra support, not to mention the extra brain power,' he said, his skin the colour of parchment. 'We had a call last night about a missing woman. It's not looking good.'

Chapter 20

Gaby

'Settle down everyone,' DCI Sherlock said, slamming his hand on the desk with enough force to rattle the legs against the floor. 'We have a lot to get through. As you've probably heard on the grapevine, we've a missing person on our hands. But before we get to that I'd like to inform you all that I interviewed Gaby for the post of detective sergeant yesterday and I'm delighted to say she was successful.' He paused until the clapping had died down. 'Anything you'd like to say, Darin, before I continue?'

Gaby shook her head, her face a picture of embarrassment. She'd never been any good at having the spotlight shone in her direction and occasions like this were torture to someone like her who just wanted to get on with the job.

'Right, back to business. Bates, what can you tell us?'

'There's not a lot to go on, sir. Tracy Price, age thirty-four years, missing since yesterday afternoon. The station received a call at 15.55 from her distraught husband, Barry, who'd had

114

a message from the school to pick up the kids, twin boys aged six. He returned to the house only to find no sign of her. Her handbag was hanging on the back of one of the kitchen chairs as usual. The family car sitting outside in the driveway. The only things missing her phone and diary.'

'Any history of marital problems?'

'Not that he'd admit to, but I wouldn't necessarily expect him to. They have a house in one of the lanes off Upper Mostyn Street. I've also been in touch with her parents and sister, but they were the first people the husband called before phoning us, which I've got to say, on paper at least, looks spot on. We're also checking CCTV footage of the area but there's quite a few spots that aren't covered that end of town.'

'What about hospitals?' Marie interrupted.

'First place I tried. No Jane Does brought in, either alive or otherwise.'

Gaby stood from where she'd perched on the edge of a chair and walked up to the front. She was still trying to process having to deal with a missing woman so soon after the murder and it was true to say, felt miffed that Sherlock hadn't allowed Owen to phone her last night but there was nothing she could do about that now. She picked up a photo from the top of the pile, ready for distribution. The face was a pretty one with rounded apple cheeks and a lively smile, but that wasn't what grabbed her attention and got her synapses going into overdrive. It was her distinctive coppery red hair, tied up in one of those messy buns that were still all the rage. Hair so like Christine de Bertrand's that, for a second, she thought they'd mixed up the photographs.

'I take it this is the missing woman,' she said after a long pause.

'Yup. Tracy Price, taken only last week.' Owen took the photo from her and added it back on the top of the pile. 'So, you've spotted it then.'

'Spotted what?' Marie interrupted with a little shake of her head.

Gaby finally tore her gaze away and turned to face the rest of the team. 'That Tracy Price could almost pass for Christine de Bertrand's sister,' she said, picking up the pile and starting to hand out the photos. 'This has just turned from a missing person's case into possibly something a whole lot more sinister. I want a widespread search started and, with the DCI's permission, extra staff begged, borrowed or otherwise from the North Wales network.' She glanced towards Malachy, who appeared to be still chewing on what looked like the remains of his breakfast. 'Devine, what was the name of that Country Park Warden who we had to contact when there was that problem with graffiti a couple of months ago?'

'That would be Dafydd Griffiths, ma'am,' he said, swallowing hard.

'Thank you. By the way next time you come in late still eating, it will be bacon sarnies all round – got it?'

'Yes, ma'am.'

She walked over to the window and fiddled with the blind, her eyes drawn to the car park outside, which was swiftly filling up with cars. The murder of Nikki Jones was spiralling out of her grasp and she didn't know what to think of this latest development. Were they linked? Possibly, although exceedingly unlikely with one being a potential victim, the other a suspect. It was that distinctive hair colour . . . surely not a coincidence? But, if not a coincidence then what? Just like Rusty the one thing she distrusted above all else were coincidences. There was no place for them in police work. She brushed a stray strand of hair away from her face before turning her head and starting to speak.

'Owen, I'd like you to coordinate the search and take the rest of the team with you,' she said, angling her head to where Jax and Marie were sitting. 'But be led by Dafydd with regards to the Great Orme. He knows the place better than anyone. I also need you to get the husband in – we'll meet him together. She snapped her fingers. 'And you'd better get Amy Potter to sit in on the interview too. We all know how astute she is. We need to push ahead with this ASAP.' She scanned round to the other side of the room and where Malachy was tilting back in his chair, his long legs stretched out before him. 'Mal, I'd like you to conduct a door-to-door of all the Prices' neighbours. All this activity will mean that we'll have to scale back a little on Nikki Jones's murder. It's not as if she's going anywhere . . .' She gathered together her notebook and phone and headed for the door, saying over her shoulder, 'We'll all meet back here at three o'clock sharp.'

Marie Morgan pushed up from her chair, her fair hair pulled off her face in a couple of plaits, which only accentuated her heart shaped face and wide-set eyes.

'I'd like to continue with looking for the knife, ma'am, if I may? I've a hunch that it might be in a car park somewhere in Llandudno.'

Gaby studied Marie's flawless complexion while she thought how best to reply. If she'd been gifted with such attributes . . . she'd probably have ended up in the same job. Her expression softened at the thought. Marie Morgan's looks were deceptive. She was usually the first in the office and the last to leave, which said a lot about her work ethic and even more about the state of her marriage. Gaby wasn't a gossipmonger and refused to listen to the rumbles that tore through the building at a rate faster than any spring tide. But she'd have to be deaf not to realise that things weren't all they seemed in Marie's garden and, just like she protected Jax with his speech impediment, she now allowed Marie the room she needed to prove herself.

'Okay. It's not a bad idea to keep our eye on the situation on the West Shore.'

'Yes and I'm happy to continue getting up an hour earlier to see if anything materialises with the dog walking,' Jax interrupted. 'After all I don't live far away and my mother's dog still has to be walked.'

Gaby nodded in his direction before focusing again on Marie. 'Okay, I'll expect you to feed back twice a day and, in the meantime, you can carry on with the interviews as well as working on finding that blasted knife. I'm not sure that we've got a handle on who Nikki was as a person yet. We still need to check with both her previous and current employers. You have my number. Keep me posted.'

She continued walking only to stop a second time, the sound of DCI Sherlock's voice ringing in her ear.

'I'd like to see you in my office.'

DCI Sherlock tilted his head for her to take a seat before speaking. 'My reasons for inviting you in for a little chat, so soon after your promotion are twofold,' he said, resting his elbows on the desk. 'Firstly, I wanted to check if you're completely happy to take the lead on both investigations?'

Gaby opened her mouth to speak but Henry stalled her with a flick of his hand. 'Now don't go thinking I have any doubts on that score. I have every faith in your ability but it's a big step.' He rubbed his hand across his chin, his gaze finally meeting hers. 'This isn't for public discussion, but DI Tipping won't be returning in the immediate future. Obviously we all hope for the best, but the super has to plan for the worst. I know that heading up two potentially huge cases will be a challenge, especially as you're brand new in the post, but I wouldn't ask if I didn't think that you were up to it.'

'You have no need to continue, sir. I view it as an honour to look after both cases until DI Tipping's return.'

'You're a good lass,' he said, slipping back into the broad Scots accent from his upbringing on the Western Isles. 'Right, back to business. I have a funny feeling about this missing woman, so I'd like all the stops pulled. I've already been in touch with the superintendent and he's arranged for additional officers to help with the search.' He picked up his pen and unscrewed the cap before continuing. 'Now, with regards to that other unfortunate incident along the West Shore. I take it you don't have enough to arrest the key suspect? As the clock's ticking, we could ask for a twenty-four-hour extension, if you think it would make any difference to the outcome?'

'I don't think so, sir. Forensics hasn't come up with any new leads we can follow yet. But Dr Mulholland's testimony is forcing me to look harder into de Bertrand's claim that there's another party involved but as to who that might be—'

'What about the husband?'

'He's certainly on the list of possible suspects,' she said. 'I plan to bring him in for questioning again but not until we've found Tracy Price.'

'Yes. Indeed.' He ran his hand over the back of his neck. 'I can't stop thinking about those poor children.'

'Neither can I.'

Chapter 21

Gaby

Tuesday 12 May, 11.40 a.m. St Asaph Police Station

'Thank you for coming down to the station, Mr Price, at such a difficult time,' Gaby began, pulling out a chair and indicating that he should do the same. 'You're already acquainted with DC Bates and this is DS Potter, our Family Liaison Officer.' Gaby inclined her head in Amy's direction.

After well over a decade in the force Gaby had thought herself one of the most astute of coppers. She'd seen most of it and heard the rest. No one was a shock just as no one person's actions could surprise her. Most members of the human race were too busy going about their lives to be bothered about others. There were, of course the minority. That small group of individuals who'd sell their granny to the highest bidder, adding their child in as a bonus. But she thought she'd had people's measure, both good and bad, right up until Leigh Clark's wife had dissuaded her of the notion. Her mind, usually so focused, couldn't help dipping back to those dark days in Cardiff when she'd taken the bait he'd been dangling of a single man about town looking for a little woman to share his life – she'd swallowed the line, hook and all. She should have known that a man like Leigh wouldn't have come without baggage. What she didn't realise was how much until his heavily pregnant wife had decided to tell her in front of the whole station. She was over him now. He rarely figured in anything that was relevant except in her reaction to a certain type of man. Barry Price was that type – she hated him on sight.

It wasn't that Price was good-looking – and he was. It wasn't that he was also tall and with a figure of a committed gym aficionado. It wasn't even his coal-black hair trailing his collar or the firm set of his jaw. It was the fact that he reminded her of Leigh – something she was struggling to forgive him for.

But for all his model looks and swaggering gait, he appeared both haggard and tense as if it had been a long time since he'd slept and, with his wife now missing for twenty hours, Gaby couldn't blame him one little bit. She watched him pull up a chair and take a seat before folding his arms across his chest, his look frank.

'I'll do anything if it will help get Tracy back. The boys . . .'

'Ah yes,' Owen said, his voice low. 'Twins, isn't it?'

'Yes, Saul and Solomon. They're staying with my wife's parents until—'

'Good plan. Best all round to try and keep things as normal as possible. So, Mr Price, can you tell me about the last time you saw your wife?'

'Yesterday morning, just before leaving for work.'

'And your work is?' Gaby said, her unopened notebook on the table in front of her. She'd rely on the microphone, set into the wall beside the table, when writing up her notes.

'I work at the family business, Price's Butchers.'

'Along Madoc Street? I know it well. Now, can you tell us exactly what happened yesterday?'

Barry raised his head from where he'd been staring at the top of the table. 'Nothing out of the ordinary if that's what you're asking. Tracy runs a mobile hairdressing business so she can still drop off and pick up the kids. I leave at seven and it was the same yesterday. She was in the kitchen messing around with the boys' lunch boxes.' He sniffed hard, running the back of his hand across his nose. 'She handed me my sandwiches and said, "See you later". That's it.'

'And was she working yesterday, do you know?'

He shook his head. 'I don't. She has a little diary, which she keeps in her handbag. It's the only thing that seems to be missing along with her mobile.'

'Okay. So, yesterday everything seemed perfectly normal. What about before yesterday? Any problems? Both of you in good health? Any financial concerns, that sort of thing?'

He held her gaze. 'Not more than most people, Detective. If you're trying to ask, in a roundabout way, if our marriage was on the rocks then the answer is an emphatic no. Oh, like most people we've had our moments, but we've always managed to kiss and make up.'

Gaby forced a smile, in the same way she forced herself to keep an open mind. Just because Leigh Clark had been a toad was no reason to suspect Barry Price of the same behaviour. She decided to end the conversation. He looked as if he'd been through enough for one day.

'Thank you once again for coming down to the station. We'll need your permission to go through her things in case there's something you may have overlooked. We'll also need to speak to your children in case they can add anything to your statement.'

'Is that really necessary?' he said, his voice sharp. 'They're only six and I don't want them to be affected by whatever's going on.'

Gaby placed both hands flat on the desk, struggling to choose the right tone of voice that spelt compassion married with authority. 'I can assure you that the wellbeing of your children will be our paramount concern during the session, which will be conducted by a police social worker specially trained in carrying out a joint investigative interview. Really, Mr Price, we do need your cooperation in the search for your wife but your consent to interview your children is something that, while desirable, isn't required,' Gaby said, nodding in the direction of Amy. 'DS Potter will escort you back to reception.' She touched Amy on the arm briefly as she passed ahead of her through the door. 'Come and find me after. I'll be in the custodial suite – I have a little job for you.'

Chapter 22

Christine

Tuesday 12 May, 12.10 p.m. St Asaph Police Station

Christine was going stir crazy. She'd already been locked up for three days – three days with nothing to do other than stare at four walls and hope the next meal would be better than the last.

She dropped the spoon back in the bowl of watery soup and picked up the hunk of bread, which at least looked and smelt familiar. Taking a large bite, more to stave off the hunger pains that had become an unwelcome friend during her days of detention, she concentrated on chewing and swallowing – anything to pass the time, which dragged with an unbearable intensity.

The faint noise, more of a vibration, didn't initially pull her out of her reverie. She wasn't expecting any visitors. That was a laugh for a start. She'd had her daily visit from her solicitor when he'd left her with the joyful tiding that there was still no news about the case, either positive or negative. Andy's final comment about *no news being good news* was far from helpful.

She only lifted her head at the sight of the door opening. The female detective walked into the room, a smile of sorts on her face. Christine had never been any good at reading expressions. Oh, she'd improved since her hearing loss, but she'd learnt the hard way that a smile didn't always mean good news just as a frown didn't always mean bad. But, after being left to her own devices for the last couple of hours, she'd welcome anyone to break the monotony – even the Grim Reaper with or without his scythe. She started to get up from the side of the bed only to pause at a touch on her arm and, lifting her head, realised that the detective was already speaking.

'Hold on a minute.' She put her hand to her hair and, removing the hearing aid from first the right and then left ear, proceeded to fiddle with the switches before reinserting them. 'I don't have any spare batteries and it's not as if I have anyone to speak to in here.'

Gaby frowned, a proper annoyed frown that stretched across her forehead in a myriad of lines. 'You should have said. Just because you're here doesn't mean we don't have a duty to look after your needs.'

'It doesn't matter, Detective . . . I'm sorry, I can't remember your name?'

'Darin, Gaby Darin.'

Christine watched her walk around the cell and, for the first time, wondered what exactly she was doing there. Even her solicitor had met with her in one of the small interview rooms at the end of the corridor and it wasn't as if there was space in here to swing a mouse let alone a cat. She was obviously here to give her some news and, with that thought, Christine's temper flared. It was one thing being left for hours on end with no idea as to what was happening in the outside world. She'd had no contact with her family. She hadn't even been allowed to read any newspapers in case she saw something she wasn't meant to about the investigation. Christine had had all she could take and suddenly she didn't care anymore if she said what she thought. After all, what could they do? They'd already locked her up and taken most of her life away. They'd certainly stripped her of her dignity – her eyes lingered on the toilet in the corner before shifting to the wall-mounted camera above her head. She opened her mouth to speak only to close it again at the detective's next words.

'I'm here to tell you that you're free to go. While our investigations are ongoing, I do need to ask you to keep us informed as to your whereabouts. I've asked DS Potter to escort you back home or wherever it is you'd like to be dropped off.'

'Please tell me that you've found Nikki's killer?'

'No, not yet. But we're doing everything we can.'

All Christine could do was stare. She'd been hoping and praying that they'd realise it was one big horrible mistake but, now that her wish had been granted, it all seemed somehow hollow.

So that was it, was it? Over? No. It would never be over until she found out what had happened to Nikki. But the worst part in all of this was that the case might be one of the many that never got solved. It's not as if the detective had given her any guarantees – far from it! The truth was she might never know.

She rested her head back against the wall. She felt drained, when her forced inactivity should mean she was bursting with energy but that wasn't the case. When she finally got home, she'd go to bed for a week—

Another thought struck, the same one that haunted her dreams. She had no home – not now. There was no way she could ever return to the flat . . . all that blood. Oh God, she felt the colour drain from her face, her gut twisting. Her beautiful home. How could she ever go back? She felt like screaming, screaming until her lungs burst. Her beautiful home, the thing that she'd scrimped and saved for, would never be the same now. She'd known from the very first sight of the shingle-laden beach with the backdrop of the Carneddau Mountains that here was a place she could call home. Christine had always loved the sea and, being brought up in Llandudno, she'd been able to indulge her passion for water-sports from kite-surfing to swimming, diving and even a little fishing. She'd poured her soul and most of her resources into turning the top floor into a light, spacious sanctuary where she could try and fill the gap left by the failure of her marriage. Now she had nowhere to go except back to her parents.

She'd all but forgotten she wasn't alone until she heard soft words spoken close to her ear. 'Is there anything I can get you?'

'Only my life back,' she said, even though as soon as the words left her lips, she realised how stupid they sounded. Her life wasn't over, far from it. She still had her small cohort of close friends and hopefully she'd still have her work; work she'd grown to love over the last couple of years. It was poor Nikki who'd suffered, not her, not really. But the last few days had changed how she viewed her life – it suddenly seemed so bloody pointless. It had only taken a second for her imperfect little world to collapse and, the worst of it was, she still had no way of knowing what exactly had happened that morning.

Detective Darin was shouldering the door, her thick roped plait hanging down the centre of her back. But for all her kindly smile and friendly words, she was still investigating the most serious of crimes, a crime Christine was up to her neck in. Struggling from sitting to standing, she brushed her hand over her hair.

'So, what happens now? I take it I'm still a suspect?'

'Currently we're following numerous lines of enquiries but, at this stage in the investigation, there's no evidence that you participated in the murder so, for now, you're good to go. That doesn't mean that we won't need to get in touch sometime in the future. There's still some forensics that we're waiting for and there are bound to be further questions.'

Gaby took one step to reach the door and, holding it open, gestured for her to precede her before following her out of the room and slamming it shut behind her. 'You'll need these,' she added, digging around in her pocket and holding out a small bunch of keys.

Christine stared at them, taking a step backwards. 'I don't think I . . .'

'It's perfectly understandable to feel anxious given the circumstances,' Gaby said, breaking eye contact briefly and looking over her shoulder. 'Ah, here's DS Potter. Amy will tell you that it's natural not to want to return home after something like this.'

'Absolutely,' Amy said, offering her a brief smile. 'But there truly won't be anything to see to remind you. The CSI team will have removed all the relevant evidence for analysis so it will be as if it never happened. How about I take hold of the keys for now and we take a drive towards the West Shore. When the time comes, if you really can't face going in, perhaps I could collect some of your things for you?'

Christine felt she was on a conveyer belt or should that be rollercoaster? Now they'd decided she was free to leave, they wanted shot of her as swiftly as possible. She scanned the wall of identical grey metal doors and suddenly her eagerness to exit the building dissipated as quickly as air leaving her lungs. They wouldn't want her back at work until the mess had been cleared up and she certainly couldn't stay at the flat with no mattress except the one in the spare room. Nikki's room. She heaved a sigh at the only option left to her, the only place that would accept her back with open arms.

Moving back into her parents' house after an absence of twelve years wasn't the best idea Christine had ever come up with, but it wasn't as if she had any alternative. At least she was free of that blasted station and, the one thing she was sure of, she'd do anything to never have to go back. After three days in captivity, where every thought and action centred around what had happened in her bedroom that morning, it felt as if she'd almost forgotten she'd led an existence outside that microcosmic spec of time.

She stood outside the station doors, taking a moment to lift her head and stare at the couple of straggly trees in the distance. The world seemed brighter somehow. The sky bluer, the clouds less imposing. She felt a laugh bubbling, a feeling that had been lost to her in recent months, outside the confines of her classroom. Her life hadn't been right for a long time, but it had taken the shock of the last few days for her to realise it. What she could do to change things was currently out of her hands but there was, at least, a determination to try. Hovering on the top step, she allowed her mind to dip into the past, a place where hurt reigned supreme. She'd learnt the same salutary lesson when the doctor had broken the news about her impending deafness. She could have rolled over and accepted what the gods or fate or whatever had thrown at her, but she'd decided to act and, with her actions, had changed not only her own life but that of Paul's too.

The weak May sunshine, warm on her face, couldn't stop a wave of icy-cold trickle down her spine. Even after a break of two years, she still regretted her decision to walk away from the one thing that had meant everything. But she didn't have the luxury of explaining her reasons for ending their marriage. Paul was one of the most honourable men she'd ever met – she knew he'd have fought to stay by her side at the expense of his own career. Her heart ached at where her thoughts were leading. Children. The very next step in their plans, plans that she'd annihilated along with her marriage vows.

'The car is this way,' Amy said, touching her arm for her to follow. 'Have you decided yet if you'd like to drop by the flat to pick up some gear? It's something you'll have to do at some point, and it will save you having to go back in a couple of days.'

'That's very kind of you but I don't think that—'

'Believe me, it's not kindness.' Amy opened the car door and, heading around the bonnet, slipped behind the wheel before turning back to Christine, her hands resting lightly around the steering wheel. 'Who knows what memories might be triggered by entering your apartment? I think you need to find out what happened that morning nearly as much if not more than we do and, for that to happen, you need to face your fears head on. It's only a flat at the end of the day. Bricks and mortar can't hurt you and I'm more than happy to be beside you all the way.'

Christine dropped her eyes to her lap while she made her decision, although the detective had already made it for her. If there was something in the flat, something that could spark the gaps in her memory, then she had to go back.

'You're right, of course you are.'

The trip from St Asaph's station to the West Shore didn't take long. Within half an hour Amy had reversed into a parking place only a couple of houses away and switched off the engine.

'If at any point you feel this is too much or the wrong decision then let me know and we'll leave immediately.'

Christine felt like telling her there and then that it was the wrong decision. She'd never felt more cowardly in her life. But instead of airing her thoughts, she followed her out of the car and through the wrought-iron gate that led up to the front door, her keys back in her hand. The one thing she'd never been was a coward and a fit of the vapours wouldn't help anyone, least of all her. If what Amy said was true, she might be about to remember something instrumental in bringing closure to this waking nightmare.

The communal hall was the same, the muted creams and browns a familiar and welcome sight after the ignominy of the police cell. She paused at the top of the stairs, looking back down before inserting the key in the door. It was too late to turn tail and run. She had to face her demons. The only big problem was she had no idea exactly what those demons were.

Chapter 23

Gaby

Tuesday 12 May, 2 p.m. St Asaph Hospital

'It never rains but it pours,' Gaby said, catching the eye of the receptionist as she shrugged off her waterproof mac. 'Half an hour ago there were only a couple of clouds in the sky.'

'Having a bad day, love? You'll find a coat-rack behind the door.'

'The worst of days.' Gaby shook her plait free of errant rain-drops before making her way across the room. While she'd visited a variety of areas in the hospital before, the children's social work department was new to her and she felt her smile growing at the sight of the brightly coloured walls displaying an array of Disney characters, a smile that quickly faded when she remembered exactly why she was here.

'I'm DS Darin by the way. I'm here to meet with a Sue Sullivan.'

The receptionist's face flashed with interest, her fingers busily tapping away on her keyboard, but all she said was, 'She's waiting for you in room two, second door on the left.'

Gaby gave her a quick smile of thanks, all her thoughts on the interview ahead, an interview she was already late for. Meeting with social workers was all part and parcel of her day-to-day job as a police officer but child interviews were tricky and a task she was happy to leave to the professionals. Susan Sullivan, the woman she was about to see, had a reputation which preceded her across the Welsh network. But she'd be no pushover and who knew what she'd be able to find out from a couple of six-year-olds.

She pasted another smile on her face before lifting her hand to knock on the door and push it open.

The room wasn't anything special, just an office with the expected desk and swivel chair. But it wasn't the office that interested her – it was the middle-aged man and woman trying to entertain a couple of book-end boys still dressed in their school uniform of blue sweatshirt, grey trousers and black lace-ups.

After another round of introductions Gaby sat back in her chair, more than happy to let Sue take the lead.

'As I was saying, Mr and Mrs Wood, all we'll do today is take the boys next door for a little play. It will only take about half an hour.'

'But we'd like to be present. Surely you can't speak to them without one of us there?' Mrs Wood, stout and red-faced, started to stand, bristling with indignation.

'It will be better if you're not,' Gaby interrupted. She didn't want to tell them that they had no choice in the matter. It would only put their backs up unnecessarily and she was well aware that it was their daughter who was missing. She softened her voice, making sure to maintain eye contact. 'The sooner we can find out any information to help find your daughter, the better. They'll be quite safe with Mrs Sullivan.'

Gaby watched the woman sink back down like a deflating balloon, her hand instinctively reaching out for that of her husband. While her heart went out to her, the stark truth was she needed this interview. The hope was the boys had either seen or heard something that she could tell the team at their three o'clock catch-up.

Sue stood and approached the two boys who were both engrossed in watching a cartoon on their grandmother's phone.

'Hello again, Saul and Solomon. Granny and Grandpa are about to have a cup of tea, which all sounds a bit boring to me. How about I take you next door? I've had a new box of Lego delivered but I'm a bit stuck,' she said, her lips turned down at the corners. 'I really need a hand from a couple of clever boys like you or my digger will never get built.'

Gaby tried and failed to settle her face into a bland mask at the immediate reaction. Susan had them at Lego but had managed to reel them in like a prize salmon at digger, the phone thrust back into their granny's lap without a backward glance.

Within seconds a tray of tea and biscuits had arrived as if out of nowhere enabling Gaby to follow Sue and the boys without any of the awkward questions she'd been expecting.

The viewing room, next door but one to Sue's office, was just that. A box of a room with four walls, one of which had been given over to a two-way mirror shrouded in a blue floral curtain. Gaby worked the string and flicked on the microphone before settling back in the only chair available.

The large playroom in front of her was set out with dolls' houses, play kitchens and shelves full to heaving with every game under the sun. But she wasn't interested in anything apart from the two identical boys leaning across the central table, their fair hair cut into a spiky cut by a loving hand; her stomach twisted at the thought. She had a bad feeling about Tracy Price. She'd had a bad feeling right from the very beginning.

Forcing her thoughts to calm, she concentrated on the conversation between the three of them as they poured over the instructions.

'I'm pretty sure I've gone wrong somewhere and I so wanted to finish it by this afternoon,' said Sue.

'Here.' A chubby finger pointed, first at the chart and then to the bucket of the digger and where it was hanging off in a decidedly lopsided fashion. 'You need a double-ended connector for that bit,' he said, searching in the large box full of pieces.

Gaby watched the petite blonde rest back on her heels, a broad smile on her face. 'You are clever. So, do you have this model at home then?'

'No, but Jacob next door sometimes lets us play with his,' the other brother answered, working on the wheels. 'I have a truck and Solly has an aeroplane. Dad sometimes comes and helps with the hard parts though,' he said, his tongue clasped between his teeth.

'Oh, dads are good at Lego. My dad is a whizz.' She wasn't looking at the boys when she spoke, all her attention on the pieces in front of her, her long slim hands deftly fitting together the axel.

'And Mum, although she doesn't have much time what with work and all.'

'Yes, indeed. And she has to run around after you too although I'm sure you're a great help.'

Gaby couldn't help a small twitch of her lips at the serious nods being made in Sue's direction. 'Does she take you to school too and pick you up or does your dad help out?'

'Only Mum. Dad has to leave really early for work and sometimes we don't even see him at night.'

'Oh, he must work really hard,' she said, her head still averted, her hand rummaging a long time in the box. 'So, who took you to school yesterday?'

'Mum, as usual,' Saul said, his little forehead puckered into a frown. 'Mondays are her old people day. She usually brings us back some sweets on a Monday.' He stopped, his bottom lip starting to quiver. 'Dad picked us up instead.'

Sue's hand stilled, her thumb and forefinger clutching onto a long yellow strip of Lego, her gaze flicking towards him before returning to her task. 'Well, I'm sure it made a nice change having your dad pick you up for once. Mums sometimes need a break. So, what kind of sweets do you normally get on a Monday then?'

'Marshmallows, one of the old ladies gives her a packet for us to share each week and sometimes we get to draw her a thank you card. I'm not very good at drawing, Solomon is much better.'

'Oh, I can't believe that. Do you think if I go and see this lady, she might give me some marshmallows too?'

'You might be too old, but you could always ask,' Saul said, his hands full of Lego.

'Do you know where she lives?'

'Mummy took us once, but I don't really remember.' Saul chose another piece with care, turning it over in his hands before replying. 'There were lots of old people, but Mrs Glynne was by far the nicest.'

Chapter 24

Gaby

'Right. Before we start . . . I have some news.'

All eyes lifted to stare at DCI Sherlock and a silence descended. There'd been recent rumours coursing through the station about pending job losses and everyone was worried. The annual budget had been cut year-on-year and, with crime figures escalating, the squeeze was on. Gaby sat back and watched as they exchanged looks, comfortable in the knowledge that, for once, she knew she had nothing to worry about.

'I had a little chat with Gaby earlier,' he continued with a smile. 'With DI Tipping still not well, she's agreed to head up both cases instead of having to bring in outside help. As I've said, it's only an interim measure and we're all hoping Stewart makes a speedy recovery.'

'Hear hear,' Owen said, lifting his mug in a mock toast before directing his drink in Gaby's direction. 'Well done, Gaby.'

'Thanks, Owen and thank you, DCI Sherlock. I'll do my best

to fill the very large shoes Stewart's temporarily vacated.' She walked across the room to stand in front of the couple of large whiteboards. 'Now back to business. As you all know, we have two cases on our hands: one a missing person's and one a murder. With regards to Nikki Jones we've had to release Christine de Bertrand, due to lack of evidence. We still need to find that blasted knife so, if anyone has any bright ideas, now's the time to speak up because I'm about to make the difficult decision of pulling all staff off the case until Tracy Price is found,' she said, inclining her head in Marie's direction. 'I know what I said only this morning but things are different now. We're already reaching the twenty-four-hour mark since she went missing and we all know what that means. We just don't have the manpower to run two such investigations fully and a missing woman has to take priority.' Gaby scanned the room only to pause briefly at the sight of Amy's raised hand.

'I do have a possible lead. It's not much but I think that Dr Mulholland might be interested in something Christine said when we were at her flat earlier.' Amy secured her ponytail back off her face before continuing. 'She's a keen swimmer and she's recently taken up scuba diving. She showed me the garage where Mrs Ellis lets her keep her tanks and diving suit rather than having to lug her kit upstairs. Apparently, there was a knife, a double-edged serrated one, particularly used by divers in case they get trapped in nets and what have you. It's missing.'

'A double-edged serrated diving knife,' Gaby repeated, picking up a felt-tip marker and adding the words to the first whiteboard. 'I'll email the doc straight after this. Thank you. Very helpful. Anything else?'

'No, not really.' Amy's brows drew together in a frown. 'She's now with her parents. I can't see her going back to the flat any time soon. She's either a very good actress or completely devastated by what's happened.'

Gaby had lost count of the times she'd heard an officer say those very same words. Criminals by nature were amongst the most accomplished liars around, something she'd learnt the hard way on her previous job. She grimaced, forcing herself to change the direction of her thoughts. Allowing herself the luxury of thinking about St David's was always risky. Her biggest regret was placing her faith in someone that turned out to be a compulsive liar and a murderer to boot. The only way she could exorcise that horrid memory was with work and with that thought, she dragged her mind back where it belonged. If Tracy was still alive, she'd find her and, if she wasn't, she'd find her killer instead.

'Anything else on the Jones murder before we go on to Tracy's disappearance?'

'Only that we're widening the knife search to all the car parks, lock-ups and garages in the surrounding area,' Marie said. 'If the tall, dark stranger exists, he had to have some means of transport. The CCTV was pretty much a waste of time but we're also checking with all bus routes in addition to the train station and taxis but with only a vague description and no photo it's going to take a miracle.'

'Okay, thank you. That all looks promising but if you haven't found it by today, Marie, I'm going to shift you onto the search.' She noted her nod with a smile before continuing. 'If no one's got anything to add let's concentrate on Tracy now.' She looked around the room before landing on Owen. 'I take it there's no news?'

'Not a dickybird,' he said, lowering his head back down to his mobile and scrolling through his messages before lifting it again. 'I have a team of twenty scouring the area but with both beaches and the Great Orme, it's an enormous task. There's only been one possible sighting and that turned out to be nothing. The newspapers are all running the story and the husband will appear on the six o'clock news later.'

Gaby nodded. 'I've just come from the hospital and the interview with her children; remember, apart from the care-home staff and residents, they're the last people to see her alive. The boys' version of events is that Monday is usually a good day for them. Their mother always picks them up from school with a bag of sweets – sweets supplied by one of her clients.' She looked up, catching Jax Williams' eye. 'It's not a completely hopeless task, Jax. We know she's a self-employed mobile hairdresser, so your first job is ringing around all the old people's homes and day centres looking for a Mrs Glynne. It will be a nice relief from all that dog walking.'

'Indeed, ma'am.' His response was nearly as glum as his expression.

Gaby turned towards Malachy, frowning at the sight of his designer stubble. 'Malachy, any joy with delving into their lives? What about finances, neighbours, illicit affairs, skeletons in their knicker drawer?'

'There's not much, ma'am and certainly no skeletons that we can find. I had the husband do a quick inventory and, as far as he can tell, nothing apart from her diary and phone are missing. So, on the surface it looks as if she returned home from the care-home around lunchtime and left again on foot in the clothes she was standing in, which doesn't make sense. What woman leaves her handbag behind unless it's an emergency?' he said, tilting his head in the direction of the board and the neat list of clothing listed: blue jeans, red jumper and flip-flops. 'With regards to finances, the house is rented. I've been in touch with the letting agent and everything looks to be above board. There are the usual standing orders going out from their joint account each month for rent and utilities but apart from that there doesn't appear to be anything out of the ordinary. They didn't have much but appeared to be coping with the odd handout from her parents. I caught up with the senior CSI a few minutes ago. They've carried out a thorough search of the property including spraying with Luminol but there's no blood traces to be found.' He took a long swig of his drink before returning the mug to his desk. 'I've also conducted a door-to-door, which has only been partially successful. The house on the left is owned by a Mr and Mrs Stevens – the husband runs Stevens' Chemist in Rhos-on-Sea – but I only got to speak to one of their kids. I'll hopefully be able to catch up with one or other of them shortly. I had more luck with the house the other side, occupied by a Deborah Miles, a retired schoolteacher. The Prices moved in a couple of years ago and, on the face of it, are ideal neighbours who keep themselves to themselves. She often hears the boys playing in the back garden on the swings and what have you. She's had more to do with the mother but not much. She occasionally meets her in the front garden when she's out tending her roses.' He looked up. 'Mrs Miles's roses, that is. The Prices aren't much into gardening apart from mowing the lawn. I tried to press her on their relationship, but she didn't have much to say. She used to hear him come in late sometimes and assumed he'd been to the pub. She rarely saw them out as a couple and less so recently.' He picked up his mug again and drained it in one before settling back in his chair. 'That's it for now.'

'Good work. Give me a buzz if anything comes from meeting with the neighbours on the other side. I'm afraid I'm going to have to ask you all to put a shift in on this,' she said, glancing down at her watch. 'You don't need me to tell you that time is running out for a happy resolution.'

The whole room fell silent for a moment before erupting into activity, each of the officers starting work on their assigned tasks.

Gaby headed to Owen's desk, laying a hand briefly on his shoulder. 'I want you to leave work at a reasonable time this evening.'

'But boss . . .'

'No buts, my lad. The next time I bump into Kate I really don't fancy my chances if I haven't at least tried to give you a modicum of family time.'

'What about you, hmm? You have as much right to downtime as any of us?' He stared up at her for so long that she was hard pushed not to put a hand to her hair. She knew she looked like shit, the lines under her eyes multiplying at an alarming rate but it was something she was able to ignore. Mirrors were to be avoided at all cost and, as long as she didn't arrive at her desk with toothpaste dribbling down her chin, she didn't care what she looked like. She'd worn her waist-length hair in the same way for nearly twenty years and was reluctant to change the easy-maintenance hairstyle for a shorter version that might need more than a twice-weekly wash and occasional brush. At some point she'd have to take the plunge and get it restyled but that wasn't going to be any time soon.

'Owen, you have no need to worry about me. I don't have a husband, partner, live-in lover or even cat or budgerigar to worry about. My life is exactly as I want it. Now hurry up and give that good lady a phone and tell her you're going to get away on time for once. Staying with her parents is all very well but what about you! I don't want to see you back in the office until tomorrow morning. That's an order, Detective.'

'I can see why you might have difficulty in securing a partner, ma'am,' he said, his deep chuckle softening the impact of his words.

Chapter 25

Marie

Tuesday 12 May, 4 p.m. Llandudno

Marie locked her car before making her way to Mostyn Street and the St Tudno Tearoom, which made the corner with Gloddaeth Avenue. The old-fashioned bell above the door made her smile as did the traditional wooden interior and exciting array of cakes. Despite being here to work she decided to treat herself to coffee and a slice of gateau, something she rarely did. Ivo liked his steak lean and his women leaner. But on this occasion, she decided to ignore his strictures and asked the woman behind the counter for a large cappuccino to go with her large slice of chocolate cake.

The café was emptying, which gave her the excuse she needed to ask the manageress to join her when she had a spare minute.

'Nikki Jones, what a terrible thing. If there's anything we can do to help?'

'Thank you, Mrs Irving.' Marie smiled at the round-faced woman before raising her mug and taking a tentative sip. 'Can you tell me a little about her? Even the smallest thing might be of some use.'

'Well, not really. She hadn't been with us long. Only a few months and she pretty much kept herself to herself. We're busy all year round so there's not much time to chat, you know.'

'What about friends or anything she talked about relating to what she did when she wasn't working?'

The woman opposite was nervous. Marie could sense it in the way she frequently looked over her shoulder, scanning the room. It was probably nothing. Feeling nervous around coppers was an occupational hazard but she'd check her up on the system as soon as she left the shop.

'No, there's nothing I can add. She was a good worker. You could tell she was educated like, not that she talked much. It was just there, a hint of the person she was underneath the mask she wore at work. I knew no more about her in the end than I did the day I employed her.'

Marie left Mrs Irving to close up the café, her words ringing in her ears. She hadn't been expecting to learn anything new and she hadn't been disappointed. Nikki was an enigma as was the location of that blasted knife.

She retraced her steps back to the side of Holy Trinity Church where she'd left her car and was soon settled behind the wheel still thinking about the knife. What she should be thinking of was the dinner party she had to prepare for. The lunchtime text from Ivo, informing her that he'd invited a couple of his colleagues over for supper, was typical. He gave no thought to the work involved and, for once in her life, she'd resorted to the freezer in Sainsbury's over the fillet of salmon and homemade pavlova he probably expected.

The day, which had started out warm and hopeful, now had a distinct chill in the air and a threat of rain on the horizon with the darkening clouds racing overhead. But Marie had more to concern herself outside of the weather and the state of her marriage. She couldn't believe that the killer would have bothered to dump the knife in the sea. For a start he could have been seen with all the early dog walkers about and why make a detour when it would be so much easier to dump it in one of the many bins that littered the streets. But she'd walked these self-same streets over and over as had Curtis and his trusty sniffer dog and they'd come up with nothing so what made her think that today would be any different.

Glancing at her watch made her nervous so she didn't. The rush hour traffic between Llandudno and St Asaph would already be starting to clog the A55 so she was going to be late whatever she did. But instead of worrying about something she couldn't change she spent the next few minutes trying to put herself in the shoes of the killer. She was convinced that he must have travelled by car and dumped the knife on the way back but that's as far as her thought processes were prepared to take her. In truth, looking for the knife was worse than looking for a needle in a haystack, the only thing missing was an excess of other knives . . .

Marie gripped onto the steering wheel, trying to snag onto the new idea fluttering on the doorstep of her mind. So where would the best place be to hide a diving knife other than amongst other diving knives? She knew that Llandudno was a huge aquatic centre with a full range of water sports available from sailing, snorkelling, wind surfing and diving. But just because she didn't know exactly where these took place didn't mean that the killer had the same level of ignorance. After that first thought it only took her five minutes to find the information she was looking for. A diving hire shop within a few metres walking distance of the main pubs along the high street. Within an hour she was back on the road to St Asaph, a carefully wrapped knife on the seat beside her and a boot full of defrosting food.

Chapter 26

Gaby

Tuesday 12 May, 6 p.m. St Asaph Police Station

It had been five-to-six when Gaby finally herded Owen out the door of the squad room, his belligerent mutterings still ringing in her ears. She'd nearly had to threaten him with a disciplinary if he didn't follow orders, the sight of his grey face and bloodshot eyes strengthening her determination to send him home instead of hanging on until they'd caught up with the remaining officers spearheading the search for Tracy.

Slipping off her shoes under her desk, she wriggled her toes, a little sigh escaping at the thought of a long hot shower and bed. But it would be a while yet before she would be able to partake in either. The only respite came in the form of caffeine, the litter of empty mugs on her desk testament to her latest addiction. But if she had any more coffee, she wouldn't be able to sleep a wink. Instead, she padded over to the water cooler behind the door and poured herself a glass, her gaze gliding to the TV, mounted on the back wall, which she'd tuned into *BBC News at Six*.

The disappearance of Tracy Price was headline news, the interview with Barry heart-breaking even for an old hand like Gaby. He could barely speak, his bottom lids heavy with unshed tears, his shoulders and head hunched. His whole body screamed defeat. In fact, he was the epitome of what a man in his position should look like. Distraught. Diminished. Defenceless.

She cast a dispassionate look at him, trying to see underneath the layers of skin, flesh and bone to discover what kind of a man hid beneath but, of course, it was an impossible task. He could be saint or sinner for all she knew. As with anything, the truth lay somewhere in the middle and only time would tell how good an actor he was.

Gaby switched the news off in disgust, placing the remote back on the shelf underneath the TV and returning to her desk, her mind on the description being broadcast into lounges around the country. She only hoped that someone would come forward because, from where she was sitting, it was all starting to look hopeless.

'Ah, I thought you'd still be here, ma'am.'

The sound of Malachy's voice had her scrabbling for her shoes and almost bumping her head on the edge of her desk in the process.

'At last. I thought you two had bunked off for the night leaving me all on my tod,' she said, throwing a tired smile at the sight of Jax and Malachy strolling into the office as if they didn't have a care in the world. She looked them over briefly. At their age they probably didn't.

Of the two, she liked Jax more with his fair hair and easy, happy-go-lucky smile. Malachy was tall, quiet and brooding with ink black hair to match his dark skin. So far there was little between them in either their work ethic or diligence. Their differences were more subtle – her mind drifted back to Malachy's unsavoury comment about lesbians. She hoped her faith in both of them wasn't about to be put to the test.

'Take a seat. I hope you've been as successful as Marie. She's found the knife. Jason, the senior CSI on the case, has volunteered to stay late to process it.'

'Where was it?'

'You might well ask, Jax. A diving shop in Llandudno which relies on the good nature of its customers to leave their hire gear in a shed around the back. It wasn't even locked but it will be now! Right then, what have you got for me?'

'To cut to the chase, ma'am, I've just come from Daffodils Residential Home situated along L-L-Llewelyn Avenue,' Jax said, the perennial notebook flipped open on his knee. 'I first spoke to the receptionist and then the manager. Tracy Price has been going along every Monday for the last couple of years. They have a small hairdressing salon, only a small room with a basin and a hairdryer, but it's a great meeting place for a good old natter. Monday morning was no different. She turned up at nine as usual and there was nothing out of the ordinary with either her manner or mood. She was full of arrangements for the twins' b-b-birthday, which falls in a couple of weeks.' He turned the page of his notebook before continuing. 'The reason it took so long is because I had to hang around for Mrs Glynne, she was out with her daughter. She couldn't believe that Tracy would up and leave like that, not with their b-b-birthday only around the corner.'

'No, and that's the problem,' Gaby said, her expression grim. 'Neither can the rest of us. Did she have anything else to say?'

'Not really. She was under the impression that Tracy was in a rush to be finished on time. She usually hangs around for a cuppa and a chat in the sitting room with the rest of the residents, but yesterday was different. She didn't say where she was off to, but Mrs Glynne thought she might have had a doctor's appointment.'

Gaby stared, leaning forward. 'What am I missing here, Jax? There haven't been any reports that she's been unwell, have there?'

'No, not unwell as such, ma'am,' he said, his face flushing. 'You know what little old ladies are like?'

'Actually no, I don't. Why not enlighten me?' she questioned softly, her eyes riveted as the blush spread to the tips of his ears.

'Well, she did say that she thought she might be . . . pregnant.'

'Pregnant? There's no record of a possible pregnancy from discussions with either her parents or her husband and it is the sort of thing they'd know before some little old lady surely?' She tried to tighten the reins on her thoughts, which were galloping ahead. If the husband didn't know, perhaps he wasn't the father? Hmm . . .

'Let's back up a minute, Jax. Tell me exactly what this Mrs Glynne said.'

She watched him peer down at his notebook and recite, word-for-word. '"She reminded me of my eldest, Ellie-Mae. I could tell weeks before, but I never let on. They always like to share the news themselves, you know. It gives them a little boost."'

Gaby let the air seep through her teeth, almost speaking to herself. 'So, it's only conjecture and supposition. The husband and parents might not have known if there was any truth to Mrs Glynne's guesswork. Sadly it's a little late to be calling her doctor's surgery even if we knew who that was.'

'Actually, I thought I'd check before heading back to the station. I didn't think you'd mind?'

'Far from minding, I'm bloody ecstatic but, hurry up, the suspense is killing me,' she snapped, sending him a quick smile to soften the sting of her words.

'Dr Hywel Turner, Mayberry Practice. It looks like there's a *Did Not Attend* annotation on her records for two o'clock, Monday. I didn't manage to see him but it's the first appointment she's made in months so it's unlikely he'll have known what the appointment was for.'

'Good work, Jax, very good indeed. For this I might see fit to pull you off dog walking duties.'

'Oh, I don't mind, really I don't,' he said in a rush. 'It's something I'm happy to continue with for a couple of d-days,' he stuttered. 'It would be a shame to give up too soon, you know . . .'

She eyed him carefully, taking in the brightening of his cheeks and the way he was now staring rigidly at his shoes. God, it was times like this that she was made to feel very old indeed, her thoughts swinging to the vegetable lasagne and small glass of wine she had planned for later – that is if she even managed to get home. It was one thing to help the likes of Owen achieve the kind of work-life balance she silently craved. Helping young lads out with their love life was something entirely different.

'So, I take it Miss Watson, her of the highland terrier fame—'

'Cairn, ma'am.'

She blinked. '*So, I take it* this Miss Watson is a hot blonde with legs up to her armpits?'

'A petite brunette, ma'am,' he said with a grin.

'Whatever. Jax. Do me a favour and at least get her phone number. I might have other duties for you after tomorrow, like helping interview Tracy's husband. He didn't mention the possibility of a baby,' she continued. 'But that in itself means very little.' She waved her hand, dismissing him. 'Okay, thanks for that. Runaway home to Mummy for your tea and remember to be back here sharp for the nine o'clock briefing.'

She didn't wait to hear his softly muttered *thank you, ma'am* before turning to Malachy. She examined his stubbly chin, smothering her smile with a cough. If she'd met him down the pub she'd have thought him cute with his wiry black hair and startling brown eyes but she must be getting old because, instead of hunky male, all she could think of was the need to have a quiet word with him about his razor usage. The uniform policy came with two distinct choices. Clean-shaven or bearded. The one thing that wasn't allowed was designer stubble simply because she couldn't have her constables looking like something the custodial officer had chucked out of his cells the morning after the night before. A thought hit, causing her to smile. She'd take great delight in passing on the little issue of Mal's facial hair over to Owen. After all, she was now his boss.

'Okay, what news do you have for me?'

'Actually, it's better than I'd hoped,' he said, crossing his legs at the ankle. 'Remember I mentioned the Stevens next door? Well, I managed to catch up with the wife. It was all a bit fraught with kids and dogs running around. Their youngest is the same age as the twins so they've seen a fair bit of Tracy and the boys, less so the husband. By all accounts Barry Price kept his distance. But she found Tracy nice and always willing to say a few words when they did see her.'

'What about rows?'

'They wouldn't necessarily hear them even if they did happen, ma'am. Built in the Fifties, the houses are quite substantial and detached.' He ran his hand over his chin, the faint rasp from his bristles filling the air. 'I have an inkling that things weren't as rosy in their garden as Barry Price would have us believe though. Mrs Stevens wasn't specific, but the impression was that Price was out late quite a lot of the time, the implication being he was down the boozer. She also said she thought there were marital problems from something her husband had said, but nothing she was prepared to substantiate with facts.'

'Mmm.' Gaby paused in the act of jotting down the bones of the conversation, twisting the pen between her fingers. 'We may have to do some more digging into the husband's private life if she doesn't turn up soon. Good work, Malachy,' she said, noting his face etched with tiredness. 'I think we'll have to invite Barry back to the station for another little chat.'

'Yes, well. I was hoping for more. Is it all right if I make tracks?'

'Yes, off you pop. And thank you. It's more than we've had since she went missing, apart from the baby rumour,' she said, watching him stroll out of the squad room, pulling the door behind him with a sharp click.

She stared down at her notebook, deep in thought. There wasn't much left for her to do tonight. She was pretty sure she'd done all she could . . . The search would continue overnight with or without her staying to await updates and, realistically, the best thing she could do right now was to get a good night's sleep. If there was no news by the morning, she'd haul the husband back in for questioning.

The seven o'clock news was starting on her car radio as she pulled up outside her house and she waited a moment, her keys clutched in her hand, listening to a rehash of the search up to now. There was nothing about the murder of Nikki Jones. After only four days, the story had sunk without trace only to be replaced with juicier bits of local gossip. She slammed the car door shut, her briefcase under her arm, her shoulder bag hanging from her fingers as she fumbled with the key fob, her mind looping back to the murder victim and whether there was any mileage in pursuing the fact that both Christine and Tracy had red hair. There was also the knife to think about—

'Damn and double damn,' she said, her voice ringing out into the deserted road, scaring next door's cat. 'Sorry boy,' she continued, casting a rueful smile in the direction of the large tabby who'd stalked away, his tail tucked between his legs. But she didn't have time to worry about upsetting Scratch. She'd suddenly remembered the one thing she should have done and hadn't.

She opened her front door and, placing her bags on the hall table, walked into the kitchen, her hand reaching for the open bottle of red on the counter – wine was the priority. Only after the first sip did she rescue her meal from the fridge and place it on the top shelf of the oven. Wandering back into the lounge, she checked her phone before resting it beside her glass on the coffee table and, slipping off her shoes, curled up on the sofa, her laptop balanced on her knees.

After booting it up, she logged onto the police network and quickly banged off an email to Rusty, including a photo of the knife that Marie had found, before copying Owen and Amy into the email and clicking send. Instead of shutting it down, she launched Google and did a quick search on the use of diving knives, only to widen her eyes at the sight of the broad, serrated-edged blades staring back at her and all only a click away. To kill someone with a knife was bad enough but to use something that had ripped and torn as it had journeyed between Nikki's ribs was quite frankly barbaric. No wonder at the amount of blood soaked up by the duvet and mattress. She picked up her glass and took a long sip, her gaze now concentrating on anywhere but the screen. Blood and guts were all very well in the day job but her evenings, such as they were, were meant to be a time to relax . . .

The ringing of her mobile cut through the air, causing her to spill her wine down the front of her blouse and, with a muttered curse, she picked up her phone. It was probably only Amy calling for a catch-up but even so.

'Good evening, Detective. Thank you for your email. I think you've solved my little mystery for me.'

She glared at the phone for a second, her mouth tightening at the sight of Rusty Mulholland's name on the screen, before jerking to her feet and starting to dab ineffectively at her blouse with a tissue, random thoughts scattering.

What the hell was Rusty doing phoning? He never phoned. She glanced down at the spreading stain with a sigh. *Thank God he can't see me wearing my glass of Barolo. The blouse is ruined, or it will be if I don't get it soaking in a vat of cold water.*

'My pleasure. You're working late,' she said, all the while thinking that the quicker she could get rid of him the more chance she had of working a miracle on her favourite M&S blouse that cost £39.99 and was worth every penny. She headed back into the kitchen and the sink, the phone tucked under her ear, trying to puzzle out his reason for phoning. There was time enough in the morning for that kind of thing, she thought, her nose wrinkling at the smell of melting cheese starting to come from the oven.

'I could say the same about you, but I hear you have a crisis on at the station?'

'You could say that. With a bit of luck, it's not something you need to concern yourself with.'

There was a pause and then. 'Never say never, Gaby. What's the Gaby for, by the way, surely not the name you were christened with?'

She continued sponging at her blouse with the nearest thing to hand, which happened to be a tea towel. Part of her was pleased that he was starting to treat her like a human being. The other part wondered at the change and what exactly he was up to. No doubt he'd tell her before the large pink stain became a permanent fixture.

'Gabriella. It's Italian.'

'Charming. Well, Gabriella Darin, if I can be of any assistance with your little problem, please let me know.' There was another pause.' I'll see you tomorrow at the station. I'm just finalising the full report.'

She returned the phone to the counter before switching off the oven and making her way upstairs, unbuttoning her blouse along the way. What she needed was an early night and not an evening thinking about the true reason for Rusty phoning – it wasn't as if he'd had anything new to tell her. Dragging on her pyjama top, she headed into the bathroom and started filling the sink before dropping her blouse into the centre. At least she knew exactly where she was with him when he was being rude. But staring at her reflection, she was still unable to completely disregard Amy's take on the situation. She flung back her head and laughed, the sound harsh in the otherwise quiet room. He needed a few lessons on how to speak to women but he'd better not look to her as a potential teacher!

Chapter 27

Christine

Christine woke with a start, her heart pounding in her chest. Lying there, staring up at the same ceiling she'd known since childhood, the dream fell away, leaving only a hazy trace of memory. She rested back into the pillow, trying to drag the strands back, trying to mould them together into something tangible, something she could work with. Something she could tell the police. But the dim figure of a man was all she had. It could be anyone, even Paul, for God's sake.

Glancing at her watch, she scrambled to her feet and headed for the stairs. If she stayed in bed any longer, she wouldn't sleep later. She'd laid down for half an hour after lunch only to fall into a deep dreamless sleep as soon as her head touched the pillow. Not surprising after three nights of being locked up in a cell.

She made her way for the kitchen, only to pause, some sixth sense making her walk to the lounge instead. Her parents had disappeared off for the afternoon so the house should be empty . . . She pushed open the door only to wish she hadn't when she saw who was sprawled out on the sofa.

'What are you doing here, Paul?'

'Perhaps I should be asking you that exact same question,' he said, his gaze never leaving her face. 'You have a perfectly good flat along the West Shore.'

She blushed, even though it was the last thing she felt like doing. But Paul here, now, was the *very last thing* she could cope with. Stepping into the room, she resisted the urge to turn and flee back up the stairs. After all, she had every right to be at her parents' house – much more of a right than he had. Instead she ignored him, giving all her attention to an ecstatic Ruby, the soft wriggling body bringing back a host of memories she was ill-equipped to deal with.

After a moment she settled her back on the rug before picking up Paul's empty mug and walking to the door. So what if she'd decided to run away on the pretext of making him a coffee? So what if her feminist alter ego was currently bashing her brain with a host of reasons why the very last thing she should be doing was making him a drink? She wasn't just making him a drink. She was making a tactical withdrawal while she regrouped – the coffee-making was a subtle form of defence, only that.

As Christine filled the kettle, she tried to count the number of times she'd been in his company since the divorce and couldn't get past two. Two times in two years and two times more than she could cope with. Paul – the man she'd met and fallen in love with, if not at first sight, then pretty much at the second. The man, if she was honest, she still loved but, knowing what she did, the man it was impossible for her to be with.

She didn't see the country kitchen with its rustic wooden beams and hand-worked pine cabinets. Plucking a couple of clean striped Cornish-ware mugs from the dresser, she only truly became aware of her surroundings at the feel of the smooth ceramic in her hands. Her parents had bought a set of six on their honeymoon and, over the years, her father had added to the collection on birthdays and Christmases so that the shelves were now heaving under the weight of the distinctive blue and white pottery. It was a tradition they'd hoped to start with her, she remembered. Her mind strayed to the set of mugs tucked away at the back of one of her kitchen cupboards. And with that thought, tears started trickling down her face, tears that felt long overdue. Now, at a time when she could least afford it, she found herself having to squeeze her emotions back down her throat while she continued making the coffee. And the worst of it was she didn't even know what the tears were for, except the realisation that she'd never have the kind of relationship that her parents had. She'd given it her best shot only to have fate screw her over at the last hurdle. Her future had been sealed that first day she'd walked into the lecture hall and found the man of her dreams addressing the audience. When she'd realised that he'd been struck by the same lightning bolt, it had taken both of their combined resolves not to act on their feelings until after she'd sat her finals.

Heading over to the sink, she scooped up handfuls of water and sluiced under her eyes before picking up the mugs, hoping the icy cold would detract from any lingering redness. She could find no excuse for not returning. There was no excuse apart from cowardice.

He was standing by the window, his fingers pleating the corner of the curtain and she took a moment to examine him. Tall and sparse, his lean frame barely had an inch of spare flesh, something that had always annoyed her. He could eat what and when he liked and yet she'd never known him put on an ounce. The last few years had been kind to him apart from his hair, which was receding on all sides, but that couldn't detract from his good looks. He was handsome when she'd first met him. He was still handsome.

He must have heard her make a noise because, before she knew it, he'd turned and pinned her with that intense blue-eyed stare he used to reserve for his students – it had been years since she'd fallen into that category.

'You look well, considering,' he said after a moment, settling onto the sofa and resting back, his legs crossed.

'Considering what exactly?' She pushed a mug in his direction before choosing a chair on the other side of the room, her gaze resting on his face. She'd always had more trouble with softly spoken words, which wasn't surprising considering the serious-ness of her head injury as a child. As his wife, she hadn't worried. She'd had normal hearing in her right ear and, apart from minor adjustments in seating arrangements, she'd coped just fine. In the early days it hadn't made any difference. She'd always been able to guess at the words he was about to utter. But not anymore. Now she was in dangerous territory and she didn't like it – she didn't like it one bit. She couldn't even put her hand up to her ear for fear he'd realise what she was doing. Being deaf in one ear was totally different to the bilateral deafness she was currently facing and something she was determined not to tell him about. He'd feel sympathy and sympathy was the very last thing she needed in her life right now.

'Considering a few nights in the cells. What else? I did try and visit, you know, but they wouldn't let me even write you a note.'

'They probably thought you were trying to help me get rid of clues.'

'Would there have been any then?' he said with a frown. 'I had hoped that you were innocent?'

'Of course I'm bloody innocent. What the hell do you take me for!'

He spread his hands. 'Well, it's not as if Nikki was your best friend or anything.'

She stared at him. 'And what exactly do you mean by that? You more than anyone must know how difficult it was for her. She was that proverbial square peg no matter how many times people tried to help her to fit in.'

'So, what happened to change all that, hmm?' He picked up his mug, taking a long sip before continuing. 'I would have thought you'd have been the last person she'd ever have turned to.'

She managed a laugh of sorts. 'I'm not that bad.'

'I never said that you were. But you must know that, to her, you were toxic.'

'Only because she thought herself in love with you.'

'Here we go again. I'm pretty sick of this, Christine. I've told you time and again that I did nothing to encourage her.'

'Just as I've told you that she didn't need any encouragement. She loved you and nothing you or anyone else said could have dissuaded her.'

'And then she disappeared off the scene only to turn up dead in your bed. A likely story. Are you sure there isn't something you're not telling me?'

The urge to turn away at the sound of his words was immense but Christine couldn't. She only had two choices here, neither of which were ideal. If she left the room, he'd most likely follow, which would defeat the object. She drew in a breath at the option left. She had to stay and argue with him at the risk of chipping away at the memories that she'd tucked deep inside, memories she couldn't afford to lose. If she lost them there'd be nothing left.

'Not that it's any of your business but no. I'm not nor have I ever been gay. And before you ask, yes, I did bring a man back to the flat but, again, what's it to you?'

His face visibly paled underneath his tan, a remnant of the walking tour he usually opted for each February half-term, a tour she used to join him on. She wondered where it had been this year. Spain? Greece? Italy? She blinked rapidly. She'd lost the right to think such thoughts when she'd decided to walk away from their marriage in the same way he'd lost the right to question who she hooked up with. She took no pleasure in knowing that she'd hurt him with her words. Her comment had been an act of desperation by someone only interested in self-preservation.

'So, what are you doing here, Paul? Rubbing salt into the wound or have you some other motive?'

'Ah. I take it your parents haven't told you then?'

'Told me what?'

'I've left the school. They've offered to put me up for a few days because of Ruby,' he said, now staring at the floor.

She scrutinised the top of his head, her thoughts ricocheting. She'd only ever wanted the best for him, and he loved working at St Gildas. She wondered what could have happened but, knowing the board, she didn't have to wonder too long. Poor Paul. Loving her was probably the worst decision he'd ever made. She heaved a sigh. This living at her parents, if only for a couple of days, wasn't going to work. She couldn't bear being in his company and, as he had nowhere else to go, she was the one who'd have to leave.

He opened his mouth to speak but she stood and held up her hand. She couldn't answer the sort of questions queuing up on his tongue. Questions like what the man's name was, in case he was able to provide an alibi. She still couldn't remember a thing about him except that there had been somebody and she'd had sex. The fact that she couldn't remember anything else was one of the things that worried her the most. No matter what she did to try and jolt her memory it still came back as a complete blank and that scared her. She'd let a man break through the protective wall she'd built after the divorce and yet she couldn't remember the first thing about him.

''Look, Paul. I'm not prepared to answer any more of your questions. You can have the house and my parents for as long as you need them. I'm more than happy to sort myself out.' She bent down and gave Ruby a quick cuddle before picking up her mug and heading back towards the kitchen, only to pause and turn. 'Did you say something?' She watched him shake his head and, with a frown, she walked out of the room, closing the door behind her.

Paul returned his now empty mug to the coffee table before resting his head in his hands, the words *I love you* still echoing across his mind, words she hadn't been able to hear.

So it was true, all of it. Not that he'd doubted for a minute what Dennis and Hazel had told him. Christine, his little Chrissie, heading towards the thing she feared the most. Total deafness. He'd known from the beginning about the riding accident that had deprived her of her hearing in her left ear, but she'd coped. She'd coped to such an extent that most people hadn't even realised.

He sat up, dragging his hand across his face, his thoughts now in the past and the dark days of the divorce. He'd tried to speak to her, tried to sort out whatever the problem was with their marriage, never dreaming for one minute what the problem could be. But she'd refused. Apart from one scrappy letter, she made sure all communication had been via her lawyer. He'd felt confused, hurt and finally angry that she could even think to throw away what they'd had together. They'd had the perfect life, both in jobs they adored – they'd even talked about having kids for God's sake!

He shivered, drawn to the multitude of photos of her dotted along the mantelpiece. He knew her better than anyone. She'd never have accepted second best and a mother that couldn't hear her child's first words, their cries, their laughter . . . He dropped his head into his hands, for once in his life at a complete loss as to how to proceed. He had no back-up plan. No *what comes next*. She'd walked away from him for the second time. He clenched his hands into fists. He was determined there wouldn't be a third.

Chapter 28

Gaby

Wednesday 13 May, 6.30 a.m. Rhos-on-Sea

After a restless night Gaby donned her running gear, her determination to continue with her exercise programme only partly the reason for her jog. She always thought better when she was active, and she might as well kill off a few calories at the same time. But with work still on her mind she propped open her laptop and started reading through her emails before heading out.

There wasn't anything of any interest except a reply from Amy.

I see that your affair with the delectable doctor is progressing nicely. You'd better watch out, my friend. It will be smoochy phone calls next.

Gaby laughed, her fingers flying over the keyboard. Amy with her hearts-and-flowers view on life needed a strong reality check – she was in the right mood to provide it.

'Ha bloody ha. I'd have to be desperate to consider dating Dr Mulholland. The simple fact is that Rusty and I aren't suited. I suggest you get on with your own relationship and stop interfering in mine.' She clicked send before she could soften her tone and, grabbing her front door key from off the table, made for the door.

It took her a good ten minutes to reach the sea-facing kiosk where she paused for breath, leaning against the railings to look across at the Welsh coastline and the changing light now the sun had started to rise. Apart from checking her emails she'd also phoned the station but there'd been no new developments, which didn't bode well. Officers learnt from day one that the longer it took for a case to break, the less chance there was of it ever being solved and missing people followed that trajectory to the letter. In her heart of hearts, she knew that the likelihood of Tracy Price turning up alive was dwindling with every passing second and there didn't seem to be a thing she, or the rest of the team, could do about it.

Glancing at the bus shelter up in the distance, she shook her head, deciding to cut her run short and head for home. She had too much on her mind, the scenic vista, for once, distracting instead of inspiring. She had two cases to solve, possibly linked. There certainly seemed to be a surplus of redheads with Christine and Tracy and even Rusty Mulholland. Her mind switched back to that phone call and part of the reason for her poor night's sleep.

Gaby walked the rest of the way, making a mental line-up of key suspects as she went, a list that perhaps surprisingly didn't feature Christine de Bertrand, simply because so far there wasn't a single strand of evidence against her that wasn't circumstantial. Any barrister worth his law degree would boot the case out on a technicality within seconds, not least because her system was floating to overflowing with booze and drugs – the deadliest of combinations. Gaby was still missing the man, the man Christine was meant to have slept with, but she did now have the knife.

Her attention was captivated by an adorable pair of poodles trotting by the side of their owner. Throwing the woman a smile, she wondered how Jax was getting on. She'd know soon enough.

At her front door, she withdrew the key from where she'd

secured it in a zipped pouch around her waist and inserted it into the lock. She had lots to do today, starting with an impromptu visit to the Prices' next-door neighbours. Malachy's report was all very well but, over the years, she'd learnt to trust her instincts and they were telling her that she still hadn't been given the full story with regards to Tracy and Barry's relationship. Statistically, he was very much under the spotlight whether they found Tracy or not.

She hurried into the kitchen and flicked on the kettle before popping a bowl of porridge into the microwave, keen now to leave for the station as soon as she'd showered, changed and breakfasted. Racing up the stairs to the bathroom, she aimed her grey leggings and sweat top in the direction of the white wicker laundry basket before climbing into the bath and turning the overhead shower on to full, taking the pain and punishment of icy cold water quickly followed by hot. Today was going to be a difficult day, she could almost taste it. Best to steal a march and get that interview with the Stevenses out of the way. She frowned, trying to decide which of the team to take. Jax would have already put a shift in with the dog walking while Marie ... work was the least of her troubles right now. That only left Malachy. Her frown deepened.

Mr and Mrs Stevens lived in a corner house just off Church Walk. The houses were all large and detached, built from the same shade of red-brick and with identical grey slate roofs. Gaby glanced at the Price house, but the curtains were pulled and, with no car in the driveway, she surmised that Barry and the twins must be staying elsewhere.

Returning her gaze back to the Stevens' property, she took time to note the well-kept front garden with its cut lawn and neatly clipped Elaeagnus hedge. It looked exactly like the Prices' and yet it didn't. Everything was better maintained and, with a family hatchback in the drive squashed between a Saab and a Fiesta, money was obviously no object. She turned in her seat, eyeing Malachy as he switched off the engine and gathered his notebook and warrant card from the dash.

'Tell me again about the Stevens?'

'Not a huge amount to tell, ma'am,' he said, resting his head back against the seat and speaking from memory. 'He runs a small chemist near the Post Office. He's a pharmacist while his wife is a solicitor. They have three kids, one in his late teens, one about to go into secondary school and the youngest, a boy, the same age as the twins. They appear to be well-to-do, owning the property mortgage-free. Mr and Mrs Average, although I've yet to meet him.'

'Okay, let's do this.' She put her fingers on the handle and opened the door, smoothing her jacket before climbing out of the car. 'If we finish in time, I'd also like a quick word with the other neighbour, the retired lady,' she said over her shoulder before heading up the drive and pressing the bell.

The door opened after one ring and Gaby looked the brown-haired teenager over in amusement as he stuffed the last piece of toast into his mouth before swallowing. She could almost forgive him his wide-eyed-stare when she introduced herself, flipping open her warrant card with a brief smile.

Shutting the door behind them, he hollered, 'Mum, the police are here to see you,' before promptly disappearing up the stairs.

She walked into the hallway, making a mental note of the décor, loving the dark-wood laminate flooring teamed with pastel blue walls and tasteful artwork.

Redecorating wasn't something she could think about anytime soon except perhaps the paint, but it was still okay to collect ideas and file them away for future reference. There'd come a time when she'd be able to do what she liked with her home but, for now, all she could afford was to keep a mental note of what she'd like to change if she had both the time and the money.

Mrs Stevens, hurrying out of the kitchen where breakfast appeared to be in full swing, was nothing like she'd been expecting.

Tracy, also the mum of a six-year old, appeared youthful in the photos scattered over her desk, her vivid hair complementing the clearness of her skin and the brightness of her smile. Gaby had never been any good at guessing ages, so she rarely attempted it. But the woman in front of her, dressed in a conservative grey shift dress, was much older than she'd been expecting, her face littered with wrinkles, her skin paler than skimmed milk. She looked smart, professional . . . and tired, her pixie cut an uncompromising iron-grey.

'Come on, Jacob, eat your cereal as quick as you can. I'll be in the lounge for a few minutes,' she said, her voice ringing out over the sound of the radio. 'Daddy's driving you all today and you know there'll be ructions if you make him late.' She headed through the archway and back into the hall, shouting up the stairs on her way past. 'Casper, the police are here for a word and can you make sure Ronan is up while you're at it.'

Gaby's inspection of the lounge was fleeting just as it was comprehensive, her decorating file full to overflowing. The room was an exercise in good taste, a place for everything and everything in its place, unlike the disorganised chaos of the kitchen. The dark wooden flooring continued throughout the ground floor, the pale blue walls echoed here but with a feature wall papered in vivid blues and greens. The twin sofas were covered in rich cream brocade and looked as if they'd never been sat in, certainly not by the jam-covered Jacob down the corridor.

After a second, she chose to sit on the nearest settee, indicating with a tilt of her head for Malachy to join her while they waited for the husband.

She'd been expecting a male version of Mrs Stevens, perhaps a little older but that wasn't what she got. Mr Stevens was both tall and handsome but in a distinguished way. There was a trace of grey at his temples and lines etched around his mouth, but these only added to the air of intelligence and charm as did the conservative grey trousers, crisp white shirt and grey-and-pink striped tie. In the same way she'd compared Mrs Stevens with Tracy, now she found herself comparing Mr Stevens with Barry Price – there was no comparison. Mr Stevens won by a mile.

She was in the process of standing up to introduce herself only to settle back in her seat at his words.

'Please don't get up, Officer. I'm sure you spend long enough on your feet as it is,' he said, his eyes twinkling. He made for the mantelpiece, resting his arm against the high wooden plinth. 'I take it this is about poor Tracy Price? A terrible business.'

'Yes.' Gaby felt herself relaxing back, taking full advantage of the comfort offered, albeit for the few brief minutes she could afford. After all, she did have a very long day ahead of her and it was a very comfortable sofa. 'DC Devine managed to have a brief word with your wife yesterday and the impression he got was that there might have been some problems with their relationship?'

'Well, I didn't know them as well as my wife but . . .' Gaby watched him lift his hand and run it over the back of his neck, his head turned to the view out of the window and the garden beyond.

'But anything you can add, sir. The longer she's not found the more difficult it gets.'

He swivelled back. 'I take it you suspect that something untoward may have occurred?'

'At this moment in time, I'm not at liberty to divulge any aspect of the investigation, but she's still missing so any information you have that could help?'

'I don't have any—'

'What about what you told me about Barry?' Mrs Stevens said, her voice sharp. 'Didn't you say you thought he was playing around?'

'Really?' Gaby shifted forward in her seat. 'Mr Stevens, if there's any information that you might have to help with the investigation, it's imperative you tell us. Obstructing the police is a serious crime and viewed in a very dim light by the courts.'

'Look, I know all that Officer but truly, it was nothing.' He pulled back his cuff to glance down at his watch before answering. 'I was putting out the bins a couple of weeks ago and I overheard the tail-end of an argument, that's all. I wouldn't even have said anything to Janice about it except that—'

'Except that he thought he heard the sound of something crashing and then what sounded like a whimper,' his wife interrupted. 'There's no use trying to protect him, Casper, not now.'

'But I wasn't sure and I'm still not.'

'You were sure enough to tell me.'

'It could have been nothing,' he continued, finally returning Gaby's stare. 'One of the twins falling – anything. It's certainly not evidence that their marriage was in any difficulty or that he had anything to do with her disappearance. To be honest, I always thought her highly strung; she wasn't past bellowing out orders on occasion. We lead very quiet lives, Detective, and the one thing we don't need is antsy neighbours always on our doorstep borrowing cups of sugar.' He moved away from the mantelpiece and collected his jacket from where it was draped across a spindle-backed chair in the corner. 'While they were a nice enough couple and their boys were good company for Jacob that's as far as our relationship went. Now is there anything else or . . .? I really do need to get to work.'

'What do you think, Mal?' Gaby said, sliding into the passenger seat while watching the top-of-the-range grey Saab.

'I think for someone so keen to get to work he's taking his time getting to his car, ma'am.'

'Ha, you obviously don't come from a large family. Even now he's probably bellowing for them to remember their lunchboxes and sports kit, while he helps Jacob on with his coat.' She turned, watching the procession of kids scrambling out in what looked like a race to bagsy the passenger seat. 'Come on, start the car or they'll get suspicious. It's a shame we won't have time to catch up with that retired schoolteacher but, with a bit of luck, all this will have been a complete waste of time. Tracy will turn up shortly, after a couple of days in a spa hotel with one of her girlfriends and wonder what all of the fuss is about.' She caught Malachy's look and pulled a grimace at the sight of his raised eyebrows. He knew as well as she did that, with over two days under their belt, the likelihood of Tracy turning up alive was now the stuff of fairy tales. She'd be found. It was all a matter of when – but the when would likely be too late.

Chapter 29

Gaby

Wednesday 13 May, 9.30 a.m. St Asaph Police Station

It was only a little after half nine, but Gaby already felt as if she'd done a day's work, as she looked at the motley assortment that made up her team. Just like her, they all looked as if they hadn't had much sleep, even Owen, despite his relatively normal finishing time. But that's how it was. Even if they did manage to have what most people would view as a good day, they still spent half the night puzzling away on the cases that, no matter how hard they tried, defied solving. She couldn't begin to list the number of coppers she'd worked with who had turned to drink in an attempt to forget the job once their shift was over, which was the very reason she always stopped herself after a couple of glasses when she was alone. Work was hard enough but with a hangover it was unbearable, as she only knew too well, her thoughts swinging back to yesterday's thumper of a headache.

No, chocolate was her fix. Dark chocolate, the 70 per cent sort that made her tongue cleave to the roof of her mouth, was at least meant to be good for her and came without the morning headache. But it was also the main reason she was in this mess, her attention shifting from her colleagues and down to her sturdy ankles. The other reason was her second-generation Italian ancestry and a life brought up to know the full benefit of a bowl of carb-filled pasta. If she closed her lids and took a deep breath, she could almost taste her mother's baked lasagne and, for a moment, wished herself back in her family home instead of having to present her miserable findings to the audience in front of her.

'Morning everyone. Thank you for all getting here bright and early,' she said, watching as Rusty pushed the door open with his elbow, a file clutched in one hand, a takeout cup in the other. She waited for him to take a seat, avoiding looking at his casual cream chinos and blue open-neck shirt, so very different from Casper Stevens's designer suit and tie. It wasn't the only difference, she thought, now concentrating on his red hair, which looked as if it hadn't been brushed in a week or cut in months. But, knowing his work ethic, he'd fit in a trip to the barber in between his workload and that's just how it should be.

'Right, let's get down to business.' She strolled over to the first whiteboard and picking up a marker, started adding to the information about the murder weapon, her words and actions focusing her mind. 'Things have moved on in the last twenty-four hours but not so you'd notice. We still have a killer on the loose, in addition to a missing woman. But we at least have some good news on the knife. A diving knife so I'm told, one that Christine de Bertrand kept in the garage along with her wetsuit and tanks. How it managed to get lodged in Nikki Jones's heart is a question yet to be answered.' She put the lid back on the pen and placed it on the desk before turning towards Rusty. 'I'm hoping that Dr Mulholland has some insights for us.'

He joined her at the front, dropping his empty cup in the bin on the way past. 'Insights are for amateurs, Detective Darin. I only deal in facts,' he said, darting her a look laced with dislike and something else she wasn't able to read. 'However, the idea of a double-sided blade such as this one—' he tapped the photo she was holding out '—is a good one. It will be interesting to hear what Jason, the CSI, finds.'

'Fair enough.' She forced a brief smile onto her lips when she'd much rather gouge out his eyes with the tip of her nails. It was as if last night's conversation had never happened which, in a way, made his current attitude all the more disappointing. She'd show him just how far from amateurish she really was but not yet. She'd bide her time until the opportunity arose to make him swallow those words. 'I believe you may have other news?'

'Yes, indeed. The rest of the lab results are back, and it makes for interesting reading.' He flipped open the folder and stared down at the first page, his square hand flat against the desk. 'As you know, the prison doctor examined Christine de Bertrand the morning of the discovery. There is evidence that intercourse had taken place but only from the presence of a silicone-based lubricant commonly found following condom use. With this lack of biological evidence, it's impossible to drill down further. But her toxicology screen does support the view that she might not have had any memory as to what took place when she got back to the flat—'

'So, she got pissed on her birthday, hooking up with person or persons unknown for the night and then what?' Gaby interrupted, the effort causing her head to pound. 'I'm afraid I don't buy that it's a case of a simple pick-up, no matter how neatly it fits with the facts. What about a date-rape scenario? You said initially there was Temazepam in her system – would that work along with the alcohol?' she said, suddenly on a roll. 'Maybe it was opportunist sex and he used what he had to hand, especially as Temazepam was found in the bathroom cabinet.'

Owen inclined his head towards Rusty, who'd taken up residence on the corner of the table. 'I take it there was no such drug in Nikki's system?'

'Now that is an interesting question, Officer,' he said, a smile flickering. 'Why incapacitate one victim only to murder the other? There was no Temazepam and nothing like the alcohol consumption. Apart from Sertraline, a well-known antidepressant, her toxicology report was clear.'

'So, where does the flatmate figure unless it was a threesome and, if Ms de Bertrand is to be believed, that's the most unlikely of scenarios,' Gaby mused, almost to herself. 'She made no secret of the fact that inviting Nikki into her home was one of the worst decisions she'd ever made.'

'Considering we found no evidence that the victim had sexual intercourse, I'd say that a threesome was highly unlikely. I do have some good news, however,' Rusty added, all trace of his smile wiped clean. 'We did find trace evidence on the sheets once they'd hung in the drying closet for twenty-four hours, when it normally takes half that time. In all my years in this job I've never come across a body more totally drained of blood.' He rubbed his hand along the length of his jaw, staring into the distance for a moment, his mind elsewhere. 'She literally bled to death in seconds.'

'Dr?' Gaby said, her eyebrows raised at his sudden silence.

'Sorry.' He shook his head briefly. 'There was some saliva that didn't belong to either of the women. It's gone off for DNA analysis and possible matching on the national database.'

'Thank you.' She took a couple of steps to the next whiteboard and stared at a photo of Tracy Price, forever captured with a laugh on her face, her hair blowing across her cheeks, her boys clutched in her arms.

It was now Gaby's turn to be silent but only for a moment.

'Right, back to our missing person's case,' she began. 'I caught up with the search team first thing this morning and, as you'll all know by now, there's no news as to Tracy's whereabouts. We've interviewed numerous family members and neighbours and even managed to track down her last job at Daffodils, an old people's home along Llewelyn Avenue. There's a variance however in the quality of information provided. If the next-door neighbours are to be believed, the Prices' marriage was in difficulty. On the other hand, there's some thought that Tracy might have been pregnant – none of which we can substantiate. Therefore I'm going to ask the DCI for more staff to widen the search—'

She stopped mid-sentence, staring now at the back of the room and where a young PC had slammed the door on its hinges even as an icy cold finger trailed down her spine. He stood there, his chest heaving, his eyes looking any and everywhere except at her. She'd seen that awful look before, a combination of horror, dread and loathing. She didn't have to listen to the words pouring out of his mouth. She knew them already.

'Ma'am. They've found a body.'

There was more. She knew it in the way his hands clenched and unclenched by his side, his head bobbing up and down like a demented puppet.

'She's at St Gildas School, ma'am.'

Gaby suppressed a groan, wondering how she could have got it so wrong.

St Gildas School – where Paul de Bertrand was headmaster.

Chapter 30

Gaby

Wednesday 13 May, 11.30 a.m. St Gildas School

Gaby knew very little about the education system in North Wales. Being childless, she had no need – a state of affairs that saw no signs of changing in the near future. Her life was set and, apart from the occasional night out with Amy, she rarely ventured past the confines of her job. She drank, ate and slept crime. The only time she didn't was when she was curled up in bed reading one of her favourite romance authors such as Sue Moorcroft and Suzie Tullett. She certainly paid little regard to schooling unless it was in relation to a case and, thankfully, serious crimes in schools were a rare occurrence.

Staring through the heavy wrought-iron gates, the first thing she noticed was the air of silence in the schoolyard, The swings still. The climbing frames empty. Despite the time, there was no sign of life apart from the CSI van and a solitary copper standing by the entrance, signing everybody in. She felt a wave of cold right down to her bones at the thought of murder, the very worst of crimes, having been committed in a place where innocent children gathered.

Her gaze wandered over the grey-stone building, before returning to the plaque attached to the gate, engraved with the date 1579, presumably the date St Gildas was founded. She stilled, suddenly aware of the emblem – a red lion sitting atop of a blue shield. So very different from her school, which had been thrown up in the 1970s. They didn't have an emblem, only the name of their school picked out in yellow against the deep blue of their sweatshirt. Her mind lingered on the crest. She could have sworn she'd seen that same badge before and recently but where? With a shake of her head, she dismissed the thought. She'd remember but not yet. Now she had more important things to think about.

She was careful to avoid the passenger seat. Instead she concentrated on the view out the window while she waited for the uniformed officer up ahead to sign them in. There was so much history here: history and elegance. The long driveway up to the grounds encroached by purple-flowering rhododendrons. The games fields in the distance mowed in precise stripes. Her thoughts returned to Liverpool and the concrete jungle that had been her local comprehensive, suddenly feeling out of her depth. But while her education wasn't bad and she'd easily managed to achieve the entry requirements needed for the force, nothing, in either her schooling or training, could in any way prepare her for the sprawling grounds of St Gildas.

'Morning, I'm DS Darin and this is Dr Mulholland,' she said, winding down her window and signing her name on the clipboard handed to her, well aware of the silent man by her side. At a time when she'd relish being alone to collect her thoughts and prepare herself for what lay ahead, she found herself in the company of the most taciturn of men.

She followed the officer's directions to the nearest available parking space and, switching off the engine, remained silent, unsure of quite what to say.

'Thank you for the lift, the garage has just texted. Mine won't be ready until later today.' Rusty's Irish lilt shattered the silence.

'It's no bother,' Gaby said, turning in her seat.

She'd never taken the time to look at him too closely and, while part of her thought of what to say, the other part was drawn to his blue eyes, now staring back. She swallowed, her mouth suddenly dry. He was attempting to be civil but only because it suited him. He'd been all ready to grab a lift in the CSI van until he realised that it was already full to bursting with officers. 'If you need a lift back it can be arranged too,' she continued with a brief smile, a smile that wasn't returned. 'Come on, we can't get this show on the road without you doing your stuff.'

Instead of replying, he stormed out the car and walked in the direction of the CSI van, leaving her to follow behind, a bemused expression on her face. It was obvious something must have happened to upset him, something that involved her, but she had no idea what. She'd never understand Dr Mulholland if she lived to be a hundred – funnily enough, that was something she was starting to regret.

'So, what have they done with all the children then?' she said, turning to one of the CSI officers and accepting the paper suit and over shoes before slipping off her jacket and stepping into the jumpsuit.

'They've sent home all the ones they could. The rest have been ferried across to St Michael's by minibus. Apparently, they have some sort of emergency reciprocal agreement.'

'Yes, well, if finding a dead body isn't an emergency then I don't know what is.'

She rested against the van to secure her over shoes before following Rusty across the car park and to the line of sheds at the back of the building, speculating for the umpteenth time what had made her decide to go into law enforcement when she hated the sight of blood. Oh, not so badly that she fainted or anything, but it was enough to make the bile rise up the back of her throat.

She could have decided on a much simpler career course – she could have even chosen to go into the family business. But with both of her brothers working for her parents, she felt the time had come to stretch her wings and a bobby on the beat was a whole lot more exciting than a job in the local Italian restaurant. The thought of food was a sharp reminder that breakfast seemed a very long time ago.

Hunger was the least of her worries when, moments later, she found herself in the very last shed, staring down at the body of Tracy Price, her unmistakable red hair chopped close to her scalp, the hilt of what looked like a kitchen knife protruding from the left side of her chest.

'Don't just stand there staring, Detective. And, if you're going to throw up, do make sure it's well out of the way of the crime scene,' Rusty snapped, before turning back to examine the body.

She lifted her brows at the CSI who was staring across at them both, his mouth dropped wide, his camera paused in the action of photographing the scene.

It was times like this that Gaby would like to have told the esteemed doctor exactly what she thought of him, but she was too busy trying not to lose the contents of her stomach.

The floor of the shed was floating with blood and, with no duvet or mattress to soak it up, it looked as if someone had strewn a few gallons of red paint over the boards. But it wasn't just the sight . . . it was the smell. Gaby struggled to heave breath into her lungs, as the heavy sweet sickly scent filled the air; she knew that it would take a very long time to get the odour out of her mind as well as her nostrils. Only seconds before, she'd been attacked by the familiar gnaw of hunger – now it felt as if she'd never feel the need to eat again. Death was an ugly business but this – this must be the worst crime scene she'd ever attended.

She clenched her fists, her nails biting deep, her arms squeezed across her chest as she continued her study of Tracy Price, so different and yet so similar to that of Nikki Jones. She tried to focus on the differences, despite the persistent feeling of nausea threatening to make her run for the door.

The victim lay naked across the middle of the floor, her hands gripping onto the hilt of the blade, her expression one of surprise. Gaby froze, appalled by that look. Tracy hadn't expected death here amongst the cricket stumps and rugby balls. She'd expected a very different experience. Her gaze finally shifted to the picnic blanket underneath, the navy and green check just discernible amongst all that red. On the face of it, Tracy had signed up to what looked like a secret assignation – one that had gone horribly wrong. But, after twelve years on the force, the one thing Gaby knew was that looks could be deceiving.

'So, what do you think then, Dr?' she said, her mind resolutely avoiding the thought of the two little boys who'd lost their mummy. She dragged in another breath, tilting her head in Rusty's direction, well aware that she hadn't spared a thought for Barry Price. She was yet to analyse whether that omission was due to the statistical probability of a close family member having been involved or for a different reason.

He glanced up quickly before continuing his preliminary examination and once again he surprised her, his voice not full of the biting retort she'd grown to expect. 'I think you need to leave me to work my magic, Gabriella, while you go and start doing whatever it is you do. I need to get her back to the morgue as quickly as possible. You can see for yourself what happened but as to why or how – that's another story.' He lifted Tracy's wrist before continuing. 'The best I can say is that she died less than four hours ago as her body is still in the state of primary flaccidity. It's also a good guess that she died at the scene and—' He shifted his attention from where he'd been looking under Tracy's lids '—it would have been only seconds. She probably wouldn't have been aware of more than a sharp pain before she died.'

'Thank you. That's something families always ask first,' she said, staring again at the remnants of that glorious hair.

Would Barry be the one to ask if his wife had suffered or would he alone know the answer to that question?

'Owen, what have you got for me,' she said, a short time later, her paper suit carefully disposed of in one of the yellow clinical waste bags, her hand patting down her hair.

'Not a huge amount, ma'am. Mr Lacey, one of the PE teachers, was setting up for athletics and he went along straight after breakfast to pick up a pile of cones to mark the course.'

Owen was concentrating on his notebook, a clear sign that he'd been affected by the news of Tracy's murder just as much as she had. After working by his side for the last three months, she'd learnt about his pretty much photographic memory and that the need to write things down verbatim, in his case, wasn't necessary. She squeezed his arm and he finally lifted his head.

'Thank God he had the common sense to lock the shed and phone us straightaway before alerting the headmaster and implementing their critical incident plan. Can you imagine a crime scene contaminated by six hundred trampling feet? Old Rusty would have had a heart attack,' he said, his chin hardening.

She rocked back on her heels a moment, her mind trying to join all the dots and failing miserably. Links. It was all about the links, no matter how tenuous. But there was nothing here that made any sense. They had two bodies in less than a week. Two bodies both stabbed to death and both linked to Christine and Paul de Bertrand. Coincidences like that didn't happen. They were made to happen. But where did St Gildas fit in and who the hell would go around chopping hair almost down to the root?

Like Christine de Bertrand, Tracy's hair would have been her crowning glory. The one thing that set her apart, turning her from pretty into a real head-turner – someone to get noticed wherever she went. Was that the link or was it a complete red herring? Gaby's lips twisted. It seemed that wherever she turned there was a redhead sneaking up behind her what with Christine and now Tracy. Even Rusty for God's sake. If she didn't know any better, she'd think that they were searching for someone with a red-hair fetish – did such a thing even exist? It was something she'd look up as soon as she got back to the station.

Gaby tried to remember a case like it and couldn't. But then maybe she was reading more into it. Maybe there was no link. Maybe the knife protruding out of Tracy's flesh wouldn't turn out to be lodged in her heart.

Throwing a final thanks to Jeff, the senior CSI present, she crunched across the gravel drive, Owen at her side. 'Come on, we have the day stretching out before of us and lots to fill it. First, we need to tell the family before any of the press get to hear. How they managed to get Nikki's story for the Sunday edition is beyond me. I wouldn't be surprised if we have someone in the department with loose lips – it would be a crying shame if those two little boys got to hear of it outside of the proper channels.'

'Not forgetting the husband, are you, ma'am? I reckon he'll be just as devastated if not more so, especially if that lady in the care home was right about her being pregnant.'

She searched his face for any tell-tale signs of a reprimand but all she got for her efforts was a bland stare.

'Thank you for reminding me of my duty, Detective Bates,' she replied, her tone sharp. 'I'll bear in mind your comments. Now, ring Amy Potter and tell her to meet me back at the victim's house in . . . let's see . . .' She pursed her lips, trying to calculate exactly how long it would take her. 'You'd better make it an hour. In the meantime, I'll leave you to check that the PE teacher has completed a written statement.' Her hand rested on the door frame, her head turned towards the outline of the shed in the distance, now fenced off with a couple of rolls of their trusty yellow tape. 'If you can check in on the doc before you go to see if he has anything more for us. With a bit of luck, and him pulling out all the stops, we should have his preliminary findings by end of play today.'

Chapter 31

Gaby

Wednesday 13 May, 1.45 p.m. Llandudno

Gaby met Amy on Barry Price's doorstep forgetting for a moment that the last time they'd been in touch was via that terse email earlier that morning. Amy hadn't.

'Are you on a death wish?' Amy grabbed Gaby's arm, preventing her from pressing the doorbell.

'Pardon?'

'I said are you on a death wish? Well, on your head be it but you seem to have forgotten that you still have to work with the man.'

Gaby's jaw dropped. 'Look, I don't have time for puzzles. Tell me what I'm meant to have done and to whom and I'll sort it.'

'Ha, sort it will you! I don't think so.' She leant forward, hissing in her ear. 'Tell me whether you meant to include Rusty in that last email you sent me. You know. The one where you said that you'd *"have to be desperate to consider dating Dr Mulholland"*?'

Gaby let out a long groan. 'Bloody hell. I couldn't have?'

'Yes, you could.' Amy stepped back, releasing her arm.

'Presumably if you didn't do it on purpose then you must have clicked "reply to all" by mistake – if it wasn't so stupid it would be funny but I'm far from laughing. He's a nice man, Gaby, who's just gone through the most horrendous of divorces. Your email will only have cemented that there's a good chance all women are like his bitch of a wife.'

Gaby felt her cheeks redden, too embarrassed to even know how to reply. There was nothing she could say, even to him. He'd never forgive her for this and the sad fact was that she'd been beginning to like him just a little. She felt Amy give her a quick hug before reaching for the bell.

'It's not the end of the world if you didn't mean it. Come on. We'll put our heads together later and see if we can't come up with something.'

This wasn't the first time that Amy and Gaby had found it necessary to break bad news and an unexpected death fell slap bang into the middle of that category. But this was the first time they'd been met with a flat rejection. Usually there was disbelief and often anger, quickly followed by a deluge of emotions that a jumbo box of tissues had no chance of assuaging. But to be greeted by a total rebuttal was new, her mind doing somersaults as to the cause.

Barry had been reluctant to open the door at first and when he did it was clear, from the bleary look on his face, that they'd woken him.

'You should be out looking for her and not haranguing me,' was the first thing Barry said on opening the hall door. He turned away, not seeming to care if they followed or not, his bare feet poking out of a pair of grubby paint-splattered jeans.

It was the sight of those feet that had Gaby pause, her gaze seeking that of Amy's. There was something almost pathetic about the way he retreated down the hall, the sound of his footsteps muffled by rag rugs strewn across the wooden floorboards, and she felt a pang of deep sympathy for what he must be going through. Oh, that didn't mean to say that he wasn't on the very top of her list of suspects. He was so far up that list as to nearly be off the top of the page. But under Gaby's stern exterior beat a heart of gold, a heart that despite all the knocks it had suffered, both in and outside of work, still hoped for the best in people. Was she about to be disappointed? It wouldn't be the first time.

They'd followed him into the lounge. There was no social etiquette in this room. No shaking of hands or waiting until they'd been seated. He stretched out the length of the sofa, his head on one armrest, his feet on the other. The television was on, some mindless daytime drivel that she no more knew the name of than the channel which hosted it, and it was on this that he was fixed to the exclusion of all else. The room was dark, stale even, the glass-topped coffee table littered with dirty plates and mugs. The rugs were sprinkled with crumbs and, despite only the passage of a couple of days, a fine filament of dust marred the sheen of the polished, dark-wood furniture.

'Mr Price,' Amy said, starting the conversation off. 'I'm afraid we have some bad news for you. We've found a body that matches the—'

'No! No you haven't. My wife isn't . . .'

'Mr Price, we need to discuss this.'

'No! No, we don't. My wife . . . Tracy isn't—' He raised both hands to his face, scrubbing his fists into his eyes like a child.

'Mr P . . . Barry. Just because you might wish for something doesn't make it true,' Amy continued, her voice soft.

Instead of a copper now, she was a parent, a parent speaking to her child. Soothing. Enticing, Comforting. 'We can't begin to tell you how upset we all are that this had to happen but now we have a murderer to find and the longer we leave it, the more time there is for the trail to go cold.'

He sat up, his shuddering breath loud in the unnaturally quiet room and lowered his hands to his lap, fisting them into tight balls. The bereaved were unpredictable and Gaby was well aware that they'd have a difficult job on their hands if he decided to turn ugly. No. An impossible one. Despite their supposed extensive training, the reality was a mandatory course on conflict resolution and breakaway techniques, which would be little use against a man of his physique if he decided to turn nasty. While sympathy bled from her veins, she still didn't like him. There was just something about him, although the sight of his bloodshot eyes and tremoring hands that no fist could completely hide was making her revise that thought.

She opened her mouth to ask him as to his exact whereabouts on Monday only to find she was closing it with a snap, his words flowing through her and changing the whole course of the conversation.

'All I want to know is that she didn't suffer. I couldn't bear it if—' His jaw hardened. 'You can ask me any questions you like but the one thing you'll never get me to admit to is the murder of my wife. You can lock me up and throw away the key. I don't care anymore.' He ran his hands over his hair, the greasy unwashed strands gathering in clumps. 'We weren't perfect, her and me, but I'd never have harmed her.' He dropped his eyes to the rug and that's where his attention remained, his voice so soft they had to lean forward to hear. 'That's not true, of course it's not. I've hurt her more times than I can remember, something that's bound to come out, especially if you go speaking to my delightful mother-in-law.' Gaby watched him trying and failing to blink back the tears even as she pushed a tissue into his hand. 'Oh God, how the hell am I going to tell the boys? They adored their mum. She was everything, absolutely everything to them.'

The whole course of the conversation had changed with those few little words.

All I want to know is that she didn't suffer.

How many times during an interview had she heard almost that exact phrase? The mouths might be different. Parents. Children. Siblings. Partners. Lovers. Friends. But the words remained the same. If you loved someone all you wanted to know was that they hadn't suffered from whatever hand that had been dealt. She still didn't trust him but, somewhere under that cynical chest of hers, gleamed a glimmer of optimism for the couple of boys that had lost their mum. She'd been led astray before in her career but, with those words, Barry Price had managed to loosen the stranglehold around his neck just long enough to let an alternative scenario creep into Gaby's mind.

The only link between the two murders was Paul de Bertrand: Christine's ex-husband and headmaster of St Gildas. But she'd interviewed him and the one thing he wasn't was stupid. He'd have known where his position was on the suspects list straight away. Unless someone was out for revenge? In the same way that a dog marks his territory, the scent of another trail was starting to streak across her consciousness.

Gaby left him in the capable hands of Amy Potter, her friend's FLO hat firmly clamped in place, the most sympathetic and understanding expression imaginable on her face. Gaby wondered for the millionth time how Amy managed to remain upbeat and in control. There wasn't a trace of the irate friend that had berated her on the doorstep less than half an hour before. Gaby couldn't think of a worse job with so little appreciation or gratitude. Time passed, emotions were glossed over, the day-to-day minutiae of life shrouded everything with new memories, leaving less and less room for the old. Family liaison officers were forgotten. They got tucked into the back of that dark cavernous mind, never to see the light of day and yet, their role was one of the most valuable to any police force. She counted herself lucky to have Amy still on her team even as she wondered what she'd made of the interview.

She walked across the road to her car. She had no idea how long Amy would stay but, if it was anything like the last time, it could be a very long time. Leaning against the door, she pulled out her phone and, scrolling down her list of contacts, picked out Susan Sullivan's number. She'd thought her job difficult – breaking bad news had to be up there with one of the worst jobs – but it had nothing on what Barry was about to do. She was determined that he'd have all the support available. Saul and Solomon's futures were about to change forever and all due to the despicable act of one person; someone she was going to catch if it was the very last thing she did.

Ending the call, her gaze shifted from the Prices' house to the house next door and the curtain she'd seen twitching out of the corner of her eye. The one thing coppers liked more than anything was nosy neighbours, the nosier the better as far as she was concerned. Neighbours always knew more than they let on, maybe even more than they thought they knew themselves. Retracing her footsteps, she tried to recall who lived on the other side. Malachy had said something about a retired teacher. Taking the time to re-interview witnesses wasn't something the force could usually afford in terms of manpower unless they were viewed as key to the investigation. But if Gaby had learnt anything about people over the last few years, it was that being a young male officer was a huge disadvantage when dealing with elderly women.

The green door was opened after one ring. If she hadn't known better, she'd have guessed the tall angular woman with salt and pepper hair had been hiding out in the hall waiting for a summons. Surely not, but there she was like that proverbial genie out of the bottle, eager to escort Gaby inside for a good old chin wag.

The lounge had seen better days, the carpet threadbare, strategically placed mats only drawing attention to the bald patches. The furniture was heavy and obviously inherited. The curtains were faded. But the tea was hot and strong, just the way Gaby liked it, and beautifully presented in dainty bone china cups, similar to the tea-set her Italian grandmother insisted on using. Settling back in the red tapestry armchair, she resisted the temptation to look at her watch. The woman in front of her, who had introduced herself as Mrs Miles, had information she needed and any hint of rushing on her part, would have her closing up tighter than any clam.

She placed the cup back in its saucer, promising herself a visit to one of the little antique shops, dotted around Craig-y-Don, on her next pay day. There were some things in life that weren't worth skimping on and sipping tea out of a proper cup was one of them.

'Thank you for the tea,' Gaby said, noting Mrs Miles's paper-thin skin and blue eyes, faded with age but still alert. There was no sign of a TV in the room, only a radio sitting on top of the bookcase and a pile of knitting on the sofa beside her. This woman had nothing to do and all the time in the world in which to do it.

Leaning forward in her chair, Gaby started to speak. 'I'm afraid I do have some dreadful news about your neighbour. I'm sure you understand that I can't divulge the ins and outs of an ongoing investigation, but I can say that Barry, Mr Price, is going to need all the support he can get over the coming weeks.'

'Of course, anything I can do. That poor man and those lovely boys.' Her face coloured, the cheeks bright, the mouth slightly open and Gaby was hard pushed not to pull a smile.

As much as she despised the human race for their morbid fascination with all things macabre, Mrs Miles was an intelligent woman and most likely kind. If all that came out of this interview was Barry being inundated with home-bakes and offerings of childcare, then her visit wouldn't be in vain. But she was seriously hoping that this woman was about to give up a whole lot more than overt signs of her sympathy.

Gaby nestled back against a tapestry cushion, choosing her words carefully. The one thing she mustn't do was let her know how much she depended on her answers.

'While I'm here I was wondering if you knew anything about the Prices' routine?' She nodded in the direction of the immaculate lawn where no weed would have ever dared show its head. 'You obviously spend a lot of time in your garden, which by the way is beautiful and—'

Mrs Miles coughed into her hand. 'I'm not sure whether I should—'

'Anything at all, even the most insignificant of things, could turn out to be a great help.'

Gaby carried on sipping from her cup as if time wasn't the most important thing. But this couldn't be rushed. She was waiting for Mrs Miles to finish the argument in her mind, hopeful that the urge to gossip would win over any misplaced neighbourly loyalty.

'Well, I don't think they got on too well. She kicked him out at one point.'

'Can you be more specific? Did you hear—'

'Oh, more than that. I saw everything – by accident, you understand.' She glanced away but only briefly. 'I was pruning my roses, let's see, so that would have been around March time last year – I always follow that nice man's instructions on that gardening programme on the Beeb. Anyway, she was shouting and screaming at him, flinging his clothes out of the bedroom window. At one point I thought about phoning the police.'

'We can't get into domestics unless there's an actual threat of violence?'

'Oh? No. Nothing like that. She took him back, more fool her. But I don't think it was quite the same.' She picked up her cup, cradling it between her fingers.

'Why do you say that?'

'I don't know exactly. I got the impression he'd learnt his lesson that last time for what it's worth. Flowers after work. More effort with the kids.' She placed her cup back down on its saucer, her lips pursed, a small frown creasing her brow into a myriad of wrinkles. 'It was her. She used to be chatty, speaking to me over the fence about this and that. It was as if someone had squeezed all the fun out of her, leaving an empty shell. I used to be able to set my watch by her routine,' she continued, ticking off each item on her fingers. 'School run. Back to the house to hang out the washing. A couple of hours out and about with that little business of hers before returning for a quick lunch and then picking up the kids in the afternoon. Then . . .' She clapped her hands. 'It all changed. I don't know where she went after work, but it certainly wasn't back to the house.'

'And when was this? After she kicked him out?'

'No, much later than that.' Her frown deepened. 'If I'd have to guess, I'd say around Christmas. Yes, that's right. When the schools broke up. I remember thinking that the added strain of that time of year must have brought home to her just what kind of a man she'd married.' She stood up, starting to gather the crockery together on a tin tray. 'If that's everything? I really must get on.'

And so must I, Gaby thought, passing over her cup and saucer, her thoughts heading in a direction that was long overdue. Rusty Mulholland and the patch-up text she needed to send him.

Chapter 32

Gaby

Wednesday 13 May, 4 p.m. St Asaph Police Station

Paul de Bertrand had visibly aged in the course of the investigation, an investigation that had only spanned five days. Gaby too had a reason for looking like something the cat had dragged in. In fact, it was probably a very good thing that the closest she ever came to animals were late night confrontations with next door's moggy. If she didn't have time to feed herself properly, she certainly wouldn't remember to feed a four-legged friend. So, what had happened in de Bertrand's life over the last week to change him so? He looked smart enough in his open-necked shirt and grey trousers and, as men went, he wasn't bad looking. With his high brow and receding hairline, he looked exactly what he was: a highly intelligent man at the top of his profession. But the lines around his eyes, forehead and mouth were etched deep and coated in shadows. He looked in need of a good meal and a full night's sleep, neither of which he was about to get in interview room four.

'Take a seat, sir.' Gaby gestured to a chair before sitting beside Owen, her hand reaching out and flicking on the microphone.

'Can you confirm for the record that DC Bates has read you your rights and, at present, you've declined the services of a solicitor?'

'That is correct.'

'And you know why you're here today?'

'Presumably because you think I had something to do with the murder.'

She eyed him keenly before returning to her notebook. She was well aware that the man sitting opposite was much cleverer than she was and, if she was going to trip him up, she'd have to unsettle him and that started by not answering any of his questions, directly or otherwise. In truth, she had no idea as to whether he was involved, and she wouldn't until Rusty got back to her to confirm, or otherwise, that the deaths were linked. But it seemed too much of a coincidence that a second body had been found at Christine de Bertrand's ex-husband's school. The only problem was that she was currently clueless as to how all the pieces fit together.

'I've been told that you've left St Gildas. That's all a bit sudden, don't you think? What about the usual notice period until a new headmaster can be appointed?'

His gaze narrowed, his face still expressionless. 'My change in career path can surely be of no interest to the investigation?'

'On the contrary. Everyone involved interests me. Please answer the question, sir.'

'Let's just say the board of directors and I had a differing in opinion as to the relevance of my former wife being investigated for murder.'

'So, you were sacked?'

'No, officer. I resigned on the spot.'

'A little over the top seeing as you're not married to her, surely?'

'Not in the slightest. I still have feelings for my ex-wife or isn't that something that's allowed?'

She decided to change tack. 'This parting of the ways with the school happened exactly when?'

'Monday morning, if you must know. As soon as the story hit the newspapers and the board realised the link.' He smiled briefly. 'If Christine had married someone with an ordinary name like Smith I'd probably still be there. The role of headmaster at a public school like that demands one hundred per cent commitment. They frowned enough when we split but the hint of a scandal, even if only by association, would have been viewed in the worst possible light.' He grimaced. 'I can't imagine the furore finding a dead body will be causing. The parents will be disassociating themselves from the school in droves. Schools like that rely on a whiter than white reputation.'

'So, you've heard of the discovery?'

'People talk. The depu . . . new headmaster phoned me first thing, probably to warn me that you lot would be heading my way.'

And therefore giving you plenty of time in which to prepare, Gaby thought, deciding to try yet another line of questioning.

'You mention your divorce and your continued feelings for Christine. If that's the case, why aren't you still together? It's not as if either of you appear to have moved on with other partners.'

She watched his throat clench and knew she'd hit a nerve. 'When are you going to stop asking that question, Detective? She was the one that filed, not me.'

Until I get an answer that makes sense. But all she said was, 'okay. We'll leave that for now. Returning to Monday, can you tell us your movements from around midday?'

'Monday was taken up, almost in its entirety with clearing out the house. I spent the first half handing everything over to Noel – Mr Barnes, the acting headmaster – and the remainder packing up boxes and squeezing them into the back of my car. Thankfully the house is furnished by the school or I'd probably still be at it.'

'And you'd be able to produce witnesses?'

He laughed. 'As the property faces the sports pitch and Monday afternoon is house games for years two and four, I'm sure I could rustle up about a hundred boys if pushed.'

'And what about early this morning from, let's say about 2 a.m. until 7?'

'In bed asleep and, before you ask, no, there were no witnesses.'

She stared at him, trying to make her mind up what to ask next. There was something in the way he'd shifted in his seat at that last question. Guilt possibly, but she wouldn't bet on it.

'Where exactly is bed currently if you've moved out of St Gildas?'

Was that slight reddening of his cheeks due to a blush or temper? She didn't know him well enough to tell but, reaching for her pen, she added a note at the top of the page. The transcript from the interview would be typed up by one of the police secretaries but the one thing it wouldn't include was changes in body language, vital to any interview.

'If you must know, Christine's parents are putting me up for a couple of days until I can sort myself out with somewhere that's willing to take animals.'

'That must be cosy as I believe she's staying there too?'

'As I said, it won't be for long and, until then Christine is staying with Kelly.'

Gaby tapped her fingers on the table, her gaze resting on de Bertrand's bland expression. While not exactly a hostile witness, he wasn't prepared to give anything away, which left her in the dark as to what questions to ask and, without Rusty's report on the second murder, she had no actual evidence that they were linked.

'Tell me about your relationship with Nikki Jones.'

His eyes widened briefly. 'Tell you about my relationship with . . .? There wasn't any relationship or, at least, not in the context I think you're insinuating,' he said, his hand moving to his lap but not before she spotted the whitening of his knuckles.

'I think you know what I mean, sir. I want to know everything I can about Miss Jones and, as her former tutor, you're an obvious choice.'

193

'I don't know what to say about her,' he said, running his hand across his jaw.

'Start at the beginning. What was she like? What were your first impressions? And take it from there.'

'Truthfully? I thought she was completely barking. A social misfit. As clever as you like but unable to harness that potential into any constructive direction.'

Gaby sat back in her chair. 'Go on.'

'There's not a lot more to tell.'

'I'm sure that's not right. Why, for instance, didn't she finish her degree? Something must have happened for her to get so far only to fall at the last hurdle?'

He took a deep sigh. 'Look Officer, you of all people will know that some people aren't as kind as they should be. I said Nikki was different but, the truth is, she stood out like a sore thumb. She kept to herself, never attending any of the social events. The other students viewed her as a hole in the ground sapping all their energy and rumour quickly spread through the other degree courses that she was someone to avoid. Being socially isolated in somewhere as large as a university campus is quite a feat, I can tell you. I tried to help only to have it thrown back in my face.'

'In what way did you try?'

'Just the normal way. Being kind. Trying to talk to her after class and helping perhaps more than I should in our one-to-one tutor sessions. If I'd realised how damaged she was, believe me, I would have thought twice about trying to befriend her. No one, least of all me, could have foreseen what would happen the last time we met.'

'And what did happen, Dr?'

Chapter 33

Nikki

2011
Cambridge

Nikki switched off her mobile and tucked it into the top of her bag. Phones were strictly forbidden in the library, a rule she was heartily in agreement with, particularly in light of the unfinished 5,000-word essay on the use of symbolism in Virgil's Aeneid. Pulling out her pen and sheaf of paper, she tried to concentrate on writing up the bibliography, the last action before summarising her work and checking for typos and punctuation, but for once her thoughts wouldn't be stilled.

Sitting back in her chair, she glanced around at the other people sharing the long table that split the room in two. She was the only one not working but there was a reason for that, her mind trying and failing not to think about tonight's ball, the culmination of three years at one of the most illustrious of universities. It seemed as if her life was a series of baby-steps forward, swiftly followed by giant leaps backward — all of them converging to this point. When her mother had informed her that she was leaving her second husband and moving to Spain, Nikki couldn't have been happier. She'd even managed to make a fleeting visit home to Barnsley to help pack up the house, putting all her mementos from her childhood into storage, not that there were many. A few photos of her and her dad before he left. A wooden bowl that had belonged to her nan. Basically, two boxes were the sum total of the life she'd lived before moving to Cambridge. Her life started and ended at the college steps – only that.

She dragged her hair off her neck, resisting the temptation to secure it with the hair bobble that was a permanent feature on her wrist. The new hairstyle had cost her more than she could afford so the very least she could do was leave it alone in the hope it would last until tonight but that was easier said than done. She'd worn her hair tied back for as long as she could remember and the weight dripping down her back was as unfamiliar as it was unwelcome.

The sound of a chair scraping against the floor forced her thoughts back to the pile of books littering her desk. She only had until tomorrow to finish the essay and, if she didn't concentrate, she'd never have the time to get ready. The long black dress and matching elbow-length gloves were hanging up in her wardrobe. But it was all the other things that couldn't be rushed like make-up, something she didn't know the first thing about. It was probably inconceivable for most people to feel frightened at the sight of the boxes and pots still in their cellophane wrappers – she felt like Cinderella trying to fulfil her destiny but with no fairy godmother to help.

She twisted her hands, the soft white skin on her wrists now faded to almost invisible silvery lines. She'd managed to conquer one fixation only to replace it with another. Paul de Bertrand.

The black dress was all she could have hoped for. Long and slinky, it emphasised her recent weight loss without showing too much bare flesh. For someone used to covering up from head to toe, the feel of cool air on her shoulders was both an embarrassment as well as a lesson in discomfort but, for once, she wasn't dressing for herself. She was dressing for him. Grabbing her wrap, she secured it across her shoulders before picking up her bag and keys, shutting the door behind her with a gentle click. With a sigh of relief, she realised that she'd timed her late exit to perfection. The halls were empty, the rooms on either side silent. The only noise the little tip tap from her four-inch stilettoes, which seemed to mirror the echo of her heart.

Nikki only stopped when she reached the double doors to the sixteenth-century dining hall, the first seeds of doubt taking breath from her lungs and courage from her heart. She could do this. She must do this. Being different wasn't a crime and she had just as much right to be here as any of the rest of them. She remembered his words and, at the memory, planted a smile on her blood-red lips before twisting the door handle, her fiery red locks catching the flickering light from the wall sconces above.

Chapter 34

Gaby

Wednesday 13 May, 4.40 p.m. St Asaph Police Station

'Well, what do you make of that then, Owen?'

'I can't really say. It does put a whole different slant on things though.'

They were sitting in DI Tipping's office, Gaby's office for the time being, comparing notes. Gaby and Owen were friends as well as colleagues and, even though they'd only been working together a few months, she'd grown reliant on his solid matter-of-fact opinions and basic common sense, something she always thought should be a pre-requisite for anyone applying for a job in the force.

'You can say that again. Nikki must have been devastated at the response she got. The laughter. The insults. The ridicule. It would have been enough to push a normal person over the edge but with her unique set of issues . . .' She shook her head, feeling a stab of deep sorrow for the girl that Nikki was. A girl not so dissimilar to her in many ways. The only difference being that she had strong parents that had been there to support her every step of the way.

'Totally misguided, if you ask me,' Owen said, checking his phone for messages. 'To think that de Bertrand or indeed any man would fall in love with her just because she changed her hair colour and tried to dress like Christine.'

'She was young, remember, and without the support of close family members. Her father deserted her before she'd even reached her teens and as for her mother . . .'

'True.' He leant forward in his chair. 'I think the question we need to ask ourselves is why she'd have then decided to move in with Christine, even if she was desperate? Surely Nikki must have hated her with a passion,' he added, now on a roll. 'Here's the woman who stole the man she loved from right under her nose only to discard him like an old shoe. But not only that. She would have also blamed her for not finishing her degree. Christine de Bertrand, the cause of everything that was wrong with her life. Most normal people would have avoided her. They'd have felt embarrassed, ashamed even about their shared history. I don't think Nikki felt either of those emotions. I don't think she could, taking into account the baggage she must have carried around since childhood.'

Gaby raised both eyebrows, the pieces of the puzzle forming in her mind, still not fitting into place – but Owen was onto something. She picked up her mug, running her finger around the rim. When the team of detectives had ganged up on her in Cardiff, when they'd tried to shame her into leaving, she'd just gritted her teeth and got on with the job, a red-hot anger building. But she'd been sensible enough to put that anger into solving cases – Nikki wouldn't have had any such outlet. Her anger would have seethed and festered like a boil, with no hope of release.

'You know what, Owen. Nikki's murder doesn't make sense and that's the problem. Now, if it had been Nikki doing the murdering and Christine the victim . . .'

'What, you're thinking of an accomplice?'

'No.' She smoothed her hand over her hair, tucking in a couple of escaped wisps. 'I'm not thinking anything other than random thoughts and that's the problem.' She sighed. 'What would you say to taking the lead instead of me?' She almost laughed out loud at the firm shake of his head. 'You're a coward, Owen. A big fat coward. After all it's not all that complex. We already know from the saliva Rusty found that there was another person in Christine's bed, presumably the same man that picked her up for sex – that is if she's to be believed and I'm beginning to come around to that idea. He probably liked it kinky or unconscious or whatever. A rummage in her bathroom cabinet would have sorted that out.' She frowned, her voice lowering. 'Now all we need to find out is what he had against Nikki.'

She pulled a face before looking down at her phone, disappointed not to find a reply to the text she'd sent Rusty. It hadn't said much, hardly anything at all but hopefully the brevity of her apology wouldn't be held against her. The problem was that she needed his expertise to move the case forward. They'd had to let Paul de Bertrand go because, just like his ex-wife, there wasn't a shred of evidence against him that wasn't circumstantial. If she had any more strands to follow, she'd seriously have to think about taking up tapestry!

'Right then. In ten minutes, we have to face the rest of them – what the hell can we tell them that isn't either speculation or guesswork?' She watched as he shook his head a second time, his mouth pulled down at the corners. 'That's what I thought.' She propped her elbows on the table and rested her chin in her cupped hands. 'I still think that both cases are linked but until our esteemed doctor gets back to us, it's all—'

'Conjecture?' Owen said, taking the word from her mouth.

'Exactly. It might have something to do with red hair but that trail isn't going anywhere. What we really need is for Jason to find a full set of prints on the knife. We also need to discover why

200

Tracy Price's body was left at that school. We know de Bertrand has an alibi for when she went missing but . . . any ideas?'

'Well, I'm sure in his job, he's come across some rum individuals in his time,' Owen said, rubbing his neck. 'Teachers not pulling their weight in addition to dysfunctional students. He might even have been knocking off one of the teachers and their husband got to hear about it.'

'Ha, I very much doubt that. I reckon Paul de Bertrand is still pining for the love of his life. I have to say I'd like to be a fly on the wall at her parents'.'

He threw back his head and laughed. 'You really do have a wicked side to you for a copper.'

'*Moi?*' She grinned, taking in the designer beard and twinkling brown eyes. He was a good man and that's what she needed by her side. Her mind flipped to Rusty. Why he couldn't be more like Owen Bates was beyond her. Working as a detective was one of the most difficult jobs, made all the more difficult if she had to watch every sentence that came out of her mouth. She wouldn't mind if he treated everyone the same, but he didn't. He was charm personified to the likes of Marie and Amy. It was only her he singled out for his irascible behaviour. It was her turn to shake her head because of course his behaviour was partly her fault.

'So, let's have a recap,' she said, standing and heading for the whiteboard that took up one wall. Picking up the duster, she scrubbed it clean and started drawing a spider diagram.

'Christine de Bertrand, out celebrating her birthday, meets a man, possibly one of the many tall, dark and handsome men roaming our streets.' She wrote Christine's name on the board. 'The next morning, she finds herself beside the body of her flatmate.' Adding Nikki's name, she continued. 'Nikki Jones, former fellow student at St Augusta's, has a difficult relationship with everybody, including her mother. The only person she felt in anyway close to was Paul de Bertrand, lecturer at the same college, now ex-headteacher of St Gildas and former husband of

Christine.' She added Paul's name, drawing thick red lines between all three. 'She liked him so much as to put herself in a position of public embarrassment by impersonating Christine, right down to the red hair. She left the following day, walking away from three years of study at one of the world's most prestigious universities.'

She turned back towards Owen, angling her head towards the board. 'Anything I've forgotten?'

He shrugged his shoulders. 'No, I don't think so. There's a mystery as to why Christine and Paul split but I can't see that it would have had anything to do with Nikki. She only came back on the scene around Christmas, didn't she?'

'Mmm, good point and, when we asked him, he neatly avoided the question.'

She faced the board again, her pen raised. 'Okay, two days later, redheaded Tracy Price goes missing, only to turn up in the middle of the sports shed at St Gildas, her hair chopped and torn from her scalp.' She drew another line, this time in green, between the names Tracy and Paul. 'There's some thought that the marriage wasn't perfect. Barry, the husband, admitted as much on interview. There's also a rumour that she might have been pregnant, something that's unconfirmed but she did have a doctor's appointment: an appointment she didn't keep.'

She stepped back from the board, recapping the green marker and placing it beside the red and the black. 'There's something staring me in the face, yet I can't seem to see it,' she said, thinking out loud. 'We have a red-haired victim and witness in addition to a wannabe redhead in Nikki but, when she died, she was brunette. With regards to Paul de Bertrand – while it might make sense for him to be involved in Nikki's murder, surely Christine would have recognised sleeping with her own husband? There's also the fact that the afternoon of Tracy's disappearance he was in plain sight, unless he had an accomplice . . . No. That's too messy a scenario.' She turned to Owen. 'What do you think? Anything to add?'

'I think I'm getting a headache, Gabs.'

'I can't imagine why,' she said, again picking up her phone only to have it ring in her hand, Rusty's name flashing across the screen. With a swish of her finger she answered in loudspeaker mode before resting it back on the table.

'Hello Dr. I have Owen with me. What have you got for us?'

The line went quiet but only for a second. 'Not a full autopsy report. I'm not a miracle worker. I'm working on it now but I thought you'd like to know I can confirm that both victims were killed by an almost identical single thrust, which ripped the heart muscle almost in two. I haven't worked out the maths yet behind the force, depth and precise angle but, putting my neck on the line, I reckon we're looking at the same person for both murders. I know you want more, but it will take a while for the lab to process the second knife and even then, I don't think it will reveal anything. There's very little evidence on the body so I can't for a minute believe that our murderer would make a mistake with the murder weapon. We'll find it's been cleaned to within an inch of its life.'

'Thanks for that. Owen, do you have anything to ask Rusty? What about chopping her hair, surely an unusual thing to do?'

'Not really, if trophies are your thing,' Rusty said. 'With two murders under his belt, perhaps he's deciding to start a little collection.'

'You say he? I take it that's not a slip of the tongue?'

'Now, Detective, when have you ever known me to not say what I mean?' Rusty carried on, not waiting for an answer. 'There was evidence of intense sexual activity before the murder so, unless you're thinking of a female accomplice, I'm pretty confident we're talking about a male.'

'But why choose the school, surely the risk of getting caught must be enormous?'

'That's a good question and one I can't answer. Maybe instead of a deterrent, the risk of being discovered by a cohort of pre-pubescent boys added to the excitement. Who knows! I can also confirm that she was pregnant but only just. So early that she might not have even known.'

Gaby stared across at Owen as if sharing a secret.

Oh, she knew all right and, if she knew, who else did?

Chapter 35

Gaby

Nearly twelve hours had passed since Tracy's body had been discovered and they were no nearer to finding the motive.

It was now heading for seven, well past the usual time for normal hard-working people to be sitting in the comfort of their own lounge and yet here she was still at her desk with her head in her hands. They had a killer on the loose and the public on high alert. Women were being advised not to walk home alone. Parents, who in the normal course of events were happy for their children to go home by bus, were cluttering the roads, making policing the area ten-times more difficult. And Henry Sherlock was on the war path. Normally the most mild-mannered of gentlemen, he was obviously on the receiving end of a great deal of criticism and the only way he could head it off was by diverting it downwards, which meant into the lap of his detective sergeant.

Gaby shifted back in her black swivel chair, having sent Owen home to his long-suffering wife, who'd decided one night back at her parents was one night too long. Her desk was clear for once, apart from her open laptop, but even that couldn't interest her. Cradling her temples between her fingers, she felt an emptiness crowd her insides. The emptiness of failure. The emptiness of defeat. She saw the future rolling out in front of her. A dead case. Two little boys who wouldn't be able to move on with their lives. The small communities of Llandudno and Beddgelert forever living under the shadow of both Nikki and Tracy's murders. She'd cry if she had the energy or inclination for tears. If she thought they'd do any good, she'd open the floodgates, but tears were the very last thing she needed. Top of the list was a carb-filled meal and perhaps a single glass of wine to aid the next part of the plan – a minimum of six hours' uninterrupted sleep. She closed her eyes briefly, the thought of pasta dragging her straight back to her mama's kitchen and her second favourite dish – sun-dried tomato and basil-drenched fettuccini. What she wouldn't give for a bowl right now instead of the ready meal she'd probably have to settle for.

'Falling asleep on the job, Detective. Whatever next!'

She snapped her eyes open to find herself staring up at Rusty, a couple of take-outs in his hands.

'If you'd had the week I've had, Dr, so would you.' She was as much in the mood for Rusty as she was her ready meal. In fact, she'd forgo both the meal and long soak in the bath for an evening without one snipe from a man she admired hugely but who she seemed destined to clash with each time they met. 'You're a little out of your way, aren't you, unless you're in need of a lift?'

He handed her a mug before settling in the chair opposite, peeling back the lid and taking a long sip. 'Sadly, it's only decaf. A little late in the day for caffeine even by my standards. And as for being out of my way I thought now was as good a time as any to start improving our relationship.'

They sipped in silence for a moment while Gaby tried to frame a response but she couldn't think of one solitary sentence that would suffice. She could always start talking about work but the one thing she'd learnt over the last few weeks was his dislike of what he termed badgering. He'd tell her only when he had something useful and not a second before. At least the silence was comfortable unlike many other silences spent in his company. However, taking a last mouthful, the coffee granular and bitter right at the end, reminded her about their relationship: satisfactory only up to a point. He'd turn on her, making her feel both inadequate and inexperienced – she had no need for someone to reinforce those sentiments. She'd been trying to overcome them most of her life.

'That was nice. Why is it that women always have to natter, do you suppose?' He stood and stretched, his fingers reaching up to the ceiling.

All she did was raise her eyebrows. If he wanted her silence, then so be it.

'Cat got your tongue?' he said, his expression turning nasty.

'You can't have it both ways, Dr.' She shut the lid of her computer, unplugging it from the charger before popping it into its soft leather case, all the time aware that he was staring at her. Well, bully for him. She knew what she looked like, her customary plait coming apart at the seams, her face devoid of the trace of make-up she'd applied earlier. 'Either you want me to be silent or you don't.'

'Harrumph.' He withdrew a folded manila envelope from his pocket, placing it on the desk between them. 'I had thought that you'd like to go through my findings this evening instead of tomorrow but if that's not the case?'

'That's not fair,' she said, rounding on him. 'You know I—'

'We're not still in the schoolyard, Gabriella,' he interrupted, picking up her empty cup and walking over to the bin. 'When did fairness have any place in a police station? Between these walls would be the very last place I'd look for any objectivity. For instance, I'd like to bet that you have both husbands on top of the list of potential suspects – am I right?'

'Well, that's because in most cases such as this—'

'But not all.'

'I know that,' she replied, trying to control her temper. If it wasn't for him having the results of the investigation, she'd storm out, leaving him to pull the door closed behind him. Instead she waved a hand in the direction of the only other chair in the room. 'Rusty, we can sit here and argue all night, or we can go through your findings *objectively* in the hope that both of us will manage to get home in time for the ten o'clock news.'

He stared back and, with that look, time suspended for a fraction only to jump forward along with her heart. Dropping her gaze, she shoved the envelope in his direction. Up until now she hadn't given any quarter to Amy's suggestion that Dr Rusty Mulholland liked her. In fact, she was convinced the opposite was true. She bit down on her lip. Now certainly wasn't the time to allow such thoughts take root in her mind – she'd step through that particular door when she'd reached the privacy of her lounge and not a moment before.

Instead of addressing the sudden tension in the room, she decided to keep to the reason for his visit, although why he hadn't picked up the phone was beyond her suddenly limited reasoning powers.

'I'm hoping you're here to solve both murders for the Welsh constabulary,' she finally said, her expression guarded.

'Hardly. I've come up with some interesting observations, only that.' He withdrew two sheets of tightly typed paper and, handing her one, continued to speak. 'These are what I view to be the main key points. I've logged the complete findings on the database.'

Gaby started reading, the room and the man fading as she took in his fact-filled findings. Two murders both by the same hand, a right-handed man of above average height due to the trajectory of the blade. She winced when she read about the blood loss and the nigh impossible task of isolating pertinent clues from such a site as a sports shed, her wince quickly turning into a frown when she read about the foetus, only six weeks old – a little girl.

'Ah, I see you're reaching the end.'

'What? Sorry.' She lifted her head in time to catch the tail end of a sympathetic look on his face. 'What's this about blood groups?' she said, in an effort to keep the conversation between the narrow professional boundaries she'd set herself. She couldn't take sympathy, not from him.

He stretched across the desk, pointing at the graph on the bottom. 'It's simple enough. The mother's blood group was B, the foetus was O. Which means the father had to have a blood type of either B or O. I've sent tissue samples off for DNA analysis but, as you know, that takes time. I also had a quick look at the electronic patient record, and it seems that Barry Price has had blood saved for group and cross matching in the past.' He raised his head, his face expressionless. 'He was AB and therefore not the father.'

Gaby's mouth dropped open. *That poor man. To lose his wife knowing full well that she'd been having an affair.* She hadn't liked him, but no man deserved that. She suddenly wished DI Tipping was there to advise her as to how to handle such news. Was she meant to break it to the husband? What would his reaction be?

'Thank you, I think,' she finally managed, pushing all thoughts out of her mind except the immediate wish to pack up and go home. 'So, when do you think we'll have the DNA to match against on the system?'

'I've rushed it through this end so hopefully days instead of weeks. You do realise that if the DNA from the foetus matches that of the saliva found on de Bertrand's bottom sheet it will confirm what I think we're all probably suspecting – that it was the same man?'

She nodded, pushing herself back from her chair. 'Thank you for this,' she said, focusing again on the report. 'Lots to think about on the way home.'

'About that.' He cleared his throat. 'Have you eaten?'

'Have I eaten?' she repeated, not quite believing her ears.

'Yes, it's a simple enough question, Gabriella. I thought that, as we both have to eat . . . that we could catch a bite together. It would be as good a time as any to continue working on our, er, relationship issues.'

Colour flooded her cheeks. What relationship issues? As far as she was concerned the only relationship they had was a working one and that didn't include dinner. She ground her teeth, trying to control the storm of feeling bubbling under her diaphragm. Amy would have a field day if she ever got to hear about this, which made her determined never to tell her.

She picked up her mobile from the desk and, slipping it into her bag, turned to grab her jacket from the back of her chair, her fingers fumbling to push the buttons through the holes.

'No.'

He was standing by the open door, his hand on the handle, presumably waiting for her to follow. Now he stilled, his expression blank.

'Excuse me?'

'I said no. No, I haven't eaten and no, I don't want to have a meal with you. Clear enough?'

'Perfectly. Am I allowed to ask why?'

'You can ask but I have no intention of answering. I don't have to explain myself to a man that, most days, can barely look me in the face and as for being civil . . . I know I was wrong to discuss you with a colleague but I've apologised for that. I'm sorry but it's how I feel. We're just not suited to anything other than a working relationship and that doesn't include dinner.'

She stood, glaring across the room, all her frustration of the last few days spilling out. She'd always had a vicious temper and, growing up with two brothers, she'd learnt from an early age to fight her own battles. But over the years, she'd also learnt that being conciliatory made for better outcomes – now she rarely flipped.

Without a word, she watched as he turned on his heel and stormed through the door, his head held high. Waiting a minute, she picked up her bag and followed, a little part of her unsettled at his lack of response. She'd expected an angry retort or even excuses for his behaviour but the numbing silence made her, for once, doubt her own judgement. She flexed her shoulders, angry for even thinking it. He was a rude arrogant git – maybe he'd be nicer to her in future and, if he wasn't, so be it.

The house had never felt darker, or more unwelcoming. Gaby pulled into the drive, regretting that she hadn't replaced the bulb in the outside light. If she'd had the foresight she'd have left a lamp burning in the lounge window like sailors' wives of old. But Gaby had no partner, no mate to share the burden of her existence. She was alone and, after her run in with Rusty, that wasn't something that was likely to change.

She slammed the car door shut, the noise echoing in the darkness, but she didn't care. She was past caring. Her life was shit with a capital S and she had neither the knowledge nor inclination to change it. Walking up the path to the front door, she remained focused, her key in her hand. This was Rhos-on-Sea, for God's sake – one of the calmest, quietest parts of Wales, and yet she felt her heart pound in her chest at the thought of a murderer on the loose. Okay, so she wasn't a redhead but then Nikki hadn't been one either.

Opening the door, she slipped off her shoes before bending to gather the post from the mat. Walking into the lounge, she headed for the three-bar electric fire and switched it on before making her way into the kitchen and where her ready meal was waiting. Pulling open the fridge, she ignored the pre-packaged dinner, instead withdrawing the screw-top bottle of white wine and pouring herself a large glass. There was a time when food was paramount but after the day she'd had, she was quite happy to manage with wine and crisps. She grabbed a couple of bags of Mini Cheddars, almost in an act of defiance. After all, with no man to please, what did it matter that her diet was about to go off the rails. For once, the weight police could go to hell.

She settled on the sofa, her mobile beside her, the mail now on her lap. Bill. Bill. Junk mail. Card from her grandmother. She took a deep sip of her wine, allowing the flavours to explode against her tongue as she studied the front of the card before flipping it over and reading the scrawl on the back. A trip to Modena was long overdue and, there and then, she promised herself to visit at the first opportunity – whenever that might be.

The knock on the door had her almost jumping out of her skin let alone the sofa and, heading into the hall, the first thing she did was secure the chain.

'Surprise!'

'Next time, Amy, a little more warning and a lot less surprise would be perfect,' she grumbled, the sight of the bottle of champagne Tim was holding doing little to calm her heart that was currently trying its hand at tap dancing. 'You do know there's a killer on the loose . . .'

'I did try and tell her, but you know Amy.'

'Yes, indeed. Come in then, if you must but I'm going to feel no compunction booting you out after drinking your champers. Mini Cheddar, anyone?' she added, a wicked gleam in her eye as she headed back into the kitchen for more glasses.

'So, what's the celebration this time? she said over her shoulder, stuffing more bags of crisps under her arm before handing out glasses and watching as Tim popped the cork.

'There doesn't need to be a reason, not with Tim's ready supply of cheap booze.'

Gaby laughed, before turning to Tim. 'So, how's the restaurant?' She took a sip of her drink, relishing the first-class bubbles on her tongue instead of the prosecco she was used to.

'Well, at least I have meat! We're using a different butcher for a couple of days until Barry gets himself sorted.'

She eyed him over the rim of her glass, choosing her words. 'So, you'll use him again then?'

'No reason not to and, if the rumours are true about his wife, he'll need all the business he can get. I'm not one for kicking a man when he's down.'

'I didn't think you would be. So, people are sympathetic towards him?'

'Absolutely. He's going to get more housewives turning up at his door with casseroles than he has freezer room for.'

'Enough about work, already,' Amy interrupted, placing her empty glass down on the table. 'I'm starving. Have you eaten? Perhaps we could order a take-out?'

'You're the second person to ask me if I've eaten,' Gaby said, the words slipping out despite her earlier determination.

'Oh? Do tell? A new man?'

'Hardly. Just Dr Mulholland having a brain freeze. I told him pretty much where he could stuff his meal.'

'You didn't, and after that email you sent him too! Gaby Darin, you're the pits. That poor man . . .'

'Poor man, my foot. I thought you said he was loaded?'

'I wasn't referring to his financial state.' Amy shook her head, her lips twisting.

Gaby glanced across at Tim and where he was pressed up beside Amy on the sofa. Perhaps a couple of hours in good company was what she needed to get her grey cells firing because sitting by herself wasn't getting her anywhere.

'Right then. Chinese or Indian?'

Chapter 36

Gaby

Thursday 14 May, 8.40 a.m. St Asaph Police Station

When Amy had suggested a curry, Gaby hadn't expected her to send Tim around the corner to pick up another bottle of champagne. The early night she'd been planning had ended with her crawling between the sheets in the small hours.

The morning came too quickly and, with the first hint of daylight peeking through the curtains, she fumbled for paracetamol before heading into the bathroom. There was no thought of an early morning jog just as the thought of breakfast, in any of its forms, turned her stomach. She didn't even have it in her to attack the pile of empty cartons littering the kitchen, something that would have caused the biggest argument if she'd still been living with her parents.

Windows down in the car, despite the early morning drizzle, blew away some of her hangover, leaving behind a banging headache and a stomach that didn't quite feel as if it belonged to her. But she'd felt worse. She'd be able to function as a serving member of the police force if she was allowed spend the first hour or so hiding away with black coffee served with a water chaser.

'Morning, ma'am, the DCI would like a word. He's in his office,' the desk sergeant said, as soon as she walked into the building.

Damping down the expletive on her lips all she said was, 'Thanks, Clancy. Tell him I'll be up after I've dropped off my things.'

She made the mistake of pulling out her compact from her bag before leaving the office. The sight that greeted her was better than she deserved after the amount of alcohol they'd consumed. At least Tim had a job where he didn't have to do much before midday, but she spared a thought for Amy and how her day was going. She'd know soon enough as she'd arranged to meet her around at Barry Price's house at ten. Pinching her cheeks added a little colour, as did a slash of lipstick. The dark shadows under her eyes were another thing but Sherlock wasn't the most discerning of individuals.

'Ah, Gaby. I do hope you have news for me,' he said when she walked in. 'I've just come from a breakfast meeting with the chief and I can tell you he's far from happy.' He pushed himself up from his desk and plonked an open newspaper in front of her. 'While I do appreciate the scaremongering tactics of the gutter press is outside your domain, this sort of trash journalism has to stop.'

'Yes, sir,' she replied automatically, her attention on the news article taking up the whole of the front page.

The Redhaired Murders, who's next?

'I don't know which bright spark cottoned on to the hair colour side of things. Especially when the first victim was a brunette.' He sank back down in his chair, propping both elbows on the desk, his stare intense. 'Please tell me you have something I can give the chief; anything will do. As we both know, he's not the sharpest knife in the drawer, but it does have to be believable.'

She held his gaze while she tried to think of something to say that would placate him. There wasn't anything – yet.

'I can assure you that the team is working flat out,' she returned swiftly, taking in the short cropped greying hair and wire-rimmed glasses, which he peered through with an intensity that matched his myopic state. 'Dr Mulholland has determined that we're looking for a right-handed male and we'll shortly be able to attempt to match DNA samples found at both crime scenes.'

'Go on, what else?'

She swallowed, the taste of stale alcohol and bile turning her stomach. What else indeed? Her mind gripped onto the first thing to hand; Paul de Bertrand, her thoughts swerving back to the school before returning to the newspaper headline in front of her. While red hair did feature, it wasn't her main interest, not now. There had to be a reason for the killer to choose that shed and, if she was a betting woman, she'd put money on de Bertrand being involved even if he didn't have the medical knowledge required to place the knife.

'I'm still looking at a line of enquiry at the school. Disgruntled parents and staff – that sort of thing. We're pretty sure that Christine de Bertrand isn't involved and, as for Barry Price . . .' She spread her hands. 'Unless he's a consummate actor, he's a broken man.'

She watched him glaring across the divide of the desk. 'That's all very well, Darin, but it's nowhere near enough. Don't make me regret my decision to promote you.'

If you feel that strongly, perhaps you should take the job and stuff it down your scrawny gullet. Instead, the coward in her, the coward that had a mortgage payment due and a car that was stuck together with gaffer tape and wishful thinking, kept silent. And with that thought she retreated out of his office, suppressing any more words with a slight inclination of her head. She'd have to make a tough decision about her future, and soon, but not until she'd put this case to bed.

* * *

Unlike many of the detectives she'd met during her career, Gaby wasn't someone to hold grudges or take her bad mood out on the officers working alongside her. After all, it wasn't their fault she'd had too much to drink or that Sherlock had decided to use her as a proverbial punchbag. She'd always believed the way to get the most out of colleagues was to treat them with respect and, apart from that unfortunate spell in Cardiff, she hadn't been disappointed. She closed her mind to thoughts of Rusty. She'd tried, she'd more than tried to treat him as a fellow professional and, as failure wasn't a concept she signed up to, she'd just have to try a different approach.

The squad room was empty apart from Owen working on his computer. But that wasn't necessarily a bad thing with most of the team out as they followed up on leads.

'Grab a car, Owen. We're meeting Amy around at Barry Price's at ten,' she said, the sight of his neatly clipped beard sparking a memory. 'And, after, I need you to have a little chat with Devine about his appearance.'

'His appearance, What!' he exploded.

'His beard, or designer stubble – whatever you want to call it. I don't care if he thinks he's God's gift. On my watch, it's clean-shaven, moustache or beard.'

'Does that also go for the women or is it only us men you're haranguing?'

She stopped, both hands on her hips, her smile softening. 'Come on, Owen. Help me out here. Better it comes from you now than Sherlock later, and I'm sure Devine would much rather that you have a quiet word than me.'

'That's your way of wriggling out of awkward situations, is it? Passing the buck.'

'You'd do the same in my shoes. Car. Five minutes if you please.'

Gaby picked up her phone from the dashboard and phoned Amy yet again, leaving another message when it went to voicemail.

'Where the hell is she? She promised she'd be here.'

'You know Amy,' said Owen. 'She'd be here if she could. She's probably been called in on a case at the last minute and has her phone switched off. With Elaine still on holiday she's having to cover her workload as well as her own.' He undid his seatbelt and opened his door. 'While I don't relish what we're about to do surely we can manage on our own for once? It's not as if we have time to waste waiting around to see if she's going to turn up.'

Telling a man that there was irrefutable evidence that his recently murdered wife was carrying another man's child was always going to be up there with the worst things Gaby had ever had to do. But, contrary to her fears, where she'd expected anger and tears all she got was complete silence.

Staring into Barry Price's face, she could see the devastation she'd caused and a quick glance at Owen confirmed that he felt the same way. The man in front of her was broken in every way possible. His life was smashed into a thousand pieces and there was nothing she could think of to say that would help. Amy's unique sense of compassion married with her professionalism was what was needed in this cold, dark room. She only wished she'd waited for her but it was too late for regrets.

There were a hundred things Gaby should be saying, phrases she'd learnt by rote during her training, but her mind was blank to each and every one of them. She didn't know his parents, his family, his friends. She knew nothing about him other than that he was now a widower with two little boys and a mother-in-law who wasn't the most sympathetic of people. The boys would be at school, which was one blessing, she thought, placing a mug of tea on the coffee table in front of him and hovering beside the sofa, not quite knowing what to do. The fact that she hadn't liked him was immaterial. Yes, he was probably a philandering type, but no one deserved what life had thrown at him.

'Look . . .'

But she didn't get any further. She'd been going to offer more

218

platitudes but all she got was Barry roaring to his feet, his pale cheeks now suffused with anger.

'Get out, now! Do you hear. Get out before I throw you out. You should have found her when I called— If only you'd listened instead of—' He broke off again, but instead of words, almost pushed them out into the hall and then into the garden. 'I don't want you here. I don't need anyone with a box of f'ing tissues and soft speech. You as good as murdered her, do you hear! Her death is on your hands,' he finally screamed, slamming the door in their faces.

Gaby glanced across at Owen, not knowing quite what to say. There was nothing she could say because, in a way he was right. If only they'd found her sooner . . . Instead of words, she sent Amy another quick message before pocketing her mobile and opening the car door, her thoughts struggling to shift from the tragedy continuing to unfold for the Price family.

It was always fatal for an officer to play the *what-if* game but in such circumstances, it was almost impossible not to. One look at Owen's set face and Gaby knew he was putting himself in Barry's position. As a single woman with no dependants, her circumstances were very different. But, one day, she planned to meet that special person and, if time was still on her side, have a child or two. She shivered, a cold shower of reality kicking in. Life wasn't a fairy-tale and happy ever afters were something the force had drummed out of her over the years. The truth was, she was a short, overweight woman with a forthright attitude that scared most men shitless. She turned her head, contemplating the Price house, the curtains still pulled. Perhaps that wasn't a bad thing. There was less chance of getting hurt that way.

It was a little over an hour to Oswestry, an hour in which Gaby rested her head back against the seat and let Owen take charge. The pneumatic drill was still pounding away inside her skull, but a couple of Alka-Seltzers seemed to have done the trick on her stomach. It wasn't the first time she'd had to function with a headache and it certainly wouldn't be the last.

The little market town, situated on the Welsh border, was new to her but she didn't ask Owen to slow down so that she could take in the sights.

'Tell me what you know about Christine de Bertrand's parents?'

He concentrated on taking the first left past St Oswald's church before answering. 'Nice couple by all accounts. Not known to us, even for a parking violation. They used to run a small hotel facing Llandudno seafront before retiring here about ten years back. Older parents – must be mid-seventies. Christine is their only child.'

'They must be pretty special to happily accommodate their daughter's ex,' she said, watching as he pulled up outside a detached red-brick house, with lace nets on the windows. 'I still can't get over he's moved in with them.' She pushed open the car door, tucking her handbag under the seat, before swinging her legs out.

The tea was hot and strong, making her wish she had the nerve to ask for a refill. But de Bertrand's ex-mother-in-law had retreated into the kitchen and the man in front of them wasn't even prepared to lift his head let alone be hospitable.

'Thank you again for agreeing to see us, Dr de Bertrand.'

'I didn't know I had any choice,' he said, folding his arms across his chest.

'No, well, we're hoping to keep this to an informal chat, unless you'd like to come back to the station?' she said, her voice hardening along with her resolve.

'No, of course not. So, how can I help?'

'I wasn't sure you'd still be here?' Her Liverpudlian accent stressed the last vowel.

He pulled a grimace. 'She's still staying with Kelly, probably best under the circumstances,' he replied, his gaze landing on the dog. 'Ruby isn't easy to accommodate.'

Gaby's eyes followed his, her expression softening. While she didn't know one end of a dog from another, adopting an animal had always been on her bucket list. The dog appeared well looked after and obviously trusted its owner. That surely had to count for something.

'Okay, perfectly understandable under the circumstances.' She'd really like to know why they'd split up, but he'd evaded that question before, and she had more important concerns to address. 'So, the reason we're here is really a fact-finding expedition. The last time we met you provided a bulletproof explanation as to your whereabouts around the time of Mrs Price's abduction,' she said, stirring in the chair, her jacket bunching around her shoulders. 'Can you come up with an explanation as to why the murderer would specifically choose your school to dump the body? Coppers don't like coincidences and I'll think you'll agree that it's too much of one not to investigate further.'

When he finally spoke his words were deliberate, reflecting the thought he must have given to this specific facet of the case. 'While I agree, I don't know enough of the facts to give an informed opinion. Christine goes on a night out, meets a man. Takes him home and he presumably then chooses to murder Nikki. There's no link to the school that I can see apart from Christine being my ex-wife, which has to be viewed as tenuous at best.'

'Hold on a minute,' Owen interrupted, turning to face her. 'What about the drinking game?'

Gaby inclined her head in acknowledgement before asking, 'Did you know about the drinking game, Dr?' Her calm expression and tone hid her budding excitement.

'The drinking game?' he repeated, shaking his head.

'Yes. Apparently, her friend—'

'Kelly, ma'am.'

'Yes, thank you, Owen,' she said, a smile breaking in acknowledgement. 'Kelly started off a drinking game, which entailed asking men how to spell de Bertrand and for each misspelling there was a forfeit where drinks were bought.'

'I have been around, Officer. What else could it be other than an excuse to get pissed?'

'Yes, but what I'm getting at—'

'What you're getting at is, my wife could have unwittingly told a stranger her surname, a surname that meant something to someone.'

'Exactly.'

He lifted his mug and drained it in one before stretching out his hand and gathering up the crockery. 'This needs some thought. If you'll excuse me a moment, I'll put the kettle on.'

As soon as the door closed, Owen burst out laughing. 'He's awfully well spoken.'

'Be quiet. I have to think.' She placed her hand on his arm and squeezed. 'You know, I'm sure you're onto something. What if there was someone in that bar who knew de Bertrand and, as soon as he heard his name, formulated a plan, a plan of revenge?' she asked, her face animated, the dull thud in her head now only a minor irritant.

'That's all very well but it wasn't Christine that was murdered.'

'Shush a minute, I'm still thinking.' The grip on his arm tightened. 'What if the plan wasn't to kill her but instead to have sex. As she said herself, hooking up wasn't something she did. So, he's standing at the bar, keeping himself to himself when he hears a name, a name he hates above all others. The getting her pissed would have been easy, she was halfway there already. He could have followed her back under the pretext of helping her, whatever. She'd have felt obliged to ask him in for a coffee and, once inside, he could have easily made his plan bulletproof by nipping to the loo and raiding her medicine cabinet. What better way to get back at De Bertrand than screwing his ex-wife senseless especially as it's clear to everyone that he's still in love with her?'

'That doesn't explain why Nikki ended up dead though, does it? And where does Tracy fit in?'

She let go of his arm, her mind trying to weave strands that didn't want to be woven. Red hair had to be key and Nikki was a brunette except for that disastrous one episode where she'd tried to impersonate Christine. Nikki, who was infatuated with Paul de Bertrand and, if her self-harming was anything to go by, not the most stable of individuals.

'She could have easily blamed Christine for everything that was wrong with her life, but would that have led her to thoughts of murder . . .?' She lifted her head, a sound from the hall having her sit back in her chair, a bland smile stapled in place.

There were no preliminaries with Paul de Bertrand. After the niceties of handing out replenished mugs was over, he sat down, Ruby settling her head on his feet and started speaking. 'In a job such as mine, one comes up against enemies all the time but most wouldn't stoop to murder or, at least, I hope not. It's hard enough attracting teachers to the profession as it is without the threat of being slaughtered.' His lips moulded into the parody of a smile. 'St Gildas is an old, revered school but, until I took up the reins as headmaster, it was falling behind in the league tables. Now it's in the top ten and rivalling the likes of Winchester and Magdalen for that top slot.' He nursed his mug on his knee, his attention now on Ruby. 'For that to happen we had to push other schools down and they wouldn't have liked that one little bit but for them to resort to murder . . .' He shook his head. 'I can't see it. So, closer to home, there's a smattering of teachers that we've had to let go, but not many and none since my divorce. Obviously, it's up to the acting headmaster to provide you with details but Mathew Diamond and Jake Seymour are two that ring a bell.' He cradled his mug between long fingers before continuing. 'Finally, there's students, not that I think for an instant that, since my tenure at the college, any of them would have committed such an act. But their parents – that's a different matter altogether. The lengths

223

some are prepared to go, to ensure their child progresses, would turn your hair grey although, it's true to say that it's more verbal than physical.' He placed his untouched drink on the coffee table. 'Being a headmaster is a little like being a guardian, diplomat and conciliator all rolled into one. For me to give you any names is against everything—'

'If you don't, sir, we can always get a court order,' Gaby interrupted, watching as he rubbed Ruby's ears between his thumb and forefinger.

'I know you can but that doesn't make this any easier.' He shook his head a second time before finally returning their gaze. 'To expel a child from a public school is rare. We don't do it unless the child gives us very little choice and that's where my thoughts are taking me. Suspending a child is different. Suspensions are two-a-penny and, after strong words from Mater and Pater, the child usually cleans up their act. But there is one that I can think of that sticks out.' He let go of Ruby to lift up his mug, his knuckles straining through the skin. 'Ronan Stevens's expulsion just after Christmas still rankles. If the mother hadn't been in hospital it might have been a very different scenario but there was nothing I could do in the end to protect the boy from the consequences of his actions. There was even talk about including the police over the assault. We were very lucky the boys' parents decided not to press charges.

Gaby caught Owen's eye, suddenly remembering where she'd seen the St Gildas school emblem before – emblazoned on the school jumper worn by one of Casper Stevens's children.

'Dr, we have to be clear here. A man's future might depend on it. So apart from the expulsion of his son, is there anything else that would lead you to conclude that Mr Stevens could be the man we're looking for? I take it you do mean Mr Casper Stevens?'

He paused a moment, as if considering her words, before giving a sharp nod. 'There's nothing else that I can think of. Up until that last meeting I have to say I liked him as a man.'

Chapter 37

Nikki

Five months ago, Llandudno

Nikki backed into the nearest doorway, the sight of the thronging masses lining the streets of Llandudno worse than her worst nightmare. So many people. Couples. Lovers. Parents with children. Everyone had someone except her, her gaze resting on the two elderly women walking in tandem ahead. Her father couldn't wait to get rid of her and as for her mother . . . She turned on her heel and headed for the pier and away from the crowds, unwilling to spend even a second thinking about her beloved mother.

She couldn't remember the last time she'd been here. They'd used to come as a family before her father had decided that his perfect little life wasn't perfect at all. They'd stayed in one of the cheap B&Bs that interspersed the posh hotels, their pastel frontages trying to cling onto a way of life that had long since passed.

Pulling on the straps of her rucksack, her back beginning to ache, she wondered yet again at the madness that had possessed her to return. It had been foolish to try and reclaim that small slice of happiness that was her life before her parents' separation and eventual divorce – before university and, finally, before Paul.

She sank down on one of the green benches that dotted the promenade, drawn to the pebble beach and blue-green sea beyond. Thinking about Paul de Bertrand, even after a span of nearly ten years, still caused a wrenching ache of regret and shame that wouldn't leave, despite the passage of time. She could still remember, as if it was yesterday, the look of reproach and, yes, it must be said, disappointment etched on his face at the sight of her dressed up like Christine. She sighed. How stupid she'd been. How naive to think that a man like him would switch his love to someone like her, even with dyed-red hair and a sexy frock. And the irony of it was, when the realisation had hit that she'd lost the man she'd never really had, it had been too late to turn back the clock. She'd blown her degree and had ended up, if not quite jobless and homeless then nearly so. She'd found employment working in a small provincial library on minimum wage. It wasn't much of a life but she'd managed.

The sea drew her like a magnet. She'd always loved water, even as a child. There was something about the way the waves edged up over the shore that fascinated her more than the cool green of a forest glade or the highest mountain peak. Not that she was a swimmer. Her mother had never been bothered enough to sign her up for the weekly lessons at the local sports centre and, when she'd been of an age to learn independently, her scars had always been the barrier that she could never overcome. But not now. Now the fact that she'd never learnt, made coming here, surrounded by the faded memories of her one pure happy time, the next step in her crock of a life. Oh, she'd have probably been content to muddle along until retirement if the library hadn't had its funding withdrawn – when that final door closed so had her willingness to continue. She was too old and set in her ways to start again, which is what she'd have had to do. Another library in another town when she barely had enough energy to get out of bed in the morning. No. This way was easier and best all round.

She stood and, slipping her rucksack off her shoulders, left it on the bench before walking across the prom to the sea beyond, her body shaking with nerves. Taking a blade to her skin was easy in comparison to what she was about to do. There'd be no sense of relief. No sense of control. But with nowhere to go and no one to turn to, it was . . .

'Hold on a minute. You've forgotten your bag.'

The words flew over her head, not one of them making a mark on her tortured mind. It was only the shocked sound of her name on someone's lips that pulled her out of the dark place that was already calling to her.

'Nikki. Nikki Jones. It *is* you.'

Even then she could have shaken her head and pleaded ignorance. After all, her future was planned, her life set in stone – the date of her death already carved. But she didn't. She recognised that voice for what it was. The voice of the woman who'd stolen her perfect future only to discard it along with the trash.

Her body turned away from the sea, a new future erasing the misery of the past, one thought uppermost.

Revenge.

Chapter 38

Gaby

Thursday 14 May, 11.00 a.m. Oswestry

'Well, what did you think of that?' Gaby said, following Owen to the car.

'I'm not sure if I'm honest.' He opened the passenger door for her before walking around to the driver's side. 'Stevens didn't look the type but then who does? And there's Tracy remember. I can sort of get him sleeping with Christine but I'm at a loss as to the rest of it. Have you considered too how he'd have the wherewithal to stab like that? Would pharmacists have the in-depth anatomy training that Rusty thinks was needed?'

'No, possibly not.' Gaby slammed the car door behind her and reached for her seatbelt. 'You do realise what this means,' she added, turning to stare back across at the house before twisting in her seat and meeting Owen's gaze. 'Ronan doesn't fit the bill. He's too young for a start. All the reports indicate a man and he's little more than a boy. But what parent wouldn't do everything in their power to protect their child . . .' Gaby's voice tailed off, her mind sweeping back to the image of Casper Stevens, standing beside the mantelpiece. 'He's a husband and father, for God's sake!'

'Just like Tracy was a wife and mother.' Owen placed his phone and keys in the cubby hole. 'Which he'd have known all too well living next door to her.'

'I can't believe that he'd—'

'We don't actually know if he did anything, and we won't until we bring him in for questioning,' Owen said, starting the car. 'Do you want me to phone for a squad car to pick him up?'

'No.' Gaby massaged her temple, trying to dispel the image of Stevens the last time she'd seen him. He was probably the last man she'd ever suspect of something like this. Where was her copper instinct if she was proved wrong? 'Before we do anything, I'd like to run a background check to see if he has any priors or any skeletons in his cupboard.'

Reaching for her mobile, she started tapping the keys only for it to come to life in her hand.

'Darin speaking.'

She stilled, her breath caught in the back of her throat, her eyes fixed on the view up ahead. After a moment she ended the call, the phone dropped in her lap, her face now paper-white.

'What is it?'

'That was Malachy. We're going to have to scratch our plans for the moment,' she said, turning to face him, her habitual bland expression nowhere to be seen. 'That neighbour of Barry Price's . . .'

'Deborah Miles?'

'Yes. She went to drop a pie off to Barry for his lunch. When she didn't get an answer, she decided to peer through the windows. She knew, you see, that we'd visited earlier.' Gaby managed a smile of sorts, a smile that never got past her lips. 'The benefit of nosy neighbours.' Her voice broke, all trace of her smile dispersed by grief. 'She found him hanging from the ceiling.'

Chapter 39

Gaby

Thursday 14 May, 2.10 p.m. Llan Clwyd Hospital

Who'd be a copper? No one who actually knew what the job entailed, that was for sure.

Under normal circumstances it took a little over an hour to get from Oswestry to Llan Clwyd Hospital, but Owen managed it in thirty-five minutes, give or take. And each one of those minutes was agony for Gabriella Darin. What could she have done differently, if anything, to prevent another tragedy? The question was swiftly followed by thoughts of those poor boys and what they were about to face.

Hanging wasn't a nice way to commit suicide, if ever the term nice could be assigned to such an act. But it was still one of the most common forms, despite the horror that awaited the poor unsuspecting individual left to find the swinging feet and engorged face. She spared more than a few thoughts for Deborah Miles, a strong woman if ever there was one. But strength and tenacity wouldn't get her very far where hanging was concerned.

Gaby had only had the misfortune to come across one such act while in uniform, but she could still remember the nightmares that ensued.

The car had barely squealed to a stop outside the hospital before Gaby wrenched open the door and raced to reception, feeling her trousers pull against her thighs as she ran up the steps.

Slamming her warrant card down, she examined the youngster decked out in his spanking brand new porter's uniform and suddenly decided to moderate both her tone and her words. Just because she was having a shit day didn't mean she had to ruin his. Instead of asking to be put through to the morgue she decided to say, 'If you could check your records for a Barry Price, please?' A small smile was the most she could manage.

Picking up her card, she resisted the temptation of tapping the edge against the top of the desk while she watched him log into the system and search their databanks, the seconds crawling into what seemed like minutes while he waited for the hospital computer to load. It was routine for ambulances to bring all victims in via the emergency department, whatever their state. She knew she was clutching at straws.

'Just arrived in ICU, which is . . .'

'I know where it is. Thank you,' she added as an afterthought, already heading for the lift, Owen by her side.

'I thought you said he'd—?'

'Obviously not!'

Intensive Care. How many times had she visited departments such as this one? How many pastel-coloured walls had she propped herself against, waiting for the harried nurses to let them in? How many smashed faces and broken bodies had she borne witness to? Far too many.

'So, how long do you think they'll keep us hanging around then.' Owen's words planted the first genuine smile on her lips in what felt like ages.

Humour, the copper's safety valve. Often macabre. Rarely in good taste. But as essential as breathing. The only problem was, after the few days she'd been having, humour was the very last thing she was up for. Blinking, she tried to think up a pithy response, but she couldn't seem to drag her mind away from the futility of it all. What man would do that and leave two little boys to face the world alone. A desperate one.

'Ha, very funny, not.' Her mouth faded back to the resident thin compressed line. 'As you very well know, the longer it takes, the better the outcome. Bagging and tagging only takes seconds. The rest—' she waved her hand towards the door '—the rest can take a lifetime of rehabilitation and recovery.'

Gaby reached up almost unconsciously to her neck, the skin butter-soft under her fingers, thanks to the nightly slap of whatever cream was on special in Asda, her mind delving through what she knew about hanging. She frowned because it didn't amount to much. She couldn't remember a case of murder by hanging and, as soon as suicide was determined by the pathologist, her team were pulled off the case. Now she realised just how lax she'd been, and her frown deepened. She could remember there was more than one type, but her brain seemed frozen on the execution hangings depicted in the spaghetti westerns her dad and brothers used to gorge on.

The door pushed open and a tall black man, dressed in faded blue scrubs, strolled out, his hands tucked in his pockets. Her first thought was based on his looks: the breadth of his shoulders, the angular cut of his cheekbones. Her second was guilt. She was old enough but obviously not wise enough if her first thought was lust. Folding her arms, she took a step back but not before indicating with a tilt of her head for Owen to lead.

'I'm DC Bates and this is DS Darin – what can you tell us about him, Dr er—?'

'McCrea.' He walked across to the powder blue chairs and took a seat, gesturing for them to follow. 'Barry Price is one lucky son-of-a-bitch. If the neighbour had been a few seconds later or a few inches shorter we wouldn't have been able to do anything. As it is, there's still only a 50/50 chance that he'll make it,' he said, rubbing his hand over the dark stubble breaking out on his chin. 'He'd strung himself up to the light fitting with one of his wife's scarves, kicking the chair away probably only moments before the neighbour looked in through the window. She had the sense to pull out her phone and call the emergency services while she ran through the door and gathered the full weight of his body on her shoulders.'

He relaxed his head back against the chair and closed his eyes, his face etched with tiredness.

'When will we be able to speak to him?' Gaby asked, almost reluctant to disturb him in his moment of peace.

His eyes flew open, his look direct. 'Not for a while, I'm afraid. We had to pop a tube down his throat to help him breathe so the best I can say is that he's unconscious but stable. Also, we've yet to eliminate the possibility of a spinal fracture or even spinal cord damage and that's not even thinking about any brain damage that might have resulted from the hypoxia, or reduced oxygen supply.' He stood, his gaze wandering over to Owen briefly before returning to Gaby. 'Well, if that's all? I'm on call tonight and I was hoping for a couple of hours' rest.' He shrugged his shoulders.

'One more thing,' Gaby said, her thoughts now with Deborah Miles. 'What about the neighbour? I thought she'd still be here?'

'She is, Detective.' He lifted his hand and pointed at the signage pinned to the wall. 'She's being patched up in the Emergency Department. That's one plucky lady, saving a life that didn't want to be saved.'

'She's all right, is she?'

'If you can call a fractured eye socket and jaw all right. For a man in the throes of death, he certainly had one hell of a kick on him. The psychiatric team are going to have a field day trying to sort him out.' He headed along the corridor only to pause at the shrill sound of his bleeper, his stroll turning into a sprint, presumably all thought of sleep forgotten.

Gaby watched him before pulling a face and turning back to Owen.

'The poor man. And we think we have it bad.' She dragged her phone out of her pocket searching for a number. 'Owen, don't judge me but I'm going to ask Paul de Bertrand to get in touch with Christine. The gutter press are going to be all over this. It's up to them if they want to avoid unwanted media intrusion but I do think they should be given the opportunity. I don't think we've ever been so wrong about a case. I'm still not sure how Stevens fits in but the one thing I do know is that those two are innocent of any wrongdoing.' She smiled briefly. 'And, after, I'm going to head down to check on how Mrs Miles is, it's the very least we can do. While I'm there, if you can round up Amy. Someone is going to have to break the news to Barry's family and I'd prefer if it wasn't me.'

Chapter 40

Gaby

Thursday 14 May, 3.15 p.m. Llan Clwyd Hospital

'Right, where is Amy going to meet us?'

'She's not.'

Gaby stopped outside the hospital entrance. There was just something in Owen's tone that alerted her to the fact that something was wrong. Very wrong.

'What do you mean she's not?' she said, staring up at him, her cheeks pale.

'Amy didn't show for work today.'

'What? She's off sick? That's unlike her.'

'She hasn't rung in sick – she just failed to show.'

She looked at him, her mouth slightly open before turning on her heel. 'Owen, you call the boys' grandparents, don't say anything about Barry, just check they're picking them up from school and taking them back to their place.'

They reached the car and, settling in her seat, she pulled out her mobile.

'Hi Tim, it's Gaby. I'm trying to contact Amy.' After barely a moment, she laid her phone across her lap and stretched for her seatbelt with unsteady fingers. 'He hasn't seen her since first thing this morning. She was going to drop into the chemist for some paracetamol on her way to work.'

'Which chemist?' he snapped.

'Which chemist do you think! The one she always uses next to Coast Café in Rhos-on-Sea. It's the nearest to Tim's. Oh God, she's been missing now for six hours and no one realised – how can that even happen?'

Gaby felt the blood drain to her feet appalled that she hadn't realised sooner that something was wrong, very wrong. It was so out of character for Amy to be late for anything and she'd at least have phoned to let her know she'd been detained. She clenched and unclenched her hands feeling powerless. They'd find Amy if it was the last thing they did – but it might be too late.

Owen started the engine and screeched out of the car park. 'Where to first?'

'Head for the chemist but I'm sending a car over – we're still a good half hour away.'

They didn't speak. There was nothing to say. As coppers they expected the worst, not because they were pessimists, not a bit of it. Coppers had to be optimists otherwise they wouldn't last five minutes in the job. The truth was that most missing people turned up alive. Either an accident had befallen them, or they'd simply had a change of plan. But Amy wasn't most people. Amy was a highly intuitive professional who rarely made a wrong judgement call. If something had happened, she'd have done everything in her power to let the station know. Out of the office, she always had her phone glued to her hand. Only last week they'd joked that she kept it under her pillow during sex just in case she missed something. So, she was either incapacitated or unable to access her mobile. Both scenarios struck dread in Gaby's heart.

Within minutes Gaby's phone jerked to life in her lap, scattering her thoughts and cementing her fears.

'That was Jax and Malachy. They spoke to the shop assistant. Casper Stevens left early. Said he had to pick the kids up from school. They've tried his mobile but he's not answering. They're about to run a background check and try and catch up with the wife. They're also going to run his number plate through the ANPR database. We'll start at the shop and take it from there.'

Her fingers drummed on the edge of her seat, her gaze on the Fiat 500 in front, weaving across the road like a maniac. In the normal course of events she'd have called it in, but she had more serious things to consider like why the hell a seemingly happily married pharmacist would go off the rails in such a devastating way. They could be wrong but, somehow, she knew that they weren't. She recognised more than most the craziness that existed in the human psyche. But unlike the driver of the grey Fiat up ahead, most people were able to control their baser urges. So, what had tipped Stevens over the edge?

'Do you want me to alert the traffic police?' Owen said as he braked suddenly in the middle of the duel carriage way, tutting his annoyance.'

'No. This is their lucky day – we have more important things than irresponsible drivers . . .'

She turned to face him, resting her head against the passenger door. There was something still shading her view, some part of the case that she couldn't get her head around and Owen was the world's best copper to talk things over with.

'Help me out here. So, are we thinking that Nikki was the instigator of her own demise? Heartbroken at losing Paul, she gives up on life only to find that Christine has ditched him. How must that have made her feel?'

'Angry? Upset?'

'More than that. I think she was devastated. He even continued to hand-deliver his ex-wife a birthday card so, in Nikki's warped mind, she probably knew he still cared. To then find another man in Christine's bed . . .' She clenched her phone, willing for it to ring. 'I think she flipped and picked up whatever she could find, in this case Christine's new diving knife, the intention being to stab them both only to end up with a six-inch blade sticking out of her chest.' Her attention was back on the Fiat as it pulled up outside a hairdresser on a screech of brakes.

'Thank God for that!' Owen said, racing past. 'Carry on, you're doing great. You're thinking that Casper Stevens picked up Christine after hearing about the link with Paul de Bertrand?'

Gaby remembered the tall, suave man that day they'd interviewed him. She'd thought then that he didn't seem to match his wife. He was more alive somehow, more vibrant. A player. But did he play away? Was that it? She'd raised an eyebrow at the time at the disparity between the way they'd looked. Pulling down the sun visor, she stole a hand to her rich brown hair, with what she liked to term the odd grey highlight. There was nothing wrong with allowing yourself to grow old gracefully, but Casper Stevens was a man fighting the onset of age with his expensive clothes and designer haircut while his wife, although smart, appeared quite happy to let nature take the lead. Gaby remembered thinking at the time that his wife's hair had been short, almost too short, her mind following a completely different trail. Maybe she wasn't viewing this from the right direction. Maybe Janice Stevens looked that way because she'd been ill.

'I'm not sure what I think and that's the problem,' she finally said, snapping the visor closed and returning to her phone. 'If he's our man, he deliberately set out to have an affair with his next-door neighbour. What was it that Mrs Miles said – something about the Prices' relationship deteriorating around Christmas time?' She twisted back in her seat. 'That's it, Owen. The catalyst. Remember de Bertrand mentioning Janice Stevens's ill health. With her in hospital, Casper had the ideal opportunity to start knocking off Tracy Price – a woman left emotionally vulnerable by Barry's infidelities.' She took out her notebook and, balancing it on her knee, scribbled a brief reminder to follow up on the wife's illness. 'I still can't see where the red hair fits, but he must have been pretty stressed with the news that Tracy was pregnant.'

'Don't forget about his son, Ronan. Being expelled from a public school like that is no joke.'

'Very true.' She grabbed his arm, her fingers shaking. 'Owen, put your foot down, there's a love. He's a desperate man and he's got our Amy.'

The chemist looked closed but all it took was a sharp knock on the door for Jax to appear and let them in. Gaby studied her surroundings but there was nothing to see apart from the usual shelves laden with toiletries and other sundry items from deodorants to corn plasters. It was the exact same as all the other chemists she'd ever visited except for one unique difference. She had no interest in anything other than the whereabouts of the owner.

'I thought it better to shut up shop, ma'am,' Jax said, gesturing for her to follow 'Malachy is with the shop assistant in the office. We haven't said anything.'

'You did right.' She went to move towards the back of the chemist only to halt at the feel of his hand on her arm.

'There's something else . . .'

She stared up at him and, for the first time, noticed his unhealthy pallor.

'What is it?' She deliberately softened her voice.

'I should have contacted you, but I thought it could wait until the briefing.' He took a deep swallow, his Adam's apple working overtime. 'This morning on my visit to the West Shore, I caught up with Rufus's mum, a German Shepherd cross – the dog that is, not the o-o-owner,' he stuttered.

Gaby screwed a brief expectant smile on her face, all the while willing him to carry on. One of her brothers had suffered from a stutter and she knew more than most that the worst thing possible was to interrupt, biting down on her tongue to prevent her doing just that.

'She's a nurse in one of the care homes – she's working nights at present,' he finally managed, taking deep, heaving breaths to help his speech. 'When she can't sleep on her days off, she often takes R-R . . . her dog for an early morning stroll. Last Saturday she saw a man racing along the path outside Christine's flat. She's adamant it was Casper Stevens – he often pops in with medications for the residents on his way home.'

She gave him a smile when all she felt like doing was grimacing. To have all her fears confirmed in such a way when the safety of one of her officers was on the line, had to be up there with having her wallet stolen. But Jax was a good cop. She knew if he could harness his enthusiasm and eye for detail, he'd make an outstanding one just as she knew that one false word or nasty remark from her would send his stutter into overdrive and his confidence into his boots.

'Good work, Jax. You weren't to know he'd come onto our radar.'

She walked behind the counter and into the office, forcing herself to concentrate on the middle-aged platinum-blonde sat in front of the desk, a glass of water on the side. The navy tunic and trousers set off the chic Fifties look as did the tattooed eyebrows and bright red lips. But Gaby wasn't here to note her attributes. She had better things to do with her time, the sense of urgency making her heart jump in her chest and her eyes smart. She was here with one thought in her mind and one thought only. Amy.

'Hello, my name is Detective Darin,' she said, flipping her warrant card open and taking a seat. 'I believe my men have asked you about the whereabouts of Mr Stevens?'

'Well, as I've been telling the young man, he's not answering his phone,' she said, a look of confusion stamped across her face. 'He said he had to pick up the boys from school, but he should be home by now.'

'Do you have any idea where else he might have gone?'

'He keeps himself to himself.'

'Thank you. If you can leave your details with DC Williams in case we need to follow up on anything.' Gaby waited until she'd been escorted out of the shop before turning back to Malachy. 'So, what have you got for us then?'

'Not a huge amount,' he said, reading from his notebook. 'Casper Stevens, forty-three. Born in Chester – moved to Llandudno and opened up the chemist about fifteen years ago. They're still looking into his education but no priors. A couple of parking tickets in his twenties but, apart from that, he's clean. We've had a quick scout around but what you see is pretty much what you get. There's a flat above but I managed to speak to the elderly woman that lives there. She's as deaf as a post and didn't hear or see anything untoward. We also had a look out the back. There's space for one car and little else. Needless to say, the parking place is empty.'

'Show me.'

She followed him out the back door, her gaze on the paved drive and the slight trace of scuff marks but nothing that could be tantamount to a clue.

Back in the office she stared at the rows of black box files and the stream of pharmacy books stretching out across the shelves in an array of colours. The desk was deep mahogany and set out with a military precision that scared the hell out of her. An empty desk was an anathema to someone like her with more work than she knew what to do with.

'Did you manage to find anything out about the wife?' she said, turning back to Malachy.

'Janice, also forty-three. They met at university. That's all they've come up with so far.' He snapped his notebook shut and returned it to his back pocket before holding out a Post-it note. 'I have her number. I was about to give her a ring before you turned up.'

'Thank you.' She wandered behind the desk and sat in the swivel chair, her mobile pressed to her ear as she quickly arranged to meet Mrs Stevens back at their house. Ending the call, she paused, compelled by some instinct to open the top drawer. Perhaps it was the absence of anything personal in the room. No photos. No trinkets. Nothing to indicate the personality of the man.

The frame was right on top and, turning it over, she couldn't fail to notice the glass smashed in a starburst pattern. The photo was of Casper and his family, taken a few years ago by the look of the toddler in his arms. But it wasn't the kids that drew her interest. It wasn't the sight of the family that dragged an expletive from her lips. It was the sight of Janice Stevens's long red hair flowing across her shoulders. She needed no further confirmation about what Paul de Bertrand had told her. Christine, Tracy and now Janice, all with the same distinctive hair colour that set them apart. Gaby hadn't really been serious in her earlier thoughts of a murderer fixated on red hair. She was deadly serious now.

Chapter 41

Gaby

The house was just as she remembered, apart from the hall cluttered with school bags. Janice Stevens led them back into the lounge, gesturing with a wave of her hand to the sofa opposite. She was wearing a similar dress to last time, this one plain navy offset by a single row of pearls, her skin free of make-up.

'We're trying to catch up with your husband. We were given the impression that he'd left early to pick up the kids?'

'As if! It's only Jacob that needs picking up and I always do that. The elder ones take the bus.'

'So, do you have any idea where he might be?'

'Casper is a law unto himself, Detective.' she said, her mouth pulled tight.

Gaby and Owen exchanged looks. 'I take it that you and your husband er . . .?'

'The last six months have been a difficult time for the both of us,' Janice said, lifting her hand to smooth over her pixie cut. 'I take it the reason you're here is something to do with Tracy's death?'

'We're not at liberty to disclose any details of an ongoing investigation.'

'Of course you're not!'

'Can you tell us your husband's whereabouts last Friday from six o'clock onwards?' Owen asked.

'Last Friday?' she repeated, shifting in her seat. 'Frankly, I have no idea. He didn't come home – I was here with the boys all evening.'

'You don't need to check your calendar or anything?'

'No, Detective. Friday night is film night in our house. I make a pile of cheesy nachos and popcorn and we all chill in front of whatever Netflix is age appropriate. Last Friday, Casper was a no-show. I don't know where he was until breakfast. He didn't even bother with an excuse. Up until that moment I thought we were just going through a rough patch – now I'm not so sure it's as simple as that. Even our eldest is starting to suspect, as if his life isn't difficult enough.'

'That would be Ronan?' Gaby said, wanting the final piece of the puzzle to slot into place.

'That's right.' She started fiddling with her wedding band. 'He's also going through a rough patch.'

'So I hear,' Gaby interrupted, watching Janice flick her a look. 'Being expelled can never be easy.'

'No. I'm not explaining my son to you but there were extenuating circumstances. If there hadn't been, the police would have been called. The two little shits that had been picking on him from day one got more than they bargained for and my son has certainly learnt a lesson.'

Gaby widened her eyes at the different take on the story that Paul de Bertrand had told them but she refrained from commenting. 'So, to get back to your husband's whereabouts. It's imperative that we track him down. What about friends? Family?'

She shook her head. 'His parents died last year and as for friends, he's fallen out of the scene in recent months. There's Jim from the golf club but I can't really see that he'd know anything.'

'Jim . . .?' Owen said, twisting his pen through his fingers.

'Mackay. He owns the Diamond Emporium along Mostyn Street.'

Gaby flicked back through her notebook at a loss as to what to ask next, her throat tightening at the thought. She was desperate to find her friend but, apart from the scuff marks outside the back of the shop, there were no leads. She'd thought the wife would be the best bet but obviously not if the *cul de sac* conversation was anything to go by. There had to be somewhere he could go. Or at least someone that had seen him with Amy, if indeed he'd taken her. It was all supposition at this stage with no clues to go on. Her mind slid back to the ANPR search they were running on his Saab, but so far there'd been no sightings. She opened her mouth to speak only to close it again at the sight of the door being pushed open and a teenager bursting into the room.

'Mum, what's this Jacob's saying about the police looking for Dad?'

Gaby studied the tall scruffy youth with interest, drawn to his skinny frame and sunken cheeks. She'd taken Janice's comment about extenuating circumstances with a pinch of salt. Now she believed everything his mother had said. Here was a young man fighting demons no kid his age should have to face.

'Ronan, you shouldn't be here . . .'

'But Dad . . .?'

'Ronan, if I may call you that?' Gaby said, her voice soft, her smile kind. 'I'm Detective Darin and this is Detective Bates. We do need to speak to your dad but it's not something that you need to worry about, unless you have any ideas as to where he is?'

'None at all. I haven't seen him since this morning when he dropped his car off at the garage.'

'Oh, that's right.' Janice jerked forward, her face colouring. 'I'd forgotten. The Saab needed a service.'

'So, your husband didn't have a car,' Gaby said, almost to herself, her thoughts confused. How the hell could he be in the frame for abduction without transport?

'No, he did,' Ronan piped up. 'He took mine. I'm still learning to drive so it's only a clapped-out Fiesta with over 100,000 miles on the clock but it's a good runner.'

Chapter 42

Amy

Thursday 14 May, 8 a.m. Rhos-on-Sea

Walking up to the shop, Amy had been pleased to see a light going on, the thump inside her skull a souvenir of the champagne she'd consumed the night before. She was far too old and wise not to know what she'd been doing but that second bottle had seemed like a good idea at the time.

She rattled the door handle, not surprised that it was still locked and, taking a step back, glanced at her watch. She had ten minutes to wait. It would mean cutting it fine if she was to reach work on time, but they wouldn't get any sense out of her unless she could sort out the hangover bashing her skull from all sides.

The sound of a key turning in the lock had her stepping forward, a weak smile on her lips at the kindness of the tall, handsome man pulling the door open and gesturing for her to follow.

'Oh God, you're a life saver. Thank you so much,' she gushed. 'A box of paracetamol please.'

'You look like you need it,' he said, walking behind the counter and, picking up a blue and white box, placed it on the top. 'That'll be ninety-six pence.'

'Cheap at double the price.' She fumbled in her pocket for her wallet before plucking out a pound coin, not caring for once if her warrant card was seen or not.

'You're a copper?'

'Detective,' she said, noting his look of interest before tearing into the box and pressing out a couple of tablets. 'But I won't be doing much detecting if I can't shift this headache.'

"Well in that case the least I can do is offer you a glass of water. Otherwise you might arrest me,' he added, a grin on his face. 'Why don't you have a seat – I'll be back in a moment.'

Amy could hardly breathe let alone speak. She also couldn't move and as for seeing . . .

She remembered back to the lectures she'd had on crisis management but all the training in the world couldn't prepare her for the reality of being trussed up like a chicken and dumped in the boot of some smelly car, the bitter taste of whatever drug he'd given her a lasting memory of what a mug she'd been. Of all the gullible fools. It had been drummed into her during her training, and on each subsequent annual update, never to enter an area alone unless there was back-up. Okay, so popping into the local chemist wasn't exactly a risk but hadn't she gone out of her way to choose Stevens' because she'd known he'd lived next to Tracy Price? That would teach her for being nosy. She struggled to keep the tears back because, if history was to repeat itself, she wouldn't be around to benefit from the lesson. She had no idea what he had planned or even if he'd just left her to die. She had no idea how long she'd been here but long enough for the pressure building up in her bladder to reach catastrophic proportions. She'd finally done the one thing she'd never imagined, the sticky stench of urine pooling between her legs a sharp reminder of her vulnerability.

* * *

She must have dropped off. One minute she was berating herself for being the worst kind of fool and the next she was blinded by the light streaming in from the open boot.

'God, you're disgusting. You stink. Couldn't you have waited.' His voice was harsh, his hands wrenching under her arms and pulling her head-first out of the car. 'Bitch. I'll bet you wet yourself on purpose.'

Before she knew it, he was dragging her along the ground, her bound feet scraping grooves into the grass. She couldn't speak because of the tape covering her lips but her vision was starting to acclimatise, not that it did her any good. She didn't know where he'd taken her and, with her watch nowhere in sight, she had no idea how long she'd been cooped up in the car. But by the changes in the light she guessed it must be heading for the evening, which meant she'd been bound and gagged for nearly ten hours. Would anyone have missed her by now? She bloody well hoped so. But even if they had . . . even if they'd called in the troops, she was in the middle of what looked to be nowhere. There were hills all around and a glimpse of sea between but no sign of life, either human or animal. No sign of anything other than the slate-roofed farmhouse in front of her, its air of neglect and *For Sale* sign telling a story she didn't want to hear.

He let her go, not caring that her head lolled back straight onto the path, but she was adamant that she wouldn't react even if her brains spilled all over the pavement. She wouldn't give him the satisfaction of knowing that he was getting to her. Her mind turned to thoughts of Tim but, heaving a sigh, she blanked him out. He couldn't help her now. She had to help herself but, with her hands and legs bound, there was little she could do.

He'd stopped speaking after those first furious words, but she knew he was angry by the way he grabbed her under the arms and yanked her over the threshold. His next words filled her with dread.

'It's the shower for you and there's no electricity – I'm sure you won't mind the cold.'

The shower was part of an *en-suite*, but that wasn't what caused her skin to crawl. It was the sight of the double bed that took up most of the room, its mattress bare and stained with age. She knew what had happened to Christine just as she knew the fate that had befallen Tracy. She'd rather die first but, with no method available . . .

Chapter 43

Gaby

Thursday 14 May, 4.45 p.m. Llandudno

Jim Mackay, owner of the Diamond Emporium, was busy serving a customer but not for long. One flash of Owen's warrant card and he swiftly handed over to his colleague before gesturing for them to follow him through a curtained door at the back of the shop.

'There's nothing worse than a copper for tightening a man's wallet, Detective,' he said with a smile that would make any dentist proud. His hair was another matter. But the wearing of a toupee wasn't currently on Gaby's list of arrestable offences even if it should have been, her gaze on the black matted rug balanced on top of his head like a crown.

'We won't keep you long, sir,' she said, stressing the sir with a brief smile. 'We need to get in touch with Casper Stevens as a matter of urgency and his wife suggested that—'

'Is everything all right?' he interrupted, his smile disappearing. 'The boys?'

'The boys are fine. Now, what can you tell us about where Mr Stevens would have gone if he's not at the shop or at home?'

He frowned, lifting his hand to his hair only to drop it back to his side, his eyes now focusing on the pale grey carpet under his polished shoes. 'I really can't say. We used to spend time together but not for a while now. If I'm honest I thought that he was avoiding me.'

'And why would he do that?'

'Janice and my wife are friends. She dropped a hint a few weeks ago that she thought they were having some marital problems.'

'What sort of problems?' Owen asked, propping himself against the nearest wall.

'Oh, the usual, I suppose. You'd really have to speak to the wife but, after Janice came out of hospital, apparently, she moved into the spare room – not that I blame her. Poor woman. Casper is a man that likes *all* his home comforts if you get my drift,' he said, sending a smirk in Owen's direction.

'Why exactly was Mrs Stevens in hospital?' Gaby pursed her lips, well aware of the silent conversation going on between the two men.

'Cancer. Again, the wife knows more but from what I understand she had to have her womb removed in the end and then chemo or was it radiotherapy? Whatever it was, she lost all her hair.' He shook his head briefly. 'Well, I'm sorry if I can't be of any other use. I haven't seen good old Casper for ages, not since his old man's funeral.'

Gaby felt the hairs tingle on the back of her neck. Janice Stevens had mentioned the death of his parents, but it wasn't something she'd thought to question.

'Tell me about his father?'

'Not a lot to tell. Didn't last two minutes after his wife died. He was a nice old boy though – used to be a GP. Casper tried to follow in his footsteps but switched to pharmacy after he failed his exams. I only went to the funeral out of respect really. They had an old stone farmhouse outside of Caernarfon I believe. You know the sort, no mod-cons. Casper was having a devil's own job trying to sell it.'

Chapter 44

Christine

Thursday 14 May, 4.45 p.m. Llandudno

'Thank you for agreeing to see me.'

Christine faced her ex-husband across the table, a cappuccino cradled between her hands.

'You didn't really give me any choice,' she said, concentrating on his lips. Despite the time Costa, along Mostyn Street, was busy and, as such, not the best of places in which to carry out a conversation with a soon to be, deaf person. Her mouth twisted at the thought, the pale shimmer of lip-gloss catching the light – lip-gloss she'd applied as an afterthought.

She hadn't dressed up for the occasion. In fact, she viewed it as an act of self-preservation to make sure she both looked and acted normally, whatever that was. So, the garment of today was a floaty dress in shades of green, which he'd seen many a time, teamed with an ancient cardigan in burnt orange. Her hair she'd pulled back off her face, securing it into a tight ponytail, a look she knew he detested. That gave her the little spark of courage she needed to stay sitting opposite a man who'd barely said two words since picking her up from Kelly's two-up, two-down halfway along Brook Street.

'No, well . . .'

He glanced down at the table and started to play with his teaspoon, his fingers twisting it over and over as if struggling to find something to say.

She heaved a sigh, reluctant to take the conversation into her own hands but if she didn't want to spend the rest of the afternoon staring at the top of his head then she'd better speak up. Being in his company was still torture and she couldn't see that changing any time soon. She loved him. She'd always love him. But fate, or whatever else you wanted to call it, had decided to interfere. She swept her lids closed at the futility of them even being in the same room together. It hurt and she was honest enough to recognise that he felt the same way. Raising her mug, she took a deep sip, trying to steady her nerves. She had to be the strong one here. She had to be strong for both of them.

'Paul. I had thought that, after the break-up, it would be best if we didn't see each other again.'

He lifted his head, his gaze sliding to meet hers with a look so bleak that she struggled not to reach out and take his hand.

'Best for whom exactly?' he said finally, lifting up the spoon again before dropping it on the table with a clatter.

'Please don't be like this. It's hard enough . . .'

'It certainly is.' She watched him shake his head and her heart broke all over again at the sight. With a sudden jerk, she pushed away from the table, the chair legs scraping along the floor. She shouldn't have agreed to see him even if it was urgent. It was too hard, too heart-wrenching. 'I'm sorry but I can't do this . . .'

He grabbed her hand, his fingers warm against her stone-cold palm, his look beseeching. 'Stay. Please. I . . . I promise I'll say my piece and be done.'

'Five minutes then,' she said, settling back in her chair.

'I have something to tell you, something that's going to be difficult. It's difficult enough for me.' He heaved his shoulders, his eyes roaming over her face before continuing. 'That Detective Darin woman has been in touch. There's been a development in the case.' He lowered his voice to a mere whisper. 'The husband of the second victim is in hospital – he's just tried to take his own life.'

She stared back, unable to break eye contact even if she'd wanted to.

'Oh God. They had kids, didn't they? What must he have been thinking?'

He shoved a pile of paper napkins into her hand. 'He probably wasn't – most likely a gut reaction to the news that he'd lost the love of his life.' His voice was dry.

She eyed him through a haze of tears, realising that he wasn't only talking about the Prices. 'Paul, you do know that I didn't want to cause you any harm?'

'Then why walk?' he said, his expression fixed. 'Did you honestly think that you going deaf would have made any difference to how I felt?' He removed his glasses, rubbing the bridge of his nose before replacing them. 'You must have a very poor opinion to think of me in that light.'

All colour left her face at his words. 'Who told you?'

'That is completely irrelevant.' He grabbed her hand again, this time his fingers tight around her wrist. 'What on earth were you thinking? I loved you, for God's sake. I loved you with every heartbeat. Hearing, sight, smell, touch, taste. You could have lost the lot and it would still have been irrelevant.' He let go of her hand and, standing, it was his turn to push away from the table, his drink untouched. 'The reality is you didn't love me enough.'

Her mouth dropped open. She'd thought she was doing what was best but, by the look of the broken man in front of her, busily slipping his arms into his jacket, she'd failed on all counts.

She stood, lifting her chin in defiance. 'If anything, I loved you too much to want you to be saddled with a—'

'And who gave you the right to make decisions on my behalf, hmm?' he said, raising his voice. 'I'm old enough and ugly enough to make my own.'

She watched him turn his back and storm out the café, her heart going with him. Her emotions surged but she wouldn't break down, not here, not now. She blinked, squeezing back the tears. Tears of regret for the mess she'd made of everything. Her thoughts shifted to what he'd said about the Prices. There was her bemoaning the loss of her hearing when those kids had lost their mother and now possibly their dad. And suddenly, tears streaming down her face, she grabbed her coat and bag and raced out of the café, not bothering who she knocked into in the process. If he still loved her, and that was a big if, she'd spend the rest of her life trying to make it up to him.

She caught him outside Billy Lal's Market and, grabbing his arm, pulled him to a halt. 'I never thought you a coward, Paul. Running out on a woman you've just professed undying love for, a woman that still loves you despite everything,' she said, her voice thick with tears.

His fingers clenched around her arm. She'd have bruises later, but the odd bruise was nothing to the fire lighting up his face. Her Paul, back where he belonged was all that mattered. Her face tilted to meet the sudden onslaught of his mouth.

She'd come home.

Chapter 45

Amy

Thursday 14 May, 6 p.m. Caernarfon

The water was freezing, just like he'd warned. She sat, huddled in the bottom of the shower, resisting every attempt to stand. It was all she could do. The only thing she could do. He hadn't even cut the strapping to her wrists and legs like she'd hoped. She knew a fair bit about martial arts and would certainly have tried to give as good as she got, despite the marked difference in both their height and physique. But he must have had the same idea. Instead of undressing her in the traditional sense, he'd grabbed a pair of scissors and cut through the seams before hurling her onto the shower tray and reaching in a hand to turn on the spray. Shampoo came next, some cheap brand smelling of lemon.

Amy was fussy about her hair. It was her one luxury. Born mousey, every six weeks she took the financial hit of having a decent cut and highlights. Brown for her spelt boring unless it was that unique shade with reddish undertones that Gaby was born with. She shut her eyelids, trying to avoid the shampoo running down her face. She didn't think she'd be able to tolerate having someone touch her hair ever again.

She knew there was more. She knew what must come next if he was to keep to his plan. The next bit would be the hardest of all, and her mind filled with Tim and the future they'd planned.

The sound of a mobile ringing dragged her back to the present and she watched as he stepped back and pulled out his phone, a frown descending.

'Ronan?'

He walked out of the room, leaving her alone for the first time since opening the boot. But fat lot of good it would do with her hands still tied. Lifting her arms up, she rubbed her wrists over her head and the shampoo that lingered before trying to loosen the strapping,

Chapter 46

Gaby

'Where the hell are we?'

'In the middle of nowhere,' Gaby said, peering out of the windscreen at the driving rain that had set in as soon as they turned left onto the A55. 'If the Satnav's right, we should see the sea in the distance.'

'In this rain? I can barely see the road let alone the horizon,' Owen said, his mouth tightening. 'If that bastard has laid a finger on her, Gaby, I swear I won't be responsible for my actions.'

'I'm right with you, Owen.' Gaby jerked forward, pointed ahead. 'There. Right in front of us. The sea, so at least we're in the right area.' She turned in her seat. 'If the Satnav's right, we're only a couple of minutes away and I really have no intention of alerting him to our presence.'

'If indeed they're there, ma'am,' Owen said. 'This eggs in one basket scenario isn't how I like to play it.'

'We had no choice, as you bloody well know. Now stop faffing and find somewhere to pull in as soon as you see the outline of the house.' She smoothed her hand over the estate agent's details resting on her lap, her stomach curling at the thought of what they were going to find. A lot could happen in the time since he'd left the chemist.

She sighed. The ANPR had tracked Ronan's car as far as the A55 and no further. So, while they had a fair idea of where Casper was heading, they couldn't be certain. They couldn't even be sure that he'd got Amy with him. The truth was they were guessing but guesses were all they had right now. Guesses and a copper's instinct.

'What's that?' she said, trying to make out the shapes between the lashing rain and busy wipers. 'Owen, pull over here – we'll continue on foot. Don't worry. There's a couple of anoraks in the back.'

'Don't tell me. I can have the pink one.'

Chapter 47

Amy

Thursday 14 May, 6.30 p.m. Caernarfon

'There's been a change of plan.'

Amy froze, her hands on her lap, the fingers of her right hand trying and failing to squeeze her left hand through its prison of tape. So close and yet so far. She had small hands and fingers, something Tim had teased her about only a couple of days ago. She'd laughed then, joining him in the joke. She wasn't laughing now.

Before she knew it, he'd doused her with cold water again, removing most of the soap before wrapping her in a towel and manhandling her into the next room and throwing her across the bed. Within seconds he was beside her, his hands now in her hair.

'Such beautiful hair, even though it's the wrong colour,' he mused almost to himself, stretching a lock so far as to make her grimace. 'Don't they say gentlemen prefer blondes but, for me, only red will do. It's never been about the woman. Tall. Short. Fat or thin. If they don't have red hair, I'm not interested. However, with you I'm prepared to make an exception.'

He moved on the bed, causing her to roll into the centre of the mattress, his voice changing, becoming almost lover-like in its tone. 'Time is one thing we don't have. I want nothing more than for us to be together.' His hand trailed a path down her cheek before spreading the towel and feasting his gaze. 'So beautiful but so little time. I had such plans when I saw you for who you are. A copper coming to snoop.' His hands wandered across her cold skin, the smooth feel of his palm forcing air from her lungs and blood from her face. 'There's so much I want to do,' he continued, his eyes hardening.

She turned her head away, focusing on the dingy wall, stained with black mildew. This tall, handsome man was mad and with that thought Amy Potter gave up hope of ever being able to free herself from his clutches. She relaxed her muscles, letting the tension ease out of her limbs while she tried to focus on the one thing that this man could never touch – her love for Tim.

She'd known the minute she'd stepped into his restaurant, three months ago that here was a man that was going to change her life for the better and nothing and no one would ever be able to take that feeling away, certainly not Casper Stevens.

Amy switched her mind off in the same way someone turned off a light, her thoughts now in the past. She didn't feel the chink of metal or the cold sliver of blade as he rested the long knife across her stomach. She didn't hear his crooning tones continuing to chant his everlasting devotion as the tip of the blade pierced her flesh between her ribs. She didn't feel the creak of the old, timber-framed bed as it shifted under their weight just as she didn't hear the muffled creak of the door as it pushed open under some invisible hand. She was in a world of her own, her thoughts filled with a future that would now never be hers, a single teardrop chasing down her cheek.

Chapter 48

Gaby

Thursday 14 May, 6.35 p.m. Caernarfon

The house was silent, dark invading all corners.

'You take the right, Owen,' she whispered, slipping off her shoes and, with the same instinct that had made her open that drawer in Stevens's office, tiptoed to the end of the hall and gently pushed open the door.

The room was dark and dingy, the only light coming from the north-facing windows. But it was still bright enough to see Amy spread-eagled on the bed and Casper Stevens bending over her, his hand clenching what looked like a hunting knife.

Gaby would be the very first to admit that in situations like this she was a coward. She'd never volunteered for anything in her life, always having the ability to weigh up situations in a heartbeat and coming up with a better plan. She was always last on those assault courses they made her go on. Time and again she was the butt of her colleagues' jokes during training exercises and the truth was no one ever wanted her on their team. She tried her best, but her best was never good enough. She was just one of those people that wasn't built to be a copper and, if it hadn't been for her sharp mind, she'd have been shown the door years ago.

But, for once, instead of thinking, Gaby acted and, with a burst of speed, which had more to do with the adrenaline soaring through her veins than the desultory jogging she was already thinking of quitting, she sprinted across the room and landed on his back, her hand clamping around his wrist, screaming at the top of her voice.

'Owen. Help!

'Get off.' Casper drew up to his full height, but Gaby held on, her legs wrapping around his thighs, piggyback style and, for the first time in her life, she felt positive about her ability to disarm him. He could twist and shake all he liked but all she had to do was hold on to his wrist for another couple of seconds until Owen . . .

The feel of the knife slicing through her arm caused her to lose grip and drop to the floor like a sack of spuds. She lay there, helpless, watching as he lifted the blade before piercing through her stomach right up to the hilt.

There was a blinding pain then nothing. Her senses dulled. Her thoughts shattered all around as the light behind her eyes suddenly switched to dark.

Chapter 49

Gaby

Wednesday 20 May, 9 a.m. St Asaph Hospital

'Completely unresponsive.'

'But for how long?'

'No one can tell. The brain shows activity but it's not an exact science. A coma can last for hours, days, weeks. Even years. The main thing is to continue to hope. The doctors and nurses here are some of the best people I've ever worked with.'

The words flickered in and out of her mind but didn't linger. She didn't recognise the harsh weeping of her mother or the sound of her father trying and failing to offer some comfort. She was unable to process that her two brothers were standing silent, unable to rationalise the deathly pale body in the bed as being that of their beautiful sister just as she was unable to read the card of thanks signed by Christine and Paul de Bertrand. She was also blind to the man sitting by her side, reaching out to squeeze her hand as he tried to provide what help and support he could to her family.

Hours passed, great swathes of time that she'd never regain, her mind in limbo while her spleen attempted to heal the damage wrought from having a seven-inch blade plunged into its depths. Day turned into night and back into day, the nurses washing and changing her, the tubes in her nose and arms providing the essential fluids, nutrients and drugs needed to maintain the *status quo*. She was unaware of Amy coming to visit, great tears streaking her cheeks at the sight of Gaby's lifeless body. She was unaware of the newspapers declaring her a hero. She'd have had something to say about that. She was unaware of all these things, her mind deciding to take a long-earned rest from a life she didn't really rate that highly.

It was the pain that did it. Not the usual pain she was used to. The stab from a tooth. A self-inflicted headache. A stubbed toe. No, this was a gnawing pain right in the centre of her gut that defied explanation. She pulled a grimace, her face wrinkling up for the first time in well over a week, a week where Rusty Mulholland had haunted ITU like a ghost, his presence telling her family and staff alike that here was a man who cared – cared desperately. But Rusty wasn't there now. Rusty was at home trying to catch up on some well-earned sleep.

Gaby's grimace turned into a frown as she tried to make sense of her situation. She was lying in bed, but something didn't feel right. The sheets certainly weren't her Egyptian cotton ones and as for that beeping . . . Her mind switched off, a sudden tiredness engulfing her. By the time the staff nurse came into the room with her next round of analgesia, she'd slipped back under the covers of unconsciousness.

It was Owen Bates who proved to be the key that unlocked her mind from the place it was resting. Owen who, despite his hatred of all things hospital, had forced himself to visit after a persistent nag from Kate.

'We're really missing you at the station, Gabs. Even Sherlock was asking after you yesterday even though he did lay into me for letting you chase up that lead without back-up.' He picked up her hand idly, continuing to speak. 'That's a laugh. As if I – or indeed any man – could ever tell you what to do. Amy's fine by the way. The best. She's taking a couple of weeks off but, apart from some bruising and scratching she'll be back to normal in no time. And as for Casper Stevens . . . Jason came up trumps in the end by matching the blood on the diving knife with the saliva on the sheets and even with poor Tracy Price's unborn child. So I'm sure you'll be delighted to hear that the bastard is under psychiatric review but, wherever he's going, it will be for a very long time.' He clenched her hand harder. 'Come on, Darin, if you'd only wake up, I promise I won't give up on the force just yet.'

Gaby drew a breath, pleased that the pain from earlier had disappeared. In its place she felt nothing. No, that wasn't quite true, the pressure on her hand was increasing. Her eyelids remained closed. She couldn't be bothered to open them – it all felt like too much effort. She listened to Owen rambling on, her memories starting to fly back into the window of her mind, tears gathering. She was pleased Amy was well. That was the only thing that mattered, her hand returning Owen's grip, tears starting to track down her face.

The pieces were finally fitting into place. She'd never know for sure exactly what had happened in Christine's bedroom but she had a bloody good idea. Nikki was damaged, more damaged than anyone could have ever guessed, the borders of Gaby's mind stretching back to include that conversation she'd had, weeks ago now, with Melanie Shaw. Nikki Jones had a huge self-destruct button hidden deep and, if it hadn't been for the actions of Casper Stevens, she'd have killed Christine de Bertrand before turning the blade on herself.

The sad fact was that no one would mourn her death, certainly not her mother. But Gaby would remember and in remembering would try and make a difference. The borders now shifted closed as sleep demanded entry but, there was still room for one final thought.

If there was ever anything she could do to help Ronan Stevens, she'd do it.

Chapter 50

Nikki

Saturday 9 May, 3.40 a.m. Llandudno

The days passed, soon running into weeks and months but still Nikki waited. She waited for the right time for her anger and disappointment to swell to such a level as to be unstoppable. It was all very well deciding on a course of action but to carry out that one perfect sweet act, something that would make up for the crock she'd made of her life, was easier said than done. Life went on, the day-to-day minutiae of work eating into her time and draining her of any inclination other than the most basic. She got up and went to work and, when she returned home, she spent the remainder of her time holed up in front of the TV. That was it.

Something needed to change, some push to make her step outside the comfort of Christine's flat. That push came with the arrival of the birthday card from Paul. Up until that point she'd almost decided on a different course. Living with Christine wasn't what she'd expected. She wasn't what she'd expected. She was kinder, softer somehow. The anger that had pulsed now only simmered – a minor undercurrent *of* resentment that probably wouldn't have escalated if the card hadn't arrived.

It wouldn't have been so bad if she hadn't seen him from her bedroom window earlier that day, his head downcast, his shoulders slumped as he turned away from the door. Paul had looked as broken as she felt and, with that thought, her anger turned into a rage.

She sat in her shoebox of a room, the knife resting across her bare skin, the blade calling to her like a siren but she resisted the temptation. Later. Later, she'd take pleasure from drawing the sharp edge over Christine's flesh . . .

Wine came first. One bottle and then two – in between mouthfuls of pepperoni pizza – while she worked on a plan. She must have slept because the next thing she knew the clock on her bedside table had shifted. Slipping out of the room, she didn't pause for her dressing gown. The night was warm, made all the warmer by the wine pulsing through her veins.

There was no premonition of what was ahead. No insight as to what lay behind Christine's partially closed door. Nikki couldn't see past her anger, which seemed to have taken on a life of its own. This wasn't about Paul or even Christine anymore. This was the final act of desperation by a woman who knew, somewhere in the dark recesses, that she had to take some responsibility for her own actions.

Pushing open the door, a scream built in the back of her throat. A war cry if you like. The culmination of twelve years of hatred. She didn't see the man shift under the duvet as she raced across the room and leapt on the bed. She didn't see him lift a hand and grab her wrist. She only saw him arching above her, the gleam of the blade matching the gleam in his eye as he drove the knife through her chest and by then it was far too late.

Chapter 51

Gaby

Walking through the doors of the station for the first time in over six weeks seemed strange. It didn't feel like that long, the days spent recuperating back in Liverpool almost disappearing before her eyes. Even the office looked the same, apart from the large bunch of flowers that tightened her throat and loosened the grip she'd been keeping on her emotions. For someone that prided themselves on never crying, she was turning into a right old watering pot.

She headed back out of the office and down the corridor to see DCI Sherlock, still unsure as to whether he'd take her to task for heading out after Stevens without backup. It wasn't mentioned during his one hospital visit but she'd put nothing past him.

'Ah Gaby, do take a seat. How are you feeling?'

She returned his smile before settling in her chair, the scar on her side still pulling despite the passage of time.

'Pretty much back to normal, sir.'

'Good. Good. Well I won't keep you long. Only long enough

272

to ask you if you'd like to continue heading up the team on a more formal footing.'

'Sir?'

He propped his elbows on the desk, his expression as unreadable as ever. 'I've been in touch with DI Tipping, Gaby and, between you and me, it's not looking that good. He agrees that we need to keep the momentum of the department by appointing an interim DI to head up the MIT and we'd both like that person to be you.' He raised his hand at the sight of her open mouth. 'No, don't say anything yet. While it might seem odd, in light of your recent appointment up to sergeant, we both know that that was a long overdue promotion. Go away and have a think.'

Gaby returned to the office, her office now, the dazed expression lingering. After Cardiff and Swansea she'd almost given up on her dream of a career in law enforcement and now this. How was she ever going to top it, she wondered, her smile only faltering when her thoughts turned to Stewart and Sheila Tipping and what they must be going through.

She'd barcly had time to look at the flowers before there was a knock on the door, which pushed open before she had a chance to say come in.

The sight of the man in front of her turned her cheeks pale before they flooded with colour. She'd heard time and again, from almost everyone she'd met, how much of a support Rusty had been during her illness – if illness was the right word. In fact, she'd threatened to leave the room the last time her family had harped on about what a splendid chap he was and how she could do a lot worse. The best she could say about Rusty Mulholland was that he confused her. Having her family nagging her only increased that confusion. She was happy the way she was, or that's what she kept telling herself. It wasn't helping.

She stood, while she tried to remember the little speech she'd worked on in case of this eventuality.

'Thank you again for all the time and support you provided my family. I hear you went out of your way to ease the situation for them.'

'I didn't do it for them, Gabriella.' He ran a hand through his hair, his gaze on her face. 'Are you sure you're fit enough to return to work? A ruptured spleen isn't a walk in the park, you know.'

'Tell me about it! Yes, I'm fine, as back to normal as I can be and it's an excuse to give up jogging,' she added, her eyes twinkling at his shocked expression. 'I might try cycling next, at least it will save on petrol and be good for the environment.'

'Yes, well, we're all pleased you're back,' he said, throwing a nod in the direction of the flowers.

She followed his gaze to the little card peeking out the top, 'Gabriella' written in a scrawl she couldn't fail to recognise. 'Oh, you shouldn't have.'

'I wanted to. We – that is I . . . Well, I'd like for us to start again?'

'Start again?'

'Yes. Look, I'm pretty useless at this relationship thing, which is clearly evident with one failed marriage but . . .'

She stopped him mid-sentence, not quite believing what she was hearing. 'Rusty, if this is your idea of a joke, it's far from funny. Most days you ignore me and, when you're not, you're plain rude.'

'I can explain all that.'

'An explanation isn't necessary,' she said, lifting her hand to her forehead. 'I'm a big girl – I know what it's like. Let's agree to differ on how we see things.' She tilted her head in the direction of the flowers. 'Thank you again for both the flowers and your assistance when I was incapacitated but I have work to do.'

She watched him walk out of the office and, shrugging her shoulders, turned the card over with a sigh. The flowers were beautiful and would look lovely in her lounge. The card . . . She stared at the bin before tucking it into her phone case instead, a small smile hovering.

It looked as if work was going to get interesting.

Acknowledgements

Writing acknowledgements is one of the hardest parts of the book writing process but never more so currently. There are lots of people to thank, my only worry being that I miss one of them out! Firstly, I'd like to thank Abi Fenton, Chris Sturtivant, Dushi Horti, Loma Halden and all the team at HQ Digital for helping to make my dream come true. The work that goes into producing a book is huge and I know that all the staff at HarperCollins, along with the rest of the world, have been working under enormous pressure since Covid-19 hit, so thank you.

I support Ernie's Angels, a local children's charity that raises funds for end of life care and funeral expenses. This book's dedication has been chosen by the winner of a competition we held last year: Jenny Palmer, Principal of Elizabeth College and a huge supporter of the charity. Thank you, Jenny, for your contribution.

Over the last twelve years I have forged strong friendships with other writers in the industry who help me almost on a daily basis. A huge thanks to my writing partner, Valerie Keogh and also to Susie Tullett, Sue Moorcroft and many others too numerous to mention but you know who you are.

Writers wouldn't get very far without readers. And book bloggers are instrumental in that process. These dedicated readers do much behind the scenes to help readers discover their next book so a huge thank you to Jo Robertson, Adele Blair, Grace Smith, Donna Maguire and Sany Garces Molina to name but a few.

I also have a very small Dream Team, a group of readers who found me through social media and love my books. Without your support my writing day would be a lonely place. So a huge thank you to Beverley Hopper, Daniela Cole, Michele Turner, Susan Hall, Elaine Fryatt, Tracy Robinson, Clare Wakelin, Madeleine Harris, Natasha Orme and Pauline Millward. You ladies rock! By the way, if this is something you might be interested in, drop me a line via social media (ScribblerJB on most platforms).

All the characters in this book only live in my imagination but I have been given permission to use a few names. FLO Amy Potter, who appeared first in *Silent Cry*, is an amazing nurse and a dear friend. Sue Sullivan, also a nurse, has left us to move to Wales. I wish her well. Christine de Bertrand (what a great name for a character) is a fellow all-year-round sea swimmer. There's also Deborah Miles, another author, who won a competition to feature as one of my characters: I hope you like her, Deborah? For the opportunity to enter one of my competitions why not follow me over on Facebook? My page is called Jenny O'Brien Guernsey Writer.

Talking of Wales, it is a while since I lived there so a big thanks to my sister, Caroline, for helping me with the research. Hope to pop home soon x

I try to keep the strands of my life separate. My writing. My nursing. My family, and rarely talk about the latter two. But as a practicing nurse, I'd like to take this opportunity to thank the team that I work with. The last few months have been particularly difficult on our ward, but my colleagues have been absolutely amazing – to put it mildly, they have worked their socks off to help keep Guernsey safe. And yet each day they come into work with a smile on their face and ask about how my book sales are doing. We have 'clap for carers and keyworkers' but this is my personal tribute to Ollie Bain-Brehaut, Sergio Ferreira, Lauren Mason, Viki Brouard, Anne Friend, Gina Billien, Vanessa Steer, Catarina Capitao, Connie Vasconcelos, Gill Barton, Sarah-Jane Walters, Shane Mechem, Annette Brazil-North, Anna Mpawaenda, Holly Allen, Bridget Martin, Paula Reid, Judith Malan, Lesley Goodenough, Tiago Pereira, Tina Bichard, Lim Kwai, Maria Andrade, Kelly Hamlin, Denise Hooley, Nadia Santos, Daniela de Silva, Claudia de Luza, Celia Ferreira, Nellie AngelKova, Cath Dyer, Kim Kyoni and, of course, Amy Potter.

With regards to Jax's speech dysfluency, or stutter. I work with an amazing bunch of speech therapists at work but also have personal experience of this issue. A special thank you to therapist, Jo Lamb. You truly are amazing.

Finally and not least, thank you to my family. Working from home is never easy but when the house is full of three teens homeschooling and a husband squirreling away on his laptop, it has been particularly stressful. We've got through it and we're still talking. I'm not sure what else there is to say about that – the usual buns for tea x

Dear Reader,

We hope you enjoyed reading this book. If you did, we'd be so appreciative if you left a review. It really helps us and the author to bring more books like this to you.

Here at HQ Digital we are dedicated to publishing fiction that will keep you turning the pages into the early hours. Don't want to miss a thing? To find out more about our books, promotions, discover exclusive content and enter competitions you can keep in touch in the following ways:

JOIN OUR COMMUNITY:
Sign up to our new email newsletter: hyperurl.co/hqnewsletter
Read our new blog: www.hqstories.co.uk
🐦: https://twitter.com/HQStories
f: www.facebook.com/HQStories

BUDDING WRITER?
We're also looking for authors to join the HQ Digital family!
Find out more here:
https://www.hqstories.co.uk/want-to-write-for-us/
Thanks for reading, from the HQ Digital team